"Magnificent read. The story exists on the land that straddles suspense, thriller, and good ol' supernatural chill-fest. The term "page-turner" has become cliched to the point of lost meaning, yet with Forsaken, we are reminded where the phrase was born: between the pages of just such a book as this. Moving the story along at a rushing river's clip, Barker braids two tales together in a dance between present and past. We begin getting the slightest feeling that the two might be more intertwined than we at first suspected, but are kept in delighted suspense until Barker lets us see. He is generous in a manner. The reader is given an omnipresent view of the world inside the covers, and this serves to build tension as we become invested in the characters, sometimes wishing to grab them by the shoulders and shake them to their good senses, other times wanting desperately to tell them what's happening just outside their line of sight. All of these ingredients are combined in a clever and delicious story, one that reads fast and fun, and with just enough darkness laying over Barker's land to make us wonder, to make us check over our shoulders one more time, to watch the shadows… they're only shadows, right?"

– *Blogger, www.princessburlap.com*

**Nominated for a Bram Stoker Award by the
Horror Writers Association – Best Debut Novel 2014**

J.D.BARKER

HAMPTON CREEK PRESS

FORSAKEN

BOOK ONE OF THE SHADOW COVE SAGA

Published by:
Hampton Creek Press
707 Lake View Drive
Shadow Cove, MA 02105

This is a work of fiction. Names, characters, places and incidents either are products of the author's imagination or are used fictitiously. Any resemblance to actual events or locales or persons, living or dead, is entirely coincidental unless noted otherwise.

Hampton Creek Press is a registered Trademark
of Hampton Creek Publishing, LLC

Cover Design by Julie Meek and Bioblossom Creative,
www.bioblossomcreative.com

Book design by Maureen Cutajar,
www.gopublished.com

Manufactured in the United States of America

ISBN: 978-0-9906949-2-2

For PB

PROLOGUE

"DIRECTORY ASSISTANCE, HOW MAY I help you?"

Rachael peered down the hallway from the kitchen. She could see light peeking out from under the door to her husband's office. He had been locked in there for hours. She cupped her hand over the receiver and spoke in a low voice. "I'm trying to find the number for a store in Maine. It's...it's like an antique shop, but different. It's hard to explain. Imagine a garage sale, but in a store. Like a thrift shop. I think it's called Needful Things."

"What city?"

Rachael had tried to remember. For days she had tried to recall the sleepy little town but it was just beyond reach, teasing her mind with slivers of recollection, then drifting back into the abyss. "Castle something," she said. "Castle Cliff, Castle Point, Castle… something."

"Castle Rock?"

Rachael frowned. "I don't know, that might be it."

She heard the woman typing. Over the years, Rachael had searched the Internet more times than she could count, but she wasn't able to locate it.

"I'm sorry, ma'am. I'm not finding anything called Needful Things in Castle Rock. Nothing at all in Maine, actually. Maybe you have the wrong name? Or maybe they've closed?"

Rachael hung up the phone without bothering to respond.

It wasn't closed.

She doubted a store like that ever closed; it just learned to hide.

A witch is a magician, who either by open or secret league, wittingly and unwillingly contenteth to use the aid and assistance of the devil, in the working of wonders or misery to those about, both friend and enemy alike.

—William Perkins,
A Discourse on the Damned Art of Witchcraft
(1608)

I woke with a start, knowing the light of morning was still hours away. I had seen her face, heard her voice. "Help me," she had pleaded.

—Thad McAlister,
Rise of the Witch

DAY 1
Charleston, SC

CHAPTER ONE

Day 1 – 1:13 a.m.

THE CHILL OF NIGHT bit at her skin as a wintry howl moaned through naked branches just beyond her window. Rachael pulled the sheets up tight around her neck and slipped over to her husband's side of the bed, searching for the warmth of his body. He wasn't there, though; she found herself alone.

"Thad?" she breathed.

With the fury of the night's storm behind it, the dark room whispered back at her—a hard, bitter whisper filled with the hollow tone of a place devoid of life, void of the safety that came with knowing a loved one was close.

Rachael watched as her breath hung in the frigid air, a white mist gobbled up by the surrounding darkness. She watched as it disappeared, replaced with her next.

Has the heater broken? she wondered. They had grown accustomed to such problems living in an older house, although the heater had never failed them before.

Outside, the wind kicked up, each bellow somewhat louder than the last as if locked in some strange contest of strength, unwilling to be outdone by one another. The thick branches of the oaks surrounding their modest home leaned in, scraping against the walls and roof.

Rachael rose from the bed, the child within her kicking in protest at the sudden movement.

"There, there, sweetie," she said. "We're just going for a little walk."

She reached for the silk robe she had draped over her dressing table chair the night before—it offered little warmth against the icy chill of the air around her.

Reaching for the wall, her fingers fumbled across the smooth surface until catching the light switch. She flicked it on, but nothing happened.

The power must have gone out, she told herself.

"Thad? Where are you, honey?" she said, this time louder than the first, but not loud enough to wake Ashley, who was no doubt snug and still curled up under her Winnie the Pooh comforter in her room at the end of the hall.

With the wall as her guide, Rachael worked her way down the hallway, pausing at her husband's office.

Why is the door open? He always closes it.

She had expected to find him, but even before her eyes adjusted to the thick darkness, she knew the room was empty. His most recent manuscript, now only half completed, stood beside the monitor of his computer. A stack of blank paper nearly as tall was piled at its side, awaiting words so it could graduate to the other. Beside them both was the antique journal in which he kept the notes for all his projects. She had found the old book for him a decade earlier in a small oceanside town. A relic of the past. Once belonging to the town scribe of some long-forgotten place, its cover was the softest of leathers, bound with thin wire.

Rachael frowned. It wasn't like him to leave the journal out like this—in fact, he rarely let it out of his sight, even for a short moment. Rachael had grown to think of it as his security blanket, his refuge from the world around him. He would spend hours at a time lost within its pages, his pen scribbling away, or sometimes just reading the faded ink of entries written long ago. Within those pages, he had found the fragments that had become his first bestseller. And now, nine novels later, his name topped the New York Times Bestsellers list again. As of yesterday, he was number one for the fourth week in a row.

Rachael knew his latest story had come from that journal, just like the others before.

From somewhere between its covers was the idea that had led to what the Chicago Tribune had called: "A masterpiece of nail-biting terror—*Diary* is a chilling glimpse into the mind of a madman eight hundred and sixty-three pages deep." He had shrugged off the write-up, not even bothering to finish reading the article. Instead, he had gone back to his office and lost himself in his current project, the journal at his side, the clicking of his keyboard shattering the stillness throughout the otherwise silent house.

It was a drug to him, it truly was.

Clickity, click, click, click... Rachael could hear the echo even now.

Clickity, click, click.

"Thad?" she uttered again, already knowing he was nowhere near.

He never left it alone... Never.

This started with that journal; it will end with that journal—that cursed antique.

The thought came into her mind as any other— seemingly fresh, although she knew in her heart it had been there for some time. Only now did she have the courage to face the truth. She never wanted to hurt him, not intentionally, but she had, she knew she had. She had hurt him in ways she couldn't even begin to explain.

Their lives were perfect. A fairy tale. She knew the truth, though, and it burned at her. Their perfect life hadn't been earned. It had been a trade, and the deal was concluding much too soon.

A deal she had made without him.

Rachael reached in and snatched the journal up without so much as a second thought, clutching it tightly against her chest.

Tonight it would end. She would make things right.

The air grew colder as she descended the stairs, carefully taking each step in the thick darkness, her bare feet shuffling across the cold, wooden steps. She came to the first landing and fell still when she heard something—her name crawling to her on the tail of the wind, a garbled voice, a snake's hiss. It had come from somewhere below.

Rachael.

The voice scratched at her.

What are you doing, Rachael?

A tingle raced across her spine and she pulled her robe tight at her neck, a feeble attempt to keep the frigid tendrils of cold air from slipping across her skin.

She grasped the journal tighter still, her knuckles turning white.

We had a deal, Rachael.

She wanted to answer, to shout out, to tell it she wasn't afraid, but when she opened her mouth her voice had abandoned her; only the slightest breath escaped her dry lips.

As she found her way down the remaining steps, the journal began to grow warm in her hands. It became hot, but she wouldn't let go. She couldn't.

Without warning or the touch of a match, the fireplace at the far end of the living room came to life. Angry flames reached halfway across the room, then pulled back with a violent roar, wrapping snugly around the few charred logs remaining from the previous night.

A deal, Rachael.

At first, Rachael shielded her eyes from the bright light but then forced herself to look, to stare into the searing red flames lapping greedily at the dark. She stared until her vision began to fill with tears, to burn, to pain her almost to the point of screaming.

She deserved to hurt.

She deserved to hurt for all she had done.

The spiral wire of the journal's binding cut at her hands as her grip tightened.

Rachael found herself approaching the fireplace, her eyes lost in the dancing flames.

His last book had come from the journal.

His last.

She would make this right.

With a deep breath Rachael threw it to the flames, flinching as they reached out, snatching it from the air. A searing heat flooded the room.

The eager fire licked at the leather binding, reaching around the journal with the hungry tongue of an unfed child, engulfing the pages within a muddled chaos of orange and red. The logs crackled and popped with excitement. Smoke bellowed forth, thick and dark, choking the surrounding air.

Then it was gone.

The hearth fell silent, filled only with the cold cinders of yesterday's burn.

She looked to her hands; Rachael found herself still holding the journal, her grasp so tight that a trickle of blood had begun to drip from where the wire binding had cut into her palm.

"I want what's mine," a woman's voice hissed from behind her.

Rachael turned to face her, the added weight of her unborn child causing her to stumble in the darkness. She grasped an end table to steady herself as her eyes found the form lurking among the shadows in the far corner of the room. The woman stepped back, slipping deeper into the dark. Rachael had no need to see her; she had seen her twice before—two times more than she wished she ever had.

The room had grown colder, filled with a numbing chill. Rachael tightened her robe, but it did little good.

"I want what's mine," the woman repeated, this time louder, angrier. Her face edged into the moonlight for one brief second, and Rachael found herself wanting so desperately to turn away, to turn from the hideous creature in the far corner, to turn away and forget what she had come down here to do, to forget it all. But she could not. She only stood still, shuddering as the voice crept up her spine. The woman sank back further, as if pained by the thin moonlight, retreating into the welcoming gloom.

Long, white fingernails protruded from her interlaced bony fingers. They made a clicking noise as she tapped them against each other at a nervous pitch.

A drop of saliva fell from her lips; it burned with a hiss as it touched the polished wood floor.

"I...I can't do it," Rachael stammered. "I can't."

The woman mumbled the angry words of a long-forgotten language, her coarse throat gritting each syllable as she spat it out. She uttered the last six words in quick succession. "The choice is no longer yours."

Rachael flinched as the journal dug deeper into her skin. She tried to drop it but found herself unable to let go.

"Three days," the woman told her. "And the child is mine."

Moonlight crept deeper into the room and the woman seemed to sink further into the corner, disappearing altogether in the night's grasp.

The fingernails remained, though, their wicked noise—

Clickity, click, click, click... It grew louder with each passing second.

Clickity, click, click... Much like her husband's typing.

A sudden pain filled her abdomen and Rachael buckled over, grabbing the edge of the doorframe. A loud moan escaped her lips.

She felt herself falling, falling.

The journal fell from her grip, quickly lost in the darkness beneath her.

I want what's mine.

"No!" she cried out, her voice lost in the surrounding ocean of murky black.

===

"Rachael? Are you okay?"

Short of breath, Rachael sat up in bed with a start, covered in sweat.

"Did the baby kick again?"

Disoriented, Rachael glanced around, her bedroom coming into focus through tear-filled eyes.

She was downstairs.

She was in the living room.

The journal, she had to find the journal.

"Oh God, you're bleeding—"

"What?" Rachael breathed.

"Your hand, it's bleeding...don't move..."

Thad jumped from the bed and bolted to the bathroom, returning with a moistened towel.

It was a dream...

It had all been a dream...

"Here," Thad said. "Let me see." He took her hand and began wiping away at the blood. "What did you do?"

"I...I don't know," she muttered. "Is it bad?"

Thad shook his head. "I don't think so; I think it's already stopped. There was just so much blood..."

Until now, she had fought the urge to look.

In the dimly-lit room, she raised her hand to the thin beam of moonlight trickling in from the window. She forced herself to examine the small red marks spanning

15

her palm from top to bottom, the trail leading from the base of her hand up through to her index finger, pink and swollen.

The pain came, and she winced.

"It's like a bunch of paper cuts," Thad stated, examining her wound in the light. "I'll see if I can find something to wrap it in—is the first aid kit still in the kitchen?"

Rachael nodded her head. "In the drawer next to the fridge."

Thad disappeared through the bedroom door, heading for the stairs.

From within her came the dull ache of the baby's kick—it had been kicking a lot lately. She wasn't the only one getting little rest tonight.

She reached for the sore spot, carefully massaging her belly just as the baby kicked again, this time even harder than before. "Shh," she told her child. "Rest now. You'll be getting out soon enough."

Outside, lightning flickered across the night sky; the gnarled hands of an ancient oak crept over the wall, a crazed shadow reaching with desperation into the room.

The clock beside the bed read 5:13 a.m.

It would be morning soon.

Rachael wanted it to be morning. She wanted that more than anything right now, but even as the clock changed to 5:14 a.m., the night seemed to close in tighter.

Her hand was throbbing now, and in the back of her mind she still felt the cold metal binder of her husband's journal biting at her. She still heard the strange clicking fingernails of the woman who had invaded her dream.

Rachael's heart pounded heavily within her chest.

Three days, the woman had said.

Three days.

Her good hand wrapped around her unborn child.

Thad came back into the room, wanting nothing more than to just help her, a silly grin across his face. "Okay, let the doctor work."

"You're so sweet," she said.

"You don't remember how you did this?"

She shook her head. "Maybe I got up in the middle of the night and cut it on something trying to steady myself. I've been so clumsy. I keep tripping over my own feet. My balance is all off. I feel like a giant Weeble."

"You look wonderful," he said, kissing her neck.

"I didn't mean to wake you."

He sighed. "I was already up. Tomorrow's trip, the book, the chance at another movie... My mind won't shut down long enough to sleep. If this deal plays out the way Del says it will, we'll be set. The numbers he's throwing around are ridiculous," he told her while dabbing at her hand with an alcohol-soaked ball of cotton. "We can sell this place and upgrade. It's time, right? A mansion in L.A., maybe an old Victorian on the cliffs of Maine overlooking the ocean. Maybe both. Whatever we want, wherever we want...no limits."

Setting the cotton aside, he picked up a roll of gauze and began wrapping it around her hand. "Nothing but the best schools for Ashley and the baby," he went on. "When we first met, I told you I'd give you the world. Now it's all ours, prime for the taking."

She forced a smile. "I'm so proud of you."

Cutting the gauze, he taped the end and held her hand up to his lips, gently kissing it. "I couldn't have done any of it without you."

CHAPTER TWO
Day 1 – 5:30 a.m.

CARVER STEPPED FROM HIS van into the thick rain and lifted his gaze to the cloud-filled dawn. "My, oh my, what a wonderful day!" he exclaimed quietly, shielding his eyes. "What a wonderful day, indeed!"

He had driven straight from Maine, and his tired old frame was aching to stretch.

The McAlister house stood in silence before him, dark and lost behind the weather. Only the light of one second-floor window crept out across the dissipating night. "Good morning, McAlisters," he smiled.

Reaching back into the van, he pulled out a small glass jar and a garden shovel from the side compartment before quietly closing the door and locking it in place.

Carver glanced both directions down the winding

road. When satisfied he was alone, he crossed their lawn with a shuffle, favoring his bad leg.

He reached the old oak and ran his hands over the thick bark. "You are a tired soul, aren't you? Hundreds of years under that belt of yours."

Carver knelt at the base of the tree and dug a hole about six inches wide and twelve deep, then reached for the jar at his side. He removed the lid and poured out the contents.

"Eko, Eko, Azarak,

Eko, Eko, Zomelak,

Eko, Eko, Cernunnos,

Eko, Eko, Aradia,

Zod ru koz e zod ru."

The white powder glowed for a brief second before it absorbed into the earth. Carver replaced the soil, rose to his feet, and wiped his hands on his jeans. "Keep her safe, my little friends," he said, and ambled back to his van. He eased into the driver's seat, tossed the empty jar and shovel into the rear, and picked up his phone, pressing the speed dial button.

The line rang twice before a woman picked up. "Is it done?" she asked.

"You bet," Carver told her.

He disconnected the call, started the van, and drove off into the morning gloom, whistling quietly to himself.

CHAPTER THREE
1692
The Journal of Clayton Stone

*T*HE DAY BEGAN DARK. *Thick gray clouds rumbled low in the sky; the air was heavy and quiet. The stillness nipped at my bones, creating an ache from deep within. Pulling the collar of my coat tight around my neck, I quickly shuffled across the cobblestone square to the church. Its doors were opened to the morning, yet darkness swelled inside.*

Thoughts of returning home entered my mind; I missed the warmth of my bed. I am not denying that such thoughts came to me, but I did not return. Instead, I crossed the square to the chapel's mouth, pausing at the font; the holy water was icy against my skin.

"We expected you earlier," a voice grumbled to my right.

I turned and studied the figure in the dim light. "Your

Magistrate," I said with a slight bow. "The hour is young enough for the likes of me."

"Sleep eluded me, I'm afraid. Thoughts of today's trial weigh far too heavy on my mind," he replied. "Come. I'll show you to your seat."

My eyes adjusted to the light as we walked through a dark corridor and entered the nave. He pointed me to a small table to the left of a desk that had been placed beside the pulpit for the magistrate. "We will begin shortly. Please make yourself comfortable."

The gallery filled quickly. Faces known to me all my life entered in nervous silence, finding seats beside loved ones and neighbors. I nodded hellos to those who passed while noting their names in the official log. When the magistrate reentered the room, he was wearing his wig and robe. The town elders followed, each taking their seats at the high altar.

Together, we then waited.

Waited for her to arrive as the morning fog burned away.

—Thad McAlister,
Rise of the Witch

CHAPTER FOUR

Day 1 – 7:00 a.m.

"**WHY CAN'T YOU STAY** home, Daddy? I don't want you to leave," Ashley pouted, scooping up a spoonful of soggy Lucky Charms and leaving a prominent trail of milk on the kitchen table. "And it's Sunday. You are not allowed to go anywhere on Sunday. That's the rule."

Thad had made a point of getting up early this morning, as he did every Sunday. Sunday was father/daughter day in the McAlister household—a tradition he cherished deep in his heart. At eight years old, she was growing up so fast. He wanted to preserve each moment, capturing them in a jar he could open years from now to relive.

They had a little game. Every Sunday, the last one out of bed made breakfast for the other (always a bowl of cereal—Lucky Charms being his daughter's current entrée of choice). The winner would get to choose the activity for the day. Reading, playing a game, or watching TV—it didn't matter; only that they did it together. He had grown up without the love of his parents; he never wanted his daughter to know the emptiness he carried inside. She simply meant too much to him.

Thad had gotten up at a little after six (not that he was able to sleep after Rachael's nightmare last night), and quietly made his way downstairs like a child on Christmas morning. He tiptoed past his daughter's door, pausing to take a wide step over the third stair (which always creaked) before descending down the remainder to the first floor.

He found Ashley wide awake and planted at the kitchen table, browsing through the comics like an investor might hover over yesterday's market activity.

Her face grew brighter still at the sight of him. He couldn't help but smile back—his little angel.

I beat you again, she had said with a laugh.

I beat you again, sleepyhead!

Thad didn't remember the last time he had actually won their little game. Sometimes he wondered if she slept at all.

Last night when he had told her he had to go to New York, she hadn't taken the news well and he considered backing out of the trip before dismissing the thought. He had too much riding on it. With the new book came a new contract and most likely a film deal; his third, if this one panned out. It was a turning point in his career, one that would surely seal his place among some of the best writers in the business. Sure, the money was great; but to be thought of on the same level as Stephen King, Dean Koontz, or Jack Stevenson—that's what he had always wanted.

The new contract spanned five books; he already had three written—a fact he had carefully omitted while speaking to Del Thomas, his agent. He had learned early on to keep him wondering when (and if) the next book would come; he then worked the one he had in his hands as his last, squeezing every drop of blood from the project. Three finished books with any agent might make them soft. Thad wanted him at his best—one hundred and ten percent, as Coach Johnson used to say back in his high school football days.

Every game's the Super Bowl, dammit!

Play to win or warm the bench…

Del Thomas did not warm the bench; he had scored some of the most lucrative deals in the industry over the past few years, but Thad didn't believe in letting others run his career. When Del had said he was going to be in New York to finalize the film rights, Thad had to be there— even on Sunday—not to step on anybody's toes but to keep them on theirs.

He had wanted to deliver the new book in person anyway. He didn't trust e-mail or the post office.

To date, he hadn't allowed anyone to read this one, not a single page—not Del, not his wife, and certainly not his publisher, but not because the novel was not ready to be read. No, that wasn't it at all. The story was too disturbing to be read.

In all of his years as a writer, Thad had never found himself reluctant to share something he had worked so hard to complete. Even now, as the finished manuscript rested comfortably in his briefcase, he couldn't help but consider replacing the tome with one of the other three he had on standby. Who would know?

He would.

He would know.

This book deserved to be published—no, *needed* to be published.

The book was filled with his sweat, his time, his life, his fears. *His fears*—what an understatement. The lead character represented what he feared most, what crept through the darkest corners of his mind, the crispy little voice he heard when alone, the bump in so many sleepless nights. He had to publish this one, put it behind him. How else could he possibly move on with his life?

He had written many stories in the past, but no other had frightened him so. Only Her story kept him up at night.

"If you stay, I'll clean my room," Ashley interrupted his thoughts, her big blue eyes staring up at him. "I promise I will." She had milk trickling down her chin and Thad couldn't help but laugh.

"I wouldn't tell your mother; she seems to be under the impression you're supposed to clean your room anyway," Thad said, running his hand through her soft blond hair. "I'd stay home if I could, sweetheart, but some very important people want to talk to me about making a movie out of one of my books. You like movies, right?"

She nodded.

"I'll make it up to you. I promise," he told her. "What do you have planned for your daddy-free day?"

Ashley shrugged her little shoulders. "I wanted to go to the zoo, but Zeke thinks it's gonna rain."

"Oh he does, does he?"

She nodded. "The zoo is no fun in the rain. All the animals hide and the smells are really bad."

Zeke was his daughter's invisible friend.

From the start, Rachael had discouraged their daughter from talking to or about Zeke at every opportunity, but Thad had always been a firm believer in invisible friends; God knew he had had his share growing up. He saw Zeke as nothing more than a way for her to express her emotions through a redirected source (a definition he had proudly stumbled upon in one of his many pop-psychology books). Imaginary friends were healthy and normal (the same book told him). Rachael felt otherwise but had kept it to herself, hoping Ashley would grow out of this phase (sooner rather than later, Thad imagined). Thad also had a sneaking suspicion Rachael was more upset over the fact their daughter's little friend was a boy instead of a girl. He had told her once this too was common (same library, different book), but she didn't want to hear it.

"So how's ol' Zeke doing these days?" Thad asked her.

"I wouldn't know," she replied in her big-girl voice. "We're not speaking today."

"But he told you about the rain today?"

"I'm not speaking to *him*," she said with a frown.

"And why's that?"

"Because he was being mean last night. He was making all kinds of noise and would not let me sleep," she said. "It was all very rude, if you ask me."

Thad chuckled. "Why wouldn't Zeke want you to sleep?"

Ashley frowned. "I don't know. Maybe he was scared of the thunder and didn't want to be alone."

"That was quite a storm last night."

She nodded.

"Lots of thunder and lightning."

She nodded again.

"The wind howled, too. It sounded like an old dog—awrooo, awrooooo." Thad hopped off his chair and padded over to her on all fours. "Awrooooo," he moaned.

"Ashley, why don't you let your father out? I think he has to go," Rachael said as she waddled into the kitchen, her hand wrapped around her round tummy, her eyes on the coffee she couldn't have.

Ashley giggled. "I'm in charge of Buster. Daddy belongs to you!"

"Wanna trade?" Rachael replied, pretending to scratch Thad behind the ear.

Buster came bouncing into the room and went straight for Thad, slobbering all over his face—it wasn't often they were on the same level, and he didn't seem willing to pass up the opportunity.

"Buster, stop—" Thad cried, trying to turn away. "That's gross!"

"He luuuves you!" Ashley clapped her hands.

"Come on, Buster—you wanna go outside?" Rachael asked.

Buster's tail excitedly flapped back and forth as he scrambled to the back door, his nails clicking loudly on the wood floor.

"Come on, Buster!" Rachael repeated, reaching for the lock. The heavy door squeaked on its hinges. A rush of damp air filled the kitchen. Damp air and—

Buster came to a stop at the opening and tensed. A soft whimper escaped his throat. His tail dropped between his legs and he slowly backed away.

"Buster, what's wrong?" Ashley asked him.

The dog fell silent.

"Thad, come here. Look at this," Rachael said, staring outside.

Thad rose to a stand and made his way over to the door; his wife's hand found his as he reached her side.

"What happened?"

Thad stepped out. His wife reluctantly released him from her grip, remaining just inside the threshold.

Their entire lawn was dead.

Every single strand of grass.

His stomach twisted as the scent crept into his lungs.

Not only dead; their lawn was rotten.

"Could it have been the cold?" Rachael asked him.

Thad shook his head. "I don't think we dropped below fifty last night—cold can't do this, not overnight, at least," he told her.

"Look over there—" She pointed at the Nelson's house.

Thad noticed, too.

Their lawn was dead, and only their lawn. The Nelson's, the Gargano's, and the Barstoke's beyond them, all were untouched. Only theirs. Not just the lawn, either. The large oak which had towered over their home for years was dark and bare, leaves dry and brown, lying lifeless at its base. Thad didn't need to inspect the tree up close to know the branches were brittle with death—he could smell the rot from here.

"What happened, Daddy?" Ashley said.

"Why don't you wait inside, honey?" he asked, his eyes following the strange line of death, which seemed to end directly at their property's edge. "I'll be right in."

He shook his head. "I watered yesterday. Everything looked damn near perfect—I don't get it," he mumbled.

"Maybe you should come back inside," Rachael said.

"Give me a minute."

"What if it's some kind of poison?" she asked him. "I don't want you to get sick."

"I don't think. . ." Thad's voice trailed off as he knelt down and ran his hand through a small pile of dirt.

He saw another to his left, and another a few feet beyond the first. As he scanned the lawn, he realized they were everywhere.

They smelled of rot and decay.

"Thad, please. . ."

He finally stood and made his way back to the door, carefully stepping over the strange piles. "Maybe call Jeff? I think we should have him come out and take a look."

"He'll blame us," she replied. "Remember when I planted those lilacs on the west side of the house instead of the east? I got a three-hour lecture on the effects of evening sunlight."

Thad shrugged. "It's his job, Rachael. Maybe he can figure out what happened. Try to keep Ashley and Buster out of the yard until we know everything is safe."

"What about when he needs to use the bathroom?"

"Toilet training for Buster!" Ashley sang.

He gestured to the newspaper. "Remember when he was a puppy?"

She frowned. "Oh boy. This is going to be a fun day."

"Mommy, you teach him to get up on the seat and I'll show him how to flush," Ashley suggested.

"See, she's got a plan." A horn beeped outside and Thad glanced down at his watch. "Crap, my cab's here. Are you okay dealing with this?"

She nodded, wrapping her arms around him. "I'll figure something out."

Thad gave her a peck on the cheek and rubbed her belly. "How's he doing?"

"*She's* doing fine," his wife retorted. "Kicking like a champ."

"I hate leaving like this but this is a huge opportunity, for both of us," Thad said.

"Did you pack your meds?" she asked.

"I haven't needed them for months. I'm fine," he snapped.

She squeezed his arm. "I'll feel better knowing you have it with you, just in case. Do you?"

His eyes met hers and held them. "In my bag. I have an appointment next week with Doctor Horton, and I'm going to ask him to take me off. I don't need it anymore and it keeps me from writing. Shuts off the creativity like a breaker switch. I don't think I ever needed to be on that stuff."

"I only want you to be okay."

He gave her a gentle hug. "I'm fine. I'm more worried about you. Promise you'll play nice with Carmen?"

She sighed. "Ah yes, Carmen."

They had been searching for a live-in housekeeper for months without success. Thad had lost count of the various candidates who had passed through their front door. Even with the help of an agency, finding someone with the right amount of experience and skill was tough. Personality clashes and language barriers further complicated the task.

How do you trust a stranger to take care of your family?

Carmen Perez had a spotless résumé and an extensive list of references, perhaps the best of the bunch, but unfortunately Ashley had not taken to her and she made

Rachael uneasy, even though she had been with them for nearly three weeks now.

Thad ran his hand through his wife's hair. "I don't want the two of you to be alone, not with the baby this close. Deal with her a few more days? I've got the agency working on a replacement."

Rachael nodded. "I'm not sure what specifically bothers me about her; something just feels off."

He kissed her forehead. "We'll find someone, I promise. Don't run her off until I get back. I'll sleep better knowing you have her here."

"No need to worry, Daddy. I'll take excellent care of her," Ashley told him, hugging his leg.

Thad lifted her off the ground. "You do that, Pumpkin. I love you both lots and lots!" Twirling her around twice, he placed her back in her chair. "I hope you work things out with Zeke," he said softly at her ear. "I hate when you kids fight."

Rachael frowned. "Come on, Thad."

The horn beeped again with an impatient double tap.

"I've got to go." Scooping up his briefcase and overnight bag, Thad headed for the door. "I'll call you tonight from the city—I wanna hear how things went at the doctor."

"Bye, honey. I love you," Rachael told him.

Within her belly, the baby kicked.

A stale scent crept past her from outside as Thad raced toward the awaiting taxi.

Buster whimpered, eyeing the yard nervously.

33

CHAPTER FIVE
Day 1 – 11:00 a.m.

RACHAEL PULLED THE THIN gown tight at her neck and shivered.

Why does it always have to be so cold in here? she asked herself.

Sitting on the aluminum table with nothing more than a flimsy paper covering didn't help much, either. Rachael shifted a little to her left and let out a sigh.

She had been waiting on the doctor for almost twenty minutes in the small examination room—it never took this long and she had so much to do today. She reached for another pamphlet from the rack beside her and flipped through "Your Normal Life With Herpes." It was almost as entertaining as the three-month-old *People* magazine she had finished a few minutes ago.

Rachael was grabbing at yet another pamphlet when Dr. Roskin poked his head through the door.

"So, how's my favorite mother-to-be doing?"

Her frustrations disappeared at the sight of him. (She had grown quite accustomed to sudden mood changes over the past eight months.)

She had known Dr. Edward Roskin for nearly nine years and couldn't imagine someone else caring for her. He had delivered Ashley, and the moment she knew she was pregnant again Rachael was certain he would be delivering this one, too.

He was an odd-looking man—short and overweight, with pink rosy cheeks and a pudgy face. He reminded her of a mall Santa who had forgotten his fake beard and mustache back at the North Pole. His thin wire glasses never seemed to stay where he wanted them; even now he was pushing them back up the bridge of his nose only to repeat the process again a moment later when they slipped back down.

"He's been kicking up a storm lately," Rachael exclaimed.

Dr. Roskin grinned at her. "What makes you think you've got a boy?"

"A girl?" Rachael beamed.

The doctor smiled. "My lips are sealed."

He placed a stethoscope under her gown. Rachael tensed as the cold metal found her skin.

"Now relax and breathe deeply," he told her.

Rachael did as he asked.

"Want to see what she looks like?" he asked.

"She?"

Roskin chuckled. "Or he."

"You're worse than Thad," Rachael laughed.

"How is Thad doing?" he asked her while tugging at the ultrasound, pulling the machine closer to the table.

"He's good. He wanted to be here today but had to go to New York again to wrap up a few things on the new book," Rachael said.

The doctor let out a sigh. "Oh boy. Just when you thought it was safe to go back in the bookstore…"

Rachael laughed. "He's really proud of this one—thinks it's his scariest one yet."

"I'm still trying to get a good night's sleep after reading the last one. I can't bring myself to go down to my basement anymore, either. He spooked me with that ending. I make Liddy do all the dirty work down there."

"Don't feel bad; I haven't been down in ours for about three months—he's got the whole floor stuffed full of props he stole from his last movie set. We've even got our very own coffin down there somewhere."

"Now that's something no home should be without," Roskin pointed out, fumbling with his glasses.

One of Dr. Roskin's nurses stepped into the room and nodded a hello, then opened Rachael's gown, exposing her belly. She applied a thin layer of jelly.

The doctor went on. "What about you? Are you sleeping well?"

Rachael nodded, even though it was a lie; she hadn't slept well in months. How did he know? Was there something in her eyes?

"Are you eating well? No cravings for ice cream with a little motor oil or a nice jar of Vick's Vapor Rub with your morning toast?"

Rachael laughed. "You're kidding, right?"

He shook his head. "I had another patient in here the day before yesterday. She's on her fourth child and can't get enough of the stuff. Some expecting mothers tend to crave oil-based products every once in a while; it's fairly common. As you can imagine, not a very healthy dietary choice."

Rachael turned to the nurse. "He's not for real, is he?"

The nurse shrugged her shoulders, fighting back a smile.

"I kid you not," he told her. "Nurse Korbin, can you please switch on the ultrasound?"

Dr. Roskin placed the sensor on her belly and gently moved the device around, staring at the monitor. The soft sound of a heartbeat filled the room. "There he is," the doctor said.

"Or she," echoed the nurse.

Rachael rolled her eyes. "Oh God."

He began working the ultrasound around in slow, tight circles until a white object appeared.

Rachael smiled at her baby.

"Looks good," the doctor said. "Two feet, two hands, all twelve toes. He's a little large for thirty-six weeks, but that's nothing to worry about."

"Just pump me full of drugs when he's ready to come out and we'll all get along fine," Rachael stated.

"Not a fan of natural child birth?" he asked.

Rachael shook her head. "I got enough of that with the first one. This time I don't even want to know what's going on down there. Hand me a healthy baby when this is all over, and I'll be fine."

The doctor smiled. "No reason we can't do that." Reaching back, he flicked off the ultrasound machine. "Why don't you go ahead and get cleaned up and dressed? We'll set you up with some more vitamins and send you on your way. Nurse Korbin, mind giving Mrs. McAlister here a hand?"

"Not at all, Doctor," she replied, already wiping away the remaining jelly.

Deep within Rachael's belly, the baby kicked.

CHAPTER SIX

1692

The Journal of Clayton Stone

I **HEARD THE SHACKLES** before I saw her. So did the others, evidenced by the hush which filled the small church. As they led her into the room, all eyes fell upon her. She looked so small and frail, her tiny frame hunched over, her flowing dark hair draping her face, long enough to near-ly reach her hands bound at her waist. Her clothing was tattered and torn, borne of the jailer's filth. She had been imprisoned for five nights now, guarded at all hours by both armed men and men of faith. Not only for fear of her but also those who followed her. To this day they remained un-known, safely hidden among us, her faithful ready to free her at the first chance. Glancing around the small church, I imagined them here now, here in numbers. The hunt for her sisters proved to be ongoing. Some believed they had fled, *somehow finding passage back to the Old World, but something told me they were still close, unwilling to abandon their blood.*

I had been told not a word had escaped her lips since capture, even though the use of torture was suspect on each of her nights. She admitted to none of her crimes, nor had she denied. In fact, it is rumored that she had laughed at the magistrate throughout, unwilling to show even the slightest weakness. Now as they led her to a bench at the front of the assembly, shackling her securely to the seat, I found it clear she walked with her head down not out of shame but only because of the restraints. This proved true, for when the men finished binding her and stepped back, she raised her head and glared at the crowd from behind piercing blue eyes and the angelic smile of a teenage girl.

—Thad McAlister,
Rise of the Witch

CHAPTER SEVEN
Day 1 – 3:27 p.m.

THAD SOMETIMES THOUGHT HE missed the city, but those feelings seemed to disappear the moment he set foot back in New York. The moment he stepped off the plane, the smog and pollution crept into his lungs. It brought on a coughing fit matched only by the older gentleman who had been sitting three rows behind him. Ten minutes later, his asthma began dropping hints that it may be time for a long overdue comeback. Thad wanted nothing more than to crawl back onto the 737 and fly it home all by himself, if he had to.

The overcrowded terminal did little to ease his tension. An overweight businessman almost knocked him over when reaching for his luggage on the conveyor belt, while an elderly woman took it upon herself to tell him of the city's fortunes.

"You must visit the Statue of Liberty while you're here," she said. "And the museums, you mustn't forget about the museums—they're world famous, you know. People come from all around..."

Thad had politely dismissed her back at the terminal, but now she had somehow ended up back at his side while waiting for her bags.

"Do you have family here?" she asked him. "I have a son about your age; he lives in Philly now. Him and that hussy, Krista or Kristi—it's all the same to me. She told my boy she was on the pill and wouldn't you know, five months later she's crying at our front door, telling me how my boy did this to her and she needs a man in her life to help her raise the damn thing. Well, we raised our son good, George and I, so he knew what he had to do. George was one lucky fella; he wasn't around to see all this, he died back in '98... Cancer from the asbestos in the buildings. He worked in construction..."

When his bag came around, Thad scooped it up and nodded politely before briskly walking toward the taxi stands outside. Behind him, the old woman went on. Not until the thick glass doors closed automatically at his back did he finally escape her.

The crowd surrounding the taxi cabs pushed forward like one large snail across the earth. Thad found himself in a line more than eighty deep, moving with the group toward the awaiting cars with little sense of urgency. He tightened his grip on his briefcase and pressed forward, his mind attempting to monitor the wallet in his back pocket and the cell phone in his jacket—both of which were ripe targets for the many pickpockets who undoubtedly made a living on this sidewalk.

Twenty minutes later, he climbed into a cab with his bag in tow and instructed the driver to take him to the Four Seasons on the Upper East Side.

Reaching into his jacket pocket, he pulled out his iPhone and pressed the power button, thankful for the couple hours of call-free time he had been granted while aboard the flight from Charleston.

No voicemails, no texts (yet another reason to give thanks). He paused for a moment, then dialed home. When he heard the steady tone of a busy signal, he disconnected the call and dropped the phone back in his pocket. *That's odd.* He couldn't recall the last time he had heard a busy signal. He'd try again later, maybe from a landline.

He rested his briefcase on his lap and settled his hands on top.

He could almost feel the manuscript inside, as if the stack of papers were somehow generating heat, a heartbeat. This was his greatest work; he had no doubts. This novel would define him; he would be remembered long after he was gone, thanks to this book.

Each page had flowed from the last with no editing to speak of. No rewrites, no drafts. It just poured from him.

There was no other way to describe it.

Poured.

He had watched the basket beside his laptop fill up like a glass of water under the tap, quick and steady without pause, until he laid down the final sheet bearing the two last words.

With that, the nightmares had stopped.

For almost a decade, She had haunted his dreams with her scarred face, guttural voice, and nails like long blades.

Clickity, click, click, click.

Even now, in the back of a cab bathed in daylight, the thought of that sound made his heart race.

Clickity, click, click.

The manuscript seemed to pulsate with heat.

He would share Her with the world.

Her.

He still couldn't bring himself to speak her true name aloud. Some might find that funny; he did not.

They pulled into the Four Seasons and Thad glanced down at his watch. He would have just enough time for a quick shower before his dinner meeting with Del and the production company on this day of days.

CHAPTER EIGHT

Day 1 – 4:32 p.m.

RACHAEL NODDED WORRIEDLY, STARING out across their dead lawn.

"I can't put my finger on it," Jeff Paskin said, scratching his head. "You say it was just like this when you got up this mornin'? No waterin' with chemicals or fertilizers from one of them depot stores?"

"Nope," Rachael said. "I swear, Jeff, we didn't touch anything."

"What about the sprinklers?"

"They've been running every other evening since you programmed them," she assured him.

Kneeling down, he scooped up one of the mounds of dirt, sniffed, then dumped the soil in a glass masonry jar. "Smells like roadkill…dirty."

"Like dirt?"

Paskin shook his head. "Not like dirt. Like something else, something filthy."

"What do you think they are, those piles?" Rachael asked. "I don't see any holes. Where did it all come from?"

"Beats the hell out of me," he said. "I've never seen anything like this."

"Could the water be bad?"

"Doubtful," he replied. "You've got city water; if that were contaminated, they'd be talking all over the news—boiling rules and whatnot. Nope, this is something different. Got to be some kind of poisoning, but I can't put my finger on the cause. You do anything to piss off the neighbors?"

"I hope you're kidding," Rachael frowned.

"Yes, ma'am."

The wind kicked up and Rachael wrapped her arms around herself, brushing off a shiver.

"You'd better get back inside; it's a little chilly out here for a woman in your condition. I'll get to the bottom of this," he said, holding up the jar to the sun for a moment before sealing the contents inside with a metal cap. "Meanwhile, I wouldn't walk barefoot out here or let your little one play outside. The dog neither, not until we know what we're dealing with."

Rachael glanced at the large oak in the corner of the yard, branches now dry and bare. "What about the tree? Can it be saved?"

"Dunno, not yet, anyway," he told her. "Once we get the soil sample back, we'll have a better idea. Don't hold your breath, though. That old lass looks pretty far gone and if she ain't gonna live, we need to cut her down quick. A big tree like that can be dangerous once she goes. I've seen them topple right on over."

"I can't believe this," Rachael told him. "Everything was fine yesterday."

Paskin threw the rest of his tools back into his truck and climbed into the cab, slamming the rusty door behind him. "Don't worry, Mrs. McAlister. I'll take good care of you. We'll find a way to fix this. You stay well now."

Rachael watched the old Ford pickup lumber down their long driveway and disappear down Border Road, heading in the direction of Dover. Behind her, Buster stood at the large picture window, his furry paws pressed against the glass, his tail wagging nervously at his back.

"I know how you feel, boy," she frowned.

CHAPTER NINE

The Journal of Clayton Stone

REVEREND DEODAT LAWSON, A visiting preacher, delivered the opening prayer. I could not help but gaze upon those around me, their eyes down or closed, some watching her with hate and fear, few actually taking in the reverend's words. When he concluded, he asked the congregation to join him in a psalm. It was then that Abigail Williams interrupted. "Now, there is enough of that." She pointed to a rat, which scurried across a beam high above them. "Her familiar is here; I imagine the spirits of her sisters are here, too. We must get on with it." Around her, the afflicted and their loved ones rattled in agreement, their voices growing from a hush to that of an angered mob in mere moments.

"Enough!" Constable Joseph Herrick shouted above them.

"Pray give me leave to go to prayer," the girl breathed her first words since capture, bringing the congregation to silence. *The court tried to ignore her request but she insisted, this time facing the magistrate directly.*

"We did not bring you here to go to prayer," Tauber replied, *"but to tell us why you hurt these children of God."* He gestured around the room, his bony finger landing on the afflicted, her accusers.

"I am an innocent person, as are my sisters. I have never had anything to do with witchcraft since I was born. I am a woman of gospel."

"Have you not witnessed their complaints?"

"The Lord open the eyes of the magistrate and minister," she commanded. *"The Lord show His power to discover the guilty."*

"If you would expect mercy of God," he told her, *"you must look for it in God's way, by confession."*

"You are a righteous, educated man. You should not believe these persons."

Tauber was in no mood to have her advise him. *"Did you not say our eyes were blinded, you would open them?"*

"You accuse the innocent. Your behavior is blindness indeed," she said.

"Yet they swear by their statements, these people of God."

She shrugged her shoulders. *"What can I do? Many rise up against me for no reason other than spite. Abigail herself has told others how she longed for beauty such as mine. Her jealousy is mindful whenever she gazes upon me."*

"That is not true!" Abigail shouted out.

"Clearly, the magistrate believes so. His fingers searched my bare skin for marks of the devil with the pleasure of a man many years his younger." She smiled up at him.

"Enough of this!" he ordered with strength enough to send her back into her chair. "Do not you believe witches are in this country?"

She smiled. "I have not made their acquaintance."

He ordered her to stop biting her lip, for the afflicted were now suggestible to her every move, some clearly chewing their own lips.

"What harm is there in it?" she asked.

But if she clenched her hands, her alleged victims felt it—and showed the bruises. If she slumped forward against the seat that served as a bar, they bore pain from that, too. When she shifted her feet, the afflicted stamped thunderously like helpless puppets. Again, she smiled.

"She dares practice witchcraft in the congregation?" Reverend Lawson proclaimed in amazement. "Tighten her bonds and put an end to this," he ordered.

I watched as Constable Herrick hurried over and tied her ankles to the chair legs and her wrists to the wooden arms. The rope was wrapped so tight her skin became pale. I feared for her, yet she seemed unfazed. Instead, the pain appeared to bring her strength. She glared out at the afflicted from behind those dark blue eyes, a hatred burning into them. It was clear they wanted to turn away, but simply did not. I also found myself unable to take my gaze from her, her image truly bewitching, intoxicating.

Although he tried to hide such, fear filled Tauber's face.

"*Who is your God?*" *he asked bluntly, knowing as well as anyone that witches worshipped Satan.*

"*The God who made me,*" *she countered.*

Although her hands were bound, she snapped her long nails against each other in such an incessant rhythm. I heard nothing else.

Clickity, click, click.

—Thad McAlister,
Rise of the Witch

CHAPTER TEN
Day 1 – 5:00 p.m.

"**HEY, DEL!**" **THAD SAID**, extending his hand across the table.

"Sorry we're late, Thad. Traffic in this city can be brutal this time of day, and our driver seemed to have a knack for picking the worst possible route to virtually every destination," the heavyset man told him with an apologetic look in his eyes. Nodding to his left, he said, "I'd like you to meet Roger Burstein. He's with Foundry Pictures."

"No worries," Thad told him. "I got here a few minutes ago." He gestured to the empty table. "Gentlemen, please make yourselves comfortable."

Del maneuvered his large frame into a chair and unbuttoned his dark gray coat. "Burstein here bugged the hell out of me for the past week to get to this table—something about wanting first shot at making your latest stack of scribble into one of those moving pictures the kids are so fond of these days. What do you think? Should we hear him out?"

Thad had known Del Thomas for the better part of a decade; he was never one to be subtle. "I don't think it would hurt to hear what he has to offer."

"I appreciate that, Mr. McAlister," Mr. Burstein said. "I promise I won't waste your time."

"Ah, famous last words," Del cracked.

The waitress arrived a moment later and took their drink orders, then proceeded to recite the catch and soup of the day before handing them menus and disappearing into the kitchen.

"She's a cutie," Del said. "Think she's into balding fat guys with heart conditions?"

"I'd tell you yes, but I decided a long time ago I wouldn't spin fiction unless I could sell it," Thad joked.

"I like you better when you're locked in your little office making me money."

"Ah," Thad said. "The truth finally comes out."

Across the table, Roger Burstein took a drink of water, the glass shaking in his hand. He was drumming the fingers of his left hand on the top of his briefcase.

Thad had a rather uncomfortable relationship with the movie studios, one that had clearly been reported to this man prior to his being dispatched. Of the three film adaptations of his novels, none had lived up to his expectations—the first, *Wicked Ways*, didn't resemble the original story at all. By the time the story made its way to film, his vision had been hacked, re-edited, and rewritten so many times by more hands than he could count—all of them opting for shock value rather than holding true to the story. They wanted a big box office on a low budget and cared about nothing other than getting a film out before the hype surrounding the best-selling novel petered out. Thad had watched the premiere with his wife in total disgust, vowing never to sell film rights again unless he had some form of creative control. For the next two movies, he had been on set each day and personally approved all script changes, ensuring they held true to the novel and the screenplay he had also insisted on drafting. While these films didn't possess the box office draw of the first, they lived up to the story and his true fans had been pleased.

"You know I'll want total creative control, right?" Thad told Burstein point-blank, watching the man's eyes for a reaction.

Burstein cleared his throat. "We assumed as much," he said. "Based on your history, I wouldn't expect anything less."

"Do you have a director in mind?"

Opening his briefcase, the man reached inside and retrieved a sheet of manila paper. After a quick review, he handed the page to Thad. "It's a rather short list. We started with the people you expressed an interest in working with on the last one, then narrowed them down to the few who will be available based on a preliminary production schedule."

"You have a production schedule already?" Del mused. "Aren't you jumping the gun a little? Hell, you haven't read it yet. What if the book is shit?"

Burstein forced a nervous smile. "We want you to know how serious we are about this project. We want to time the film release with the paperback in roughly nine months, which doesn't allow much time for preparation."

"I don't want to rush this, Del," Thad told his agent.

"And you won't have to," Burstein fired back before Del Thomas could reply. "We'll work with you at your own pace, even if it means missing the paperback release—that just happens to be an ideal release date."

"What kind of money are we talking about?" Del broke in.

"Not everything's about money, Del," Thad countered.

Del smirked. "Don't kid yourself, Thad. It's always about money."

"We're prepared to offer you four million for the screenplay and film rights, along with points on the back end," Burstein replied.

Thad had never received points before, but he understood how lucrative they could be. On his last film, he had been paid one million for the screenplay and film rights, which he thought was pretty good considering the one before that only paid two hundred thousand. However, the film had gone on to make nearly forty-five million in box office and DVD sales. If he had received points, he would have stood to make nearly six million more than he had. At this stage in his career, he had been prepared to forego up-front-money in order to get a portion of the profits. He wasn't expecting to receive both—four million plus points was much more than he had ever anticipated.

"Seven million plus points," Del shot back. "We all know this picture is going to make at least fifty million based on the performance of Thad's previous three films. Hell, we may even hit sixty million. The publisher is planning one of the largest print productions for a work of fiction in the past decade. Thad's e-book sales are through the roof. At seven plus points, you're still stealing this deal."

Burstein fell silent for a moment, his hands once again drumming the top of his briefcase. "I'm prepared to go as high as five million, but that's the best I can do."

Del shook his head and placed his napkin on his lap as the waitress arrived with their drinks. "Well, Mr. Burstein. I suggest you enjoy your meal today, because the only thing you're going to see us sign is the credit card receipt."

"This is a very good offer," Burstein told him.

"I agree," Del replied. "But it's not the most lucrative offer we're entertaining right now, and frankly I don't feel like playing Let's Make a Deal. You've got our terms; if you can't match them, I'm afraid our business today is over." To the waitress, he said, "I think I'll go with the clam chowder—I've been craving seafood all day. Thad, what'll you have?"

Thad stared at him for a moment before breaking out of his reverie. "Ah, yeah, I think I'll get a sirloin; medium-well, please."

The waitress eyed Burstein, whose face was bright red as he held back his anger. "The sirloin is fine. Rare, please," he told her. Turning to Thad, he said, "Excuse me, gentlemen. I need to make a call."

With cell phone in hand, he left the table and hurried to the lobby.

The waitress picked up their menus, told them someone would return momentarily with their salads, then disappeared toward the kitchen.

"Del, are you high?" Thad exclaimed. "That man's head is going to explode! You don't really think we can get seven million plus points, do you?"

Del shook his head. "Naw, we're going to get six. If this guy can't cough it up, I'm sure somebody else will. Don't you read the trades? You're holding the most anticipated manuscript of the decade in that briefcase of yours."

"Christ," Thad replied. "I need a drink."

"We'll make it a celebratory toast when this guy signs on the dotted line," Del told him, nodding toward Burstein, who was pacing the sidewalk just outside the restaurant now, his cell phone pressed firmly against his ear.

Less than a decade ago, he had been holding down two part-time jobs while trying to draft his first book. In his wildest dreams, he couldn't have possibly imagined…

"Rachael is never going to believe this," he marveled.

"Is the book any good?" Del asked while buttering a roll. "Never mind; don't answer that. It doesn't really matter at this point, and I don't want you to diminish my mojo."

"Your mojo?"

Del smirked. "What? You don't think you got here on talent, do you? My mojo paved this road, baby."

"It's different."

"Huh?"

"You asked me if the book was good, and it is," Thad told him. "But this one is different from anything else I've ever done. Honestly, Del, I don't know how the story will play out as a movie, I really don't."

"You got the manuscript on you?" Del asked. "Your publisher wanted me to drop it off tomorrow."

Thad hesitated, then reached into his briefcase, removing the manuscript. The tome felt warm. "Guard this one with your life; I don't want to see excerpts in the National Examiner."

"You got it," Del said, his pudgy fingers wrapping around the text.

"I'm not kidding," Thad told him. "I don't want a word of this novel getting out until publication. The whole world needs to read this story at once—no favors or sneak peeks this time, not for anyone."

Del pulled the manuscript to his chest. "I will eat this treasured stack of dead trees before I will allow it to fall into the hands of the enemy, Scout's honor."

"No eating the manuscript, Del."

"Yes, sir."

Del locked the novel in his own briefcase, then glanced up as Burstein returned to the table. "Hey, look who's back! So, did your boss dig some cash out from under his mattress or are we going to have to raid somebody else's coffer?"

Burstein took a drink and sighed. "I can offer you six million up front and points on the back end, but that's as high as we can go without digging into the promotional budget. That wouldn't help any of us."

Del winked at Thad. "So, what do you think, buddy? You wanna make a movie?"

CHAPTER ELEVEN

Day 1 – 5:05 p.m.

CARMEN PEREZ MOVED THE chair a little to the left and swore under her breath as she found another small pile of dirt hidden beneath. She had found eight others like it under other pieces of furniture; she even found some at the back of one of the cabinets in the kitchen.

"Messy little child," she said. "Bringing such filth in from the outside."

With a dust pan and small brush, she swept up the dirt and deposited the waste in the trash can she had been carrying around. "She wouldn't make such a mess if she had to clean up after herself," she complained.

"What's wrong, Carmen?"

Perez turned to find Rachael standing at the living room's doorway.

If this woman could control her child, I wouldn't spend the day cleaning up after her.

"Miss Ashley is bringing filth into the house," she blurted out. "This has been going on for a few days. Today I found dirt in cabinets, under furniture; I do not know where else she has put such filth, but this must stop. This is not the behavior of a respectful child."

Rachael stepped into the room and eyed the trash can. "Phew," she breathed.

"Very filthy," Carmen agreed.

"If that's from outside, you need to be careful," she told her. "Mr. Paskin thought the yard might be contaminated—you should wash your hands and be sure you're wearing gloves if you find any more."

"Oh, so now she is going to make me sick with her little games," Ms. Perez stated flatly.

Rachael rolled her eyes. "I'm sure she didn't mean anything. Kids sometimes do strange things to entertain themselves. Do you know where she is?"

"No, Ms. Rachael," Perez said.

"Ashley!" Rachael yelled, her voice echoing through the large home. "Come here, baby!"

A moment later, Ashley poked into the room, toting her stuffed Winnie the Pooh.

Rachael knelt down beside her and pointed to the chair. "Ms. Perez found dirt underneath that chair and in a few other places; did you bring it in from outside?"

Ashley shook her head.

"Now, what did I tell you about telling the truth?"

Ashley pouted. "I didn't do it, I don't like dirt. It's messy and yucky and stinky."

Rachael took a deep breath. "Ashley, I didn't carry dirt in here, and Ms. Perez certainly didn't. If not you, then who? Buster?"

She shrugged her shoulders. "The outside smells yucky. Daddy told me not to play outside and I haven't."

Ms. Perez voiced something in Spanish under her breath, then went back to cleaning up the mess.

Rachael brushed the hair from her daughter's eyes. "Okay, honey." She wasn't in the mood to argue right now. The baby was kicking again and she wanted to get off her feet. "Just stay in the house like your daddy said until we figure out what happened, okay?"

"I said I was," Ashley insisted.

"Okay, sweetie. Go wash up for dinner; we're going to eat soon."

Behind her, Ms. Perez smirked and left the room, heading back to the kitchen with the broom, dust pan, and trash can in tow. *That woman has no clue who is paying whom,* Rachael thought.

The odor filled the air. The same nasty, putrid scent as their lawn. Nausea crept up from her stomach and Rachael ran toward the bathroom, not feeling much like eating dinner.

CHAPTER TWELVE

1692

The Journal of Clayton Stone

*J*ONAS TAUBER SHUFFLED THROUGH *a number of papers before removing his glasses, rising, and approaching the bench.* "You are the husband of one Elizabeth Knapp, are you not?"

"I am," the man in the pulpit replied.

"She is maid to the Willard household?"

"She is."

"Very well," Tauber said, pausing for a moment. "Can you tell us how she came to see the doctor of Groton in the month of October, Anno, 1691?"

Ned Knapp wiped the perspiration from his brow, his eyes scanning those in attendance.

"Mr. Knapp?"

"Right," Knapp said. "She took after a very strange

manner, sometimes for days on end. Weeping, laughing, even roaring hideously with violent motions and agitations, crying out in the wee hours of the night, then forgetting all at first light. Our children are frightened still."

"Rightfully so," Tauber told him. "But there came more?"

Knapp nodded. "Her torment did not stop; it only grew worse. The doctor was not able to offer the cause; he only advised much rest."

"Did this help?"

Knapp shook his head and wiped the sweat from his brow. "In November following, she fell ill. A sleep came upon her like no other, not so much as a stir came from her for nearly six days and nights. It worried me so; I soon found myself unable to rest. I stayed at her side, her hand in mine, watching her slip away from me." A tear welled in his eye and he bowed his head for moment, his eyes avoiding those in the gallery.

Tauber walked back over to him. "What came next, Mr. Knapp?"

"It was when Pastor Willard arrived that a demon took possession of my beloved," Knapp confessed.

Concerns rushed through the crowd. I myself felt my stomach tighten at the mere mention of such an event.

"A demon?"

He nodded. "On the sixth night, a heat came upon her and a voice grew within her without any movement of her lips. Words came in a voice not her own, words unknown to myself and the others in the room. It was then that her tongue had drawn out of her mouth to an extraordinary *length and the demon began manifestly to speak from with-in her; some words were spoken from her throat while her lips were sealed, others came with her mouth wide open without the use of any of the organs of speech."*

"The demon belched forth most horrid and nefandous blasphemies, exalting himself above The Most High. These words were unknown to my wife; they were clearly the tongue of the devil himself. I dare not repeat them here."

"And Pastor Willard, he witnessed all of this?"

"He did," Knapp nodded.

Tauber walked back to his table, no doubt noting the pastor as a future witness. Without turning, he added, "What were the pastor's thoughts on all this? Did he share them with you?"

Knapp looked down, his hands anxiously kneading at the rim of his hat.

"Mr. Knapp?"

A hush had fallen upon the crowd, one that only allowed the cry of the wind to be heard. It brought with it a chill like no other, a chill deep within the bones of all those now watching Knapp with intense interest.

"The pastor, sir," Tauber pushed. "What were his thoughts on your wife's affliction?"

"She had become a child of Hell," Knapp breathed.

The crowd went silent for a moment, then came to life in a burst of conversation. The magistrate slammed down his gavel. "Silence!"

Knapp wiped his damp eyes and continued. "She cried out in one of her fits that a woman had appeared to her. She *claimed to be the cause of her possession and only she could remove such a spell. Then my beloved was taken speechless for some time. She remains such to this day."*

"And her accused, the woman, you know of her?"

Knapp nodded. "I do."

"This woman, is she among us?"

I watched as his eyes fell upon the blue-eyed girl in the pulpit before turning away in haste. He needn't have said more.

—Thad McAlister,
Rise of the Witch

CHAPTER THIRTEEN
Day 1 – 7:00 p.m.

THAD HIT THE CALL button on his iPhone and pressed it to his ear, cursing under his breath when a busy signal played for the fourth time in the past three hours.

Del chuckled at his side. "The pool boy must still be at the house; I can't think of any other reason for a woman to have the phone off the hook for that long."

"We don't have a pool," Thad replied, staring at the bottom of his empty glass.

"Mailman, plumber, massage therapist, tai chi instructor—any one of them could be shtuping your wife right now. Probably got the kid locked in the closet while your maid works the video camera for some website she hasn't told you about."

"You're full of encouragement, aren't you?"

"I'm full of this, too," he slurred, holding up an empty shot glass. "Are you ready for another?"

They had spent the past few hours celebrating the film deal at the hotel bar, and Thad felt as if he had more alcohol than blood flowing through his system. He probably couldn't stand and walk a straight line if his life depended on it. Not that it mattered; he was determined to have a good time tonight. He had signed the largest deal of his life and he deserved a good time. If Rachael was too busy to pick up the phone, so be it. He wasn't about to let anything bring him down. Not now.

"Absolutely," he slurred. "...another beer, too."

"Ah, Christ," Del said. "I need to catch a red-eye home and it's after seven. Thank God for cabs and my sensible packing habits."

"You're going to abandon your number-one client? I'll remember that at contract renewal time."

"I'm sure you'll be fine, Sparky. You're a big boy," Del told him. "Just don't forget to stumble back to the airport tomorrow to catch your own flight. You don't want to be stuck in the big city. Their way of life might warp those small-town values of yours."

"I think we're past setting boundaries. Consider me warped," Thad said as the bartender set two tall glasses of beer on the bar in front of them followed by two shot glasses, which he promptly filled with tequila.

How many was that now? Thad had lost count. He vaguely remembered something about liquor making you sicker before reaching for it.

Del slid his shot and beer down the bar to Thad. "All yours, buddy. I gotta go. I'll give you a call early next week once I get all the details on this thing. Meanwhile, you have a good time. Serious congratulations are in order!" Pulling out his wallet, he handed two crisp hundred-dollar bills to the bartender. "Keep them coming until he falls off the stool, then pour them on his head until the cash runs out."

The man nodded with a grin and shoved the money in his pocket. Thad quickly found he had no problem drinking alone. He downed Del's shot, shivering as the liquid burned his throat, then took a sip of beer as a chaser. The bartender returned a moment later with a bowl of peanuts. "Dinner is served," he said. "Our finest imported nuts from the great land of Planters."

Thad dug into the bowl, scooping a fistful and dropping them into his mouth.

"I heard a rumor floating around that you're someone famous."

Thad turned to find a young girl standing at his side. No more than twenty or twenty-one, she had long dark hair that fell over her shoulders and halfway down her back. She wore a white button-down blouse, short black skirt, and heels which easily added four inches to her height. She was smiling at him shyly, her dark blue eyes glistening in the soft light of the bar.

Did he know her? Something about her...familiar. His mind was awash in alcohol, unable to string together a cohesive thought.

"A pretty girl like you shouldn't talk to strangers," Thad said, doing his best to keep from slurring his words.

"Some would say a handsome young man shouldn't sit alone in a bar unless he wanted to be talked to," she replied. "Do you mind if I join you?"

Thad hesitated for a moment before nodding at the empty stool beside him.

She looks like—

If she had seen him remove his wedding ring, she didn't acknowledge it. Instead, she leaned toward him and breathed her name in his ear, her hand casually resting on his thigh.

CHAPTER FOURTEEN
Day 1 – 8:30 P.M.

RACHAEL HUNG UP THE phone with a frown. She had been trying to reach Thad for hours and his phone kept going to voice mail. She checked online and found out that his flight had touched down on schedule. He always called, particularly this late in the day.

Del.

Fucking Del.

She had never been a fan of her husband's agent. The overweight prankster disgusted her. While she believed his constant advances were nothing more than crude attempts at humor, his drinking and lack of any moral sense left much to be desired. If the man didn't do such a good job, she would have asked Thad to fire him years ago.

She debated calling the hotel; she'd leave a message

with the front desk. She decided against it, though—he would think she was checking up on him.

That's exactly what you want to do, right?

All alone in the city, how much do you really trust him?

When he was with Del, there was no telling what he might do.

She wanted to trust him, she did.

There had been one time, only that one time.

Once a cheater.

Rachael shook away the thought and set down the phone.

She wouldn't.

He would call home. He must have gone straight from the airport to his meeting. The meeting just ran a little longer than planned, that's all.

He always called.

Except when he didn't.

Maybe the pregnancy was making her anxious. She had been emotional throughout. Mood swings, hormones...now with the baby's constant kicking at her abdomen. She had to contend with Ms. Perez, the problems with their lawn, Ashley acting strange...

She was juggling so much.

When was the last time you made love to your husband? the voice taunted. *Four months, five months...*

A long time.

You're thirty pounds overweight and haven't dressed up or touched so much as a mascara wand in nearly two months. Do you honestly think he's attracted to you?

How long, really?

Rachael didn't remember.

How long since she had even wanted to?

How long since he had wanted to?

Rachael glanced in the mirror near the front door and ran her hand through her hair, watched it fall limply back against her shoulders.

She could be beautiful.

When you want to be.

She hadn't felt beautiful in so long.

After the baby she'd bounce back; she had after Ashley. She'd hit the gym as soon as her doctor gave her the green light. She always watched her diet. A couple months, tops.

She'd bounce back. He'd wait.

He didn't wait the last time. What's he really doing in New York, Rachael?

A tear welled up in her eye as she pondered being alone, raising two children by herself as her husband trotted the globe promoting his latest book and probably another movie.

Something clicked at her ear and she turned, finding nothing but an empty living room behind her. It was the third time she had heard the sound today, and each time her mind drifted back to the dream which had filled her nights for weeks.

Rachael couldn't shake the image of the old woman standing in the shadows at the corner of the room, a twisted smirk playing at her lips as she rattled her long, sharp nails against each other with a clickity click.

She didn't want to be alone—not now, not ever.

Rachael just wanted her husband to come home.

She wanted him to come home and hold her in his arms until all these feelings washed away.

CHAPTER FIFTEEN

1692

The Journal of Clayton Stone

"*TELL ME ABOUT THE Book of Red,*" Tauber said. "*Your collection of signatures, where is this tome now?*"

"*I know not of this book you speak.*"

"*It has been said you are collecting souls in exchange for freedom from your torment of late,*" he told her. "*Subjecting those around you to afflictions until, unable to take anymore, they willingly signed your book.*"

"*Her familiar bit me!*" Mary Walcott shouted from the gallery. "*Just now, on my arm!*" She jumped and raised her arm. The others gasped at the site of a fresh bite mark, blood dripping to the floor. Elizabeth Hubbard stood and wrapped the wound in a cloth with haste. "*I saw it!*" she shouted. "*For only but a moment. A creature struck and disappeared under the chairs!*"

At that, those in attendance came to their feet, most flee-ing while a few of the men cautiously searched beneath the seating.

"What do you say to this?" Tauber shouted above the noise.

The magistrate slammed his gavel down. "Quiet!"

"What do you say!"

She only smiled, her fingers unconsciously clicking together.

When finally satisfied that the familiar was gone, the crowd returned to their seats, watching the floor with wary eyes.

"Tell me about this book."

"There is no book."

"She lies!" Carol Bender shouted. "Before the eyes of God, she lies!"

Tauber turned. "What knowledge of this have you?"

"I signed her book," she confessed. "On the lives of my children, she made me sign."

"I too was made to sign," Abigail Rawling told them.

Through the confessions, my eyes remained on her. One would believe their words would draw fear, but that is not what I witnessed; instead, I found delight in her as she leaned back in her chair.

"Where is it?"

"I do not know of what you speak."

"Is the book with your sisters?" Tauber pushed.

Silence.

Tauber pounded the table, then turned to the gallery. "Will anyone among you testify to this book?"

Without hesitation, Mercy Short stood. "I will testify against this witch! I too signed this book."

"So be it," Tauber said.

—Thad McAlister,
Rise of the Witch

CHAPTER SIXTEEN
Day 1 – 11:48 P.M.

THUNDER CRACKED IN THE distance followed by a web of lightning that reached across Ashley's room like the gnarled fingers of an old man, scratching at the corners of her walls, long nails inching toward her bed, toward her.

Ashley pulled the sheets over her head and brought her knees up to her chest.

"One one-thousand, two one-thousand, three one-thousand, four—"

Another rumble filled the night and she caught her breath before it had a chance to escape and give away her hiding place; every little girl knew that was how the monsters found you—the slip of your breath always gave you away.

Buster whimpered at her feet and she poked her head out for one brief second. "Quiet," she instructed before disappearing again under her grandmother's heavy quilt.

He grumbled and plopped down to the floor, letting out a loud sigh.

"They're gonna hear you!" she scolded.

Across the room, dozens of stuffed animals stared back at her, their black beady eyes glistening with hunger in the crackling light, their mouths moving in the shadows. Their arms and legs seemed to shuffle ever so slightly, mocking her, inching a little closer. She imagined that they planned their attack while she slept, each toy dropping the charade of lifelessness the moment she drifted off, stretching their tiny limbs, taking their places among the army of plastic and fur to await instruction.

"Buster, you'll protect me, right?" she asked.

The dog raised a floppy ear and grunted, then closed his eyes again, content to sit this battle out at the side of her bed.

The dolls sat in silent patience.

Outside, the storm grew. The wind howled in defiance as viscous clouds suffocated the moon, taking the night as their own. When the rain began to fall, drops pelted the window, millions of tiny spears and rocks thrown by unseen hands at the glass.

Would it hold?

Ashley couldn't be sure.

She watched, glancing away only long enough to revisit the army of stuffed animals. They wanted the

79

window to break. They wanted the rain and wind to get into the room so they could make their move under the cover of the storm. They didn't fool her, none of them. She had caught on to them about a week ago.

She had thought Elmo was clumsy, the way he always fell from the shelf on which he sat with the others. After all, each morning he'd be lying on the ground while the rest of her toys remained still. When a tiny hand reached out from behind Winnie the Pooh and pushed, she gasped. She witnessed Elmo tumble to the floor, the little hand then disappearing back behind the other toys. Buster had seen it too and padded over to investigate, his tail slapping against his hind legs, his nose in detective mode. After about a minute, he gave up and returned to his favorite spot beside her bed, his eyes fixed on the toys until sleep overcame him.

The entire event had happened so fast and with so little noise that Ashley wasn't sure she had witnessed anything at all. She couldn't tell her mommy or her daddy; they wouldn't believe her. There was only Zeke—with intent, he had listened to every word, nodding on occasion, offering his support. In the end, he had agreed there was a problem and volunteered to guard the animals while she slept or was out of the room until they determined the cause of the uprising.

Tonight, Zeke was missing.

Sometimes he liked to hide, but tonight Ashley felt certain he wasn't in the room. She didn't think he was even in the house. She quietly called his name and there was no reply. He had good ears; he usually responded regardless of where he hid. If close, he would surely have come to her, wouldn't he?

Did she do something to make him mad?

Ashley was doubtful, but he could be temperamental at times. Sometimes he got angry and she didn't know it.

Thunder grumbled with anger outside and Ashley tensed. When lightning flooded the room a moment later, she stole another glance at the toys.

Did they move again?

They looked different.

Gerber, her favorite teddy bear, was sitting to the left of a tall, stuffed parrot; she thought she had left him on the other side. Her small pony was lying on his side—she remembered standing him up before she went to bed.

Of course, he might have fallen over (as stuffed ponies were often known to do). This wouldn't be the first time, Ashley reassured herself. He fell lots. All the time.

Thud.

From the toys.

Ashley peered through the darkness through a small opening in the folds of her quilt, her heart pounding so hard each beat echoed against the fabric of the mattress.

Buster had heard too; he lifted his head and stared at the army of toys. Ears back, he bared his teeth and a low growl escaped from deep within his throat. He stood with caution, hunched low, his eyes fixed on the stuffed bear.

"What is it, Buster?" she asked him. "What do you see?"

Buster inched closer, his nose sniffing at the darkness.

Ashley crawled out from under the comforter and lowered herself to the floor, falling in behind him. "Get 'em, boy," she coaxed.

The dog shuffled to the stuffed animals and grew tense. He examined the teddy bear, then the parrot, his nose moving from one toy to the next as he dismissed each, working through them all. When he reached SpongeBob, Buster barked and leapt back with a yelp. He shook his head and wiped his paw against his nose.

He was bleeding.

Ashley stared at him for a moment in disbelief, then bent down to examine his nose. She found two small puncture wounds at the tip.

"What happened, Buster?" she asked.

He whimpered back at her before shaking his head again.

Ashley turned back to the stuffed animals.

The angry storm rumbled outside.

When the lightning came, she caught her breath with a hush as something stared back at her, not from the stuffed toys, but behind them, peering out from between. A small hand reached up and wiped a speck of blood from pointy little teeth before retreating into the shadows, leaving a trail of dirt in its wake.

DAY 2

CHAPTER SEVENTEEN
Day 2 – 12:15 a.m.

"SHHH," SHE BREATHED.

Thad let the young girl kiss him. Her lips found his and his heart fluttered like a teenager. When she told him she didn't want to go up to his room but instead wanted to make love to him under the stars, he didn't question her. Instead he followed as she led him through the lobby, out the front door, toward the edge of the park just to the east of the grand hotel.

The chill of night reached for them, holding them, gently guiding them deep into the trees. Within moments, the city skyline disappeared, lost beyond the canopy of trees and interlaced branches.

Thad stumbled, his drunken feet tripping over a protruding tree root. He recovered his balance. "Stealthy like cat," he slurred.

The girl laughed. "Almost there."

His vision blurred and he shook clear. Those last two shots had been a mistake. His mind was lost in fog. His movements were those of a marionette whose strings were a little too long. He shouldn't be here; he should be alone. Not this, he shouldn't be doing this.

Something about this girl. She reminded him of—

The decision was not his to make.

The forest opened on a small clearing and she turned to him, her dark blue eyes glistening under the moonlight. Taking his hand, she guided him beneath the folds of her skirt, along the back of her thigh. Thad felt her warmth burning beneath his touch, a heat unlike any other coursing through the tips of his fingers. She pressed tightly against him, her breath warm, sweet, drifting from her mouth as he found the nape of her neck.

Thad wanted to pull away and leave this girl where she stood. Instead, he flicked the clasp of her skirt and tore it free.

A soft giggle escaped her lips as he frantically tugged at the buttons of her blouse, unsnapping some, breaking others, until the garment fell from her shoulders to the ground beneath. She stepped back from him and eased her fingers beneath the waistband of her panties, slowly sliding them off. She removed her bra a moment later and watched him with those eyes, her naked body glowing softly in the pale moonlight before lowering herself to the earth and reaching to him with an outstretched hand.

This girl.

Nothing existed but her.

Thad fell to his knees and ran his hands down the length of her.

She curled her fingers, digging them into the damp earth, a soft sigh escaping her. "Fuck me," she moaned softly. "Oh God, fuck me…"

He ran his hand over her thighs, gently spreading them apart. He found her hand on his, guiding, leading him, until he brushed against the moistness between her legs. A chill raced up his spine as she arched her back in ecstasy, his touch drawn closer by her movement.

Thad shed his clothes. The wind howled wildly around them, and the large oaks danced with their long shadows as the moon looked down upon their pale, sweat-covered bodies. The young girl's fingertips dug deeper into the dirt as his tongue slid across her nipples, her chest, moving lower ever so slowly. With strong arms, he reached under her and gently raised her to his lips as the chilled night air wrapped around them, sending a frenzy of electricity from fingertips to toes.

Do you want me? The words found him, although nothing was spoken aloud. *Do you want to be inside me?*

"Yes," he groaned.

Not yet, she replied. *There is something you must give me first. Then, only then…*

"Anything. . ."

Ahh, yes. I only want what is already mine, nothing more.

Her fingernails were long and sharp; they dug into his back as she pulled him closer. *I want you to help me,* she told him, her fingers digging deep, drawing blood.

"Yes," he told her.

You owe me.

"Yes," Thad said. "I owe you."

I want the box; will you get it for me?

"What box?"

You know of what I speak, Thad. They buried it so long ago but there it remains, waiting for you to bring it to me. You know where you must go, don't you, Thad? Where those men hid my treasure? Those evil, nasty men? My precious Rumina Box.

He pressed his lips to hers and ran his hand through her hair. A clump came away with his touch, and at first Thad thought he had pulled it out. Then he felt the wetness under his other hand. He raised his fingers to the light only long enough to see blood dripping from the tips.

Beneath him, the young girl giggled before wrapping her legs tightly around him, locking him in an embrace. Thad looked to her eyes only to find they were gone, replaced with dark, empty sockets within the skull of the creature beneath him.

You will bring my box back to me, won't you? You will bring my treasure to me? You haven't much time, you simply don't. Less than three days, I'm afraid.

He looked up and found an old woman and a large, burly man staring down at them, mere feet away. How long had they been there? The entire time?

Thad tried to pull away but couldn't break away. Instead, both of them sank deeper into the earth as the dirt grew moist with her decaying form.

She said something else to him before they disappeared into the ground, but he wasn't able to hear her words. Her voice was lost behind his screams.

━━━━━━

Thad woke to the buzzing of his portable alarm clock on the hotel nightstand. He reached over and slapped the device silent. He then cursed under his breath and glanced around the luxurious room.

Just a bad dream, he told himself.

Another one.

"I guess Ashley isn't the only one with imaginary friends," he mumbled aloud while rubbing his aching temples.

He had set the alarm for four in the morning in order to make his six o'clock flight from JFK.

Thad felt one hell of a headache coming on—a common occurrence after a night out drinking with Del.

Swinging over the side of the bed, Thad slowly rose from his slumber. He didn't notice the moist dirt clinging to him until he stood and looked down at his legs.

"What the—"

Glancing back, he found the sheets black with mud.

It was in his hair, on his arms—

Thad crossed to the bathroom and flicked on the light.

He was covered in dirt, some dry, some still wet. A sour, sickly odor.

Like feces.

It smelled like rotting feces.

Turning to his left, Thad froze when he saw his back.

Dozens of small, red slash marks.

Her nails.

She had scratched him.

A dream, nothing more. There was no doubt in his mind. Nothing happened. He had sleepwalked many times when he was a child; maybe he had again. Sleep-walked and gotten scratched by branches.

But where?

Could he have wandered into the park? Was that possible?

Somebody would surely have stopped him, wouldn't they?

They're from her, you know they are. You stink of sex under all that dirt—deny all you want. That won't change what happened.

His briefcase was on a table at the far side of the room. He went over, threw back the lid, and rifled its contents until he located his journal near the bottom. He flipped through the pages until he found it.

The Rumina Box.

A rough sketch at best; he had never claimed to be much of an artist.

The scratches on his back began to ache, but Thad forced himself to ignore the pain.

He often sketched the items, people, and relevant locations from his books. The exercise helped him visualize during the writing process. When describing a house, for instance, he would map out each floor, sometimes in great detail. This ensured that his characters' movements and experiences when maneuvering through that house remained consistent. Sometimes, these things would evolve with the story and he would find himself returning to previous chapters in order to amend them with the changes. Objects would sometimes change in the same manner, but that was not the case with this box. Like everything else in this story, he understood exactly what this object looked like from the moment he had begun.

The drawing depicted the box to be about six inches wide and four deep. Although you couldn't tell from the rough sketch, Thad was certain it had been carved from one solid piece of mahogany, taken from a tree fallen by lightning on the very night of its creation. The interior was lined with nearly an inch of lead. It had been melted shut on the first and only occasion the lid had been closed, sealing its contents for eternity.

You will bring my treasure to me, she told him. *You haven't much time.*

Thad traced the edge of the drawing with his finger.

You know where you must go, don't you Thad? Where those men hid it?

The box was hidden at the end of his novel, buried, to be precise.

Buried beneath an old, gnarled oak tree in a fictional forest on the outskirts of a town that did not exist.

He flipped two more pages, stopping at the picture of a girl, no more than a teenager. Her long dark hair flowed down her back and over her simple black-and-white Puritan dress. She stood at the mouth of a cabin deep within the woods, a forest not unlike the one in his dream.

This wasn't the first time he had dreamt of her. He had hoped the dreams would stop when he completed the book.

For months, she had dominated his thoughts. He'd wake to the sickly sweet scent of her breath lingering in the night air. The moisture of her kiss at his neck. She had guided him as he wrote the book, her siren's song calling him back to blank pages, her words helping to fill each of them. Then she was gone, if only for a little while.

He had hoped he'd lost her when he wrote that last page. But here she was, invading his night once more.

Thad closed the journal.

He vaguely remembered the bartender and a bellhop carrying him back to his room.

"You lush," he mumbled to himself. "That's how you got back up here."

He could only hope pictures didn't end up on the Internet. The last thing he needed right now was to get tagged in a Facebook picture—*This famous fuck drank himself silly in my bar! Found him outside playing in the mud!*

The sound of his cell phone drifted in from the other room, the broken ring gnawing at his throbbing head.

CHAPTER EIGHTEEN

1692

The Journal of Clayton Stone

COME TO ME.

Her voice drifted to me on the howl of the wind, muffled by a relentless rain and the crackle of the fire I had made earlier, now dying in the hearth. When I heard her, I thought sleep had finally found me and that she was but a dream. Then thunder struck outside and I realized I wasn't lost to slumber at all.

I sat up with a start, my eyes scanning the dark room.

"Are you here?"

Only silence responded. I found no one, yet I felt a presence.

When her voice came again it seemed to reach from all around me, yet nowhere in particular. The disembodied cry of a specter seeking me out, a siren's call.

Her call.

I had no choice but to go to her; I wish to make that clear for anyone who may read this. My mind never allowed me such decision; I couldn't say no any more than I could choose to stop breathing.

I dressed with purpose and pushed out into the cold, dark night, crossing the town square with nothing but a sliver of moonlight to guide me. At this late hour, all was quiet.

The church was not locked. I pulled open the heavy oak door and went inside, closing it behind me. As my sight was poor, her hand somehow guided me across the floor to the back hallway and down the narrow steps. Reaching the door at the bottom, I watched in silence as the lock cracked open by unseen hands and fell to the ground. There was a faint click and it opened before me. I stepped into the hallway, lit only by the flickering light of candle at the far end. The door closed with a bang. I did not turn to investigate; my eyes were fixed on her cell and my feet knew no other course.

I found her sitting on the bed, a thin smile playing across her lips as I reached the bars and finally stood still. Her beautiful skin glowed in the dim light, smooth as the most expensive of porcelain.

"I hoped you'd come."

"The choice was not mine," I said. "But you already know that, don't you, witch?"

The comment didn't sound as harsh as I had wished; she only smiled, then ran her fingers through her long dark hair. "I saw the way you looked at me in court; you glimpse the truth. You believe I am not guilty of that which they charge."

"I know no such thing."

Standing from the bed, she came to the bars. Her fingers brushed mine, sending a shiver over me.

I turned and raced for my home.

I spent the remainder of the night at the fire, hoping the flames would warm my chilled bones.

They did not in the slightest.

—Thad McAlister,
Rise of the Witch

CHAPTER NINETEEN

Day 2 – 1:20 a.m.

DEL THOMAS HAD BEEN on the plane for at least fifteen minutes before his curiosity got the better of him. Much to the dismay of the old woman at his left, he rose from his seat and plucked his briefcase from the overhead compartment, his overweight frame pressing against her as he wrestled the bag free from the crowded mess holding it prisoner. Falling back into his seat with the briefcase in his lap, he worked the locks with his thick fingers. He smiled with satisfaction as they clicked open. The woman beside him mumbled something to herself before returning to her magazine.

"You're not exactly thin as a rail either, lady. Good luck landing a husband with those saddlebags in tow."

Her eyes widened and she reached for the attendant

call button.

"Good idea. Maybe they'll move you to the back of the bus with the rest of the cattle."

She gathered her things, unbuckled her belt, and stomped away, her face red as a beet.

Del raised the armrest between the two seats and stretched out.

The manuscript stared up at him, stark white, bearing nothing more than the book's title and the name of the author in bold block letters.

This simple stack of papers would make him a very wealthy man, he thought to himself with a smile. Words could not express how much Del loved his job.

With the manuscript in hand, Del sealed the briefcase and placed it under the seat in front of him, settling in for the flight. He had about an hour before he'd be back in Boston, plenty of time to peruse Thad's latest.

As the plane passed through turbulence, he turned the page and found himself lost in the words.

CHAPTER TWENTY

Day 2 – 5:00 a.m.

THAD REACHED FOR THE phone and hesitated for a moment before answering the call.

"I had a wonderful time last night," she teased, her sultry voice slipping across the line, the warmth of her breath finding his ear.

"Who is this?" he heard himself ask, although he already knew the answer.

She sighed. "That hurts, Thad. It really does," she said. "How could you not recognize me? We've been so close over the past few months while you wrote your book—practically kindred spirits. I would have thought you'd be glad to see me after everything we've been through together."

"You can't be—" Thad stammered.

"Can't be what?" she asked. "Can't be real? Am I, Thad? Am I real?"

The blood drained from Thad's face. "It's fiction," he said. "It's just a story, she's not real...you're not—"

"You sure know how to make a girl feel welcome. I bet next you're going to tell me I'm a lousy lay, too, right? What a great way to tie a bow around our little tryst."

"This isn't happening," Thad sat on the corner of the bed, cradling his head.

"Poor baby. Feeling a little guilty, are you?"

Thad remained still, his mind racing. "This can't be..."

She giggled. "...happening?" she said. "You already said that. Believe me, it did happen, and you were very much a part of it, my dear Mr. McAlister. Would you like to fill in your wife, or would you rather I made the call?"

Thad felt his grip on the phone tighten. "So that's what this is about, some kind of blackmail?"

"Some kind..."

"What do you want from me?"

"I want you to call me by my name," she breathed. "I want you to call me Christina."

"Cut the shit. What do you want?"

"I want you," she giggled softly, "to help me find Her box."

CHAPTER TWENTY-ONE
Day 2 – 5:00 a.m.

"**M**OMMY!"

Ashley stared at her stuffed animals in horror and shouted her mom's name for the third time. Beside her, Buster rubbed his nose with a front paw. The bleeding had stopped, leaving two small puncture wounds at the tip of his snout.

Ashley jumped when her bedroom door swung open, then breathed a sigh when she saw her mother standing in the doorway.

"What happened?" Her mother frowned. "What's wrong?"

She pointed at the toys. "There's something behind them. It bit Buster!"

Rachael crossed the room, eyeing the stuffed animals.

"What kind of something?"

"A monster with red eyes, Mommy," she breathed. "Tiny little red eyes and hands!"

Rachael gently raised Buster's head and examined the small wounds. He whimpered, then backed up and sneezed, shaking his head.

"Thanks, Buster," Rachael wiped her wet face with her sleeve.

She hoped to God they didn't have rats. This was an older home and although their exterminator visited every other month, the occasional mouse or rat would get inside—this time of year in particular as the weather began cooling down in anticipation of winter.

"It might still be back there, Mommy!"

Rachael pushed the stuffed animals aside one at a time, ready to pull away in an instant if she spotted something looking back at her. The smell hit her a moment later, and nausea crept up her throat.

Ashley covered her nose. "Pewwy, what is that?"

When she moved the large teddy bear, she found a number of small dirt piles hidden behind it, a trail leading to a four-inch hole in the drywall.

"Rats," Rachael grumbled under her breath.

Ashley shook her head. "Not a rat, Mommy; it didn't look like a rat, it wasn't…it was something else!"

"Of course it's a rat, dear. It was dark; your eyes were probably playing tricks on you, that's all."

Again, Ashley shook her head. "It…it stood up. Rats don't stand up in real life, only in cartoons."

Rachael pushed the remaining stuffed animals aside and examined the hole a little more closely. It didn't have that rough, chewed appearance typically left by mice and rats; instead, its edges were smooth. The four-inch circumference was almost perfect. She found no debris, no dust or chunks of drywall around the hole, as if whatever had cut it out had also taken the time to cart away the resulting waste.

"Go get me a flashlight, honey."

Ashley wandered out of the room with Buster on her heels. She returned a moment later with the emergency flashlight they kept in the hall closet. Rachael switched it on and aimed the beam at the hole.

The opposite wall and the edge of a 2x4 stud on the right was visible but little else. Lying down on her side, she tried to get a better view but didn't have enough room. She cursed her oversized belly. Rachael took a deep breath and reached into the hole, cautiously feeling around.

"Mommy, don't—the monster is gonna bite you like it did Buster!"

Ignoring her daughter, she groped around inside, her fingers tracing the drywall to the wood stud on the right, then reversing directions until she found the stud on the left. If something had been in there, it was gone now. But to where? She saw no other holes and with only eighteen inches between the studs, there was little room to maneuver, no place to hide. Then she felt something on the left stud, a groove of some sort. There was another about two inches above the first; another above that—Rachael couldn't get her hand high enough to look for a fourth, but she suspected one existed.

Like a ladder. A ladder carved into the wood leading up.

To the attic?

Rachael knew they had a small crawlspace between the first and second floors and the attic above. Once they gained access to one or the other, the rats would have the run of the house, able to reach any section undetected.

If they were indeed rats.

What else could they be?

Grabbing a large Dr. Seuss book from the bookcase beside her, Rachael pressed it flat against the hole, then stacked a handful of other books in front, blocking access.

"Let's see them get through that," she said with confidence. "I'll call the exterminator first thing in the morning, honey. Don't worry; we'll send him packing!"

Ashley frowned. "They won't hurt him, though, will they? I don't want them to hurt him, only help him move to a new house."

"That is exactly what they'll do," Rachael reassured her. "Just like a moving company."

"Can I sleep in your bed? I don't want to be in here," she pouted. "Buster doesn't either, and Zeke went away somewhere, so we're all alone."

"Of course you can, honey," Rachael said, brushing her daughter's long blonde hair from her damp eyes. "We'll have ourselves a sleepover, only us girls!"

Ashley smiled and took her mother's hand. "When is Daddy coming home? I miss him."

I wish I knew, Rachael thought.

"Soon, honey," she told her. "Soon."

As she led her daughter out of the room, a movement caught the corner of her eye from beyond the window. Even though the night was deathly still, she told herself it was just a shadow from one of the trees outside, unwilling to give her subconscious the satisfaction of a glance back.

CHAPTER TWENTY-TWO

1692

The Journal of Clayton Stone

"*PLEASE PROVIDE YOUR NAME for the record.*"

"*Mercy Short,*" she said.

She had been removed from the room, no doubt returned to the small cell at the back of the church.

I have no firsthand knowledge of Mercy Short, having only met her once some time ago. I believe her to be around twenty-five years of age, a few years older than myself. She has a husband and two children, both of whom were led away by elders from the church moments earlier, sparing them from the testimony of their mother.

Mercy Short was clearly nervous, her eyes fluttering across those in the gallery before settling on her hands, which were folded in her lap.

Tauber smiled down at her. "*There is no need to fear,*

child. You are among friends here. You are among those who want to hear your story."

Mercy forced a smile and nodded. "It began about a month ago; of the exact night I am not certain. I awoke deep within the night to the sound of a brewing storm. My husband was not at my side; I assumed he went to the barn to tend the horses. This is often the case when lightning is afoot," she explained. "I reached for the lantern at my side; only then did I realize I could no longer move."

"Were you bound?"

Mercy shook her head.

Tauber appeared puzzled. "What held you still?"

She took a deep breath, her eyes gazing briefly across the crowd before returning to her lap. "The grip of unseen hands held me still."

Those behind me mumbled softly. The magistrate silenced them with a glare.

"I felt long fingernails digging into my limbs with even the slightest of movements, but I saw no one."

Tauber turned and faced the gallery. "You knew this presence, though, didn't you?"

She nodded. "Her scent betrayed her; the fragrance of wild lilacs filled the room. I found it unmistakable. I called her name but no reply came, only her scent. Then there was her warm breath at my ear as she spoke."

"What did she say?"

"You will sign my book," she said. "By the blood of your children, you will sign."

"I tried to protest, but another hand held my mouth."

"Did all end with that?"

Mercy fell silent, her eyes again darting briefly to the elders seated at the high altar.

"Did it end there, Mrs. Short?" Tauber's voice echoed through the wooden hall.

"No," she breathed. "It did not."

"Continue, then; tell us all."

With a deep breath, she went on. "The hands, so many yet none at all, they pulled the covers aside and tore at my gown until my legs were bare. The room grew so cold I remember wanting nothing more than to cover myself, but they held me firm. Another hand brushed against my leg and I felt a sharp pain as something pierced my skin. I screamed silently, for they still held my mouth. Then I lost myself to the night, waking only as the morning light crept across the room."

"You were alone?" Tauber asked. "When morning came?"

"My husband slept soundly at my side. I found myself back beneath the covers. I would have believed all to be a dream but not for the cut on my leg."

Tauber walked back to his table and glanced down at his notes. "This proved to be the first of many nights, was it not?"

Mercy Short nodded. "They returned nearly every night thereafter."

"And the cuts?"

Mercy Short's eyes glistened with tears. "I have many now, one for each night that followed."

"What of this book?"

Mercy fell silent and Tauber grew impatient. "Mrs. Short! What of this book?" he shouted.

She startled and wiped the tears from her eyes.

"Mrs. Short!"

"I signed it!" she cried. "I signed her damned book, but she didn't stop! She will never stop!" Standing, she tore up her sleeves, revealing dozens of slash marks. "They will bleed me until I stand at death's door!"

Tauber slammed his fist against the desktop. "Who betrayed you, Mrs. Short? Who did this to you? Was it the accused?"

Mercy Short dropped back into her seat, her eyes welling with tears.

"Was it the girl on trial?!" he shouted.

Mercy could only nod her head.

—Thad McAlister,
Rise of the Witch

CHAPTER TWENTY-THREE

Day 2 – 5:01 a.m.

"**YOU'RE CRAZY,**" **THAD SAID** before disconnecting the call.

The phone began to ring almost immediately, but rather than answering, Thad threw his iPhone across the room. A moment later, the hotel phone beside the bed tore through the silence. Thad swore under his breath and scooped up the receiver. "Leave me the fuck alone!" he shouted.

"You don't want to break your phone, Thad. Think of that iPhone as your family's lifeline, your only lifeline to your treasured wife and daughter. They miss you so much. I'd hate to see your family apart any longer than necessary."

"What are you talking about?"

"Family is such a precious thing, don't you think? So precious and so fragile, like delicate glass in a thunderstorm."

Last night had been a dream, right? Had to be.

He had been so drunk.

"You're so silly, Thad. You and your doubts. After our little adventure, the bartender did bring you upstairs with the help of one of his friends. You did some nasty things to me; I really enjoyed it. But then you passed out. I couldn't wake you, I simply couldn't. I asked him to help you get back to your room."

Thad sat on the corner of the bed and ran his hand through his hair. "Whatever happened between us, if anything happened at all," he drew a deep breath, "was a mistake, mine and yours—you don't have to involve my family."

"My dear Thad, they're already involved. You dragged them in the moment your lips touched mine. I've got no doubt you'll help me find Her. We'll do this thing together. Your family and mine. Won't that be fun?"

Thad felt his face begin to burn with anger. "She's not real!"

"Oh, but She is. You're kidding yourself if you don't believe it," Christina said. "And She has so many friends, so many just like me, wanting nothing more than to help her come back. People who are willing to do anything to help bring her back. I do mean anything, Thad. Her family is strong, Thad, much stronger than yours. We've waited hundreds of years for this day to come. I honestly can't wait a moment more. We really need to get started—there is little time left."

"This isn't real," Thad said. *I'm imagining it, all of it, I must be.*

"We have your wife, Thad. We also have your daughter," she told him. "I'm going to say this next part very clearly, Thad, because I don't want there to be any misunderstandings. Are you listening, Thad?"

"Yes," he nodded, the word barely escaping his lips.

"They will die if we don't find Her, if you don't—"

Thad nearly let the phone slip from his fingers as his breath caught in his throat. He had no reason to believe her, this voice on the phone, yet he did, he believed every word. "What have you done with them?" he breathed.

"You need to focus on your task, Thad. I don't want you to be distracted, so I'm going to tell you they're fine and they will stay fine as long as you help me, as long as you help *us*."

"Help you find Her…," Thad pointed out. "A fictional character."

"Come on, Thad. Aren't we beyond your trivial denial by now? The story, Her story came to you so easily for a reason. There are forces at work here much greater than either you or I can possibly understand, forces which compelled you to tell Her story." She paused for a second, then added, "I know you researched Her, Thad. After you started the book, you went back and pulled every periodical you could get your hands on. Quite the diligent little library patron. Weren't you surprised to find the legends and tales about Her in those old texts? Stories so close to the ones you thought came out of your sexy little head. She lived long before you stumbled into Her world, lover boy. You get that, don't you? If I were you, I would try to recall just how you came into possession of the journal. It started there, didn't it? With that journal?"

Thad remembered—his wife had found the journal in an antique shop. "The perfect place for an old story to be reborn," she said.

"You must wonder, Thad. Did the story come from you, or from the journal? I think you've known the answer to that little question for a long time," Christina pointed out.

"How?" he heard himself ask.

"Her world is one of magic, the unexplained. She knew the journal would one day tell Her story. She also understood that story would lead the world back to Her...would lead her back to the world. She has many followers, Thad. We've been waiting for Her; we've been waiting a very long time. Now it's up to you to bring Her back to us."

Thad lowered his head and ran his hand through his hair. "She's evil," he finally said.

"The clock is ticking, Thad. Your family doesn't have much time. You must find Her and bring Her home."

"Where do I start?"

"Where do you think, Thad? You need to start where your story ends, with a very special box."

The box.

Thad had tried to forget about the box after completing the book. He wanted to forget everything it stood for, but the box never left his thoughts—nor did its resting place.

He stood from the bed and went to his suitcase. He found a small pill bottle resting between his socks. Popping the cap, he palmed two. Risperidone. He hadn't taken them for months, but they had helped with the voices before; they had helped silence them.

"She won't let you forget," Christina said. "Not yet. You've got work to do."

"I want to speak to my wife and daughter," Thad told her, staring down at the pills.

"We're watching you, Thad. You need to hurry. No calls to anyone."

The line went dead.

Thad found himself sitting in perfect silence, the image of this girl burned in his mind. He swallowed the medication dry, wondering if a couple little pills could keep this girl from coming back.

CHAPTER TWENTY-FOUR

1692

The Journal of Clayton Stone

*M*Y HOUSE SEEMED STRANGELY cold as I arrived there after the long day of trial. I piled wood into the hearth and stoked a fire. I had little for dinner but such things didn't matter; my appetite had left me.

The trial had concluded for the day about four hours earlier, as nobody was willing to stay past dusk. Mercy Short was taken home by her husband against the advice of Doctor Groton, who thought she was in too fragile a state to return to the very place in which she had suffered her horrors. Mercy herself had silenced him, convinced the witch would find her tonight regardless of where she slept. Only God offered protection, she said. At her insistence, Father Lawson would keep watch.

The warmth of the fire called out to me and I went to my

favorite chair. Pulling a warm blanket down over me, I watched the flames dance over the logs and lost myself in the steady hiss and rasp of the hearth.

I woke moments later to a hand on my shoulder and warm breath at my ear.

"Don't be startled," a voice instructed.

Such warning did little good. I jumped from my chair and turned around.

Although my eyes were adjusted to the darkness, I found it difficult to perceive the form before me, her face cloaked beneath the shadows of a dark hood.

"Reveal yourself!" I commanded, doing my best to hide my fear.

Reaching behind me, I grabbed the fire stoke.

"Wait."

Her long, delicate hands went to her cloak and pulled the hood back.

As her face found the light, my heart froze within my chest.

The girl had escaped from the confines of the church.

"How did you free yourself?"

She shook her head. "You speak of my sister. The magistrate holds her in that tiny damp cell, not I."

I suspected twins, for no sibling resembled another quite so remarkably unless such was true. "You are wanted, too," I pointed out. "The charges faced by your sister were brought upon the entire family."

She nodded. "It bothers me so to be free when she suffers at their hands, but I must help her and I cannot if I am shackled at her side."

"As a servant of the court, I am obligated to report you," I told her, the fire stoke still gripped firmly in my hand. "I am obligated to bring you to them."

"If that is what your heart tells you, then you clearly have no choice."

Her sad eyes filled with desperation and defeat.

I realized I was staring and looked to the floor. "Why have you come to me?"

She took a step forward. Her warm breath caressed my face. "You are of a good heart, and you know these accusations are untrue."

"I have said no such thing."

"What you feel and what you speak are clearly at conflict, but we both know the truth."

For that, I held no answer. There had been much testimony against her sister. I had even witnessed events firsthand, but a part of me truly did find innocence there, despite the evidence against her.

"Like the others in town, you are afraid the magistrate will charge you as a conspirator if you were to voice your true feelings."

It was true.

She reached out to me, her delicate fingers wrapping around my hand. "You must help us," she pleaded. The words to put her touch to paper elude me, for I have never before nor after experienced such a thing. An energy escaped her and found its way to me, slipping across my skin much like rain falling from the heavens. Exquisite, entrancing. I forced myself to pull away and took a step back.

"Are you what they accuse you to be?" I asked, not sure that I wanted to hear the answer.

"I am no more dangerous than you."

"Do not evade me. Are you what they accuse you to be?" I repeated, no longer concealing the anger in my voice.

"Please, you must help us," she pleaded.

"I cannot."

She looked to me, her eyes filled with sorrow. "For that, I am so sorry."

Her hand came up with such speed, a movement faster than I could have imagined possible. I felt her fingers brush my forehead. "Dormious," she breathed.

My eyes became heavy; my mind clouded with sleep as my legs disappeared beneath me.

I saw her smile as I fell. I couldn't help but long for the beauty of it as all went black.

—Thad McAlister,
Rise of the Witch

CHAPTER TWENTY-FIVE

Day 2 – 9:30 a.m.

R ACHAEL WOKE TO A CRASH.

Beside her Ashley stirred, then looked to her as she wiped the sleep from her eyes. "What was that, Mommy?"

Rachael shook her head and pulled back the covers, shivering as the cool morning air found her. "I think it came from outside."

Rising from the bed, she went to the window and glanced out over their front yard, peering through the unforgiving thick rain. "Damn."

The large oak tree had succumbed to whatever had killed their lawn the day before and toppled over. Brittle and splintered branches littered their yard, lying atop a pile of brown, dead leaves. "Our tree fell over, sweetie. It's sick, like the grass."

———

Thirty minutes later, they had showered and made their way to the kitchen, where they found Ms. Perez fussing over a quick breakfast. "I already called Señor Paskin and he will be on his way with a crew to remove the old tree as soon as the rain stops, so you just sit and relax and I will take care of everything!"

As soon as the rain stops, right. Rachael took a seat and poured herself a cup of decaf. "Any messages?"

Ms. Perez set a plate of toast and eggs in front of her and shook her head. "No calls, Ms. Rachael. I'm sorry."

Where was he? Why hadn't he called? What was he doing?

"I'm hungry, too!" Ashley explained as she pulled herself into her favorite chair.

Ms. Perez brought her a plate. "I didn't forget about you, little one. Here you are."

"Ms. Perez, do you think we have rats?" Rachael asked.

Ms. Perez's eyes grew wide. "Rats! Oh please, no rats. They are foul, foul rodents."

"You haven't seen anything?"

"No rats, no mice; this house is very clean all the time," Ms. Perez protested.

"I'm not blaming you, Ms. Perez. You do a great job. But this is an old house and sometimes they can get in."

"Maybe with the weather?"

Rachael nodded. "Especially with bad weather."

Ms. Perez stopped wiping the counter and came over to the table. "Then perhaps I did see something."

"What?"

"Yesterday, when vacuuming, I thought something ran behind the couch in the living room, but I found nothing when I looked closer," she said.

"A rat?"

"It was so fast, I cannot be sure," she told her.

Rachael hesitated for a moment, then stood and went to the living room, the housekeeper following close on her heels.

"I think the light played a trick on me," she said.

Someone had drawn the drapes in an attempt to block out the dismal weather, leaving the room in a dark gloom all its own. With the windows closed, the space had taken on a musty scent that was bound to awaken her allergies if she remained too long. The stench found her as soon as she neared the couch.

"It stinks, Mommy."

Rachael turned to find Ashley at the doorway with Buster close on her heels. "You should finish your breakfast, honey. We'll be right back."

"I want to chase the rats, too," she pouted.

Rachael rolled her eyes. "Okay, but stay behind us, all right, sweetie?"

Ashley nodded and sat on the floor. Buster fell to the ground beside her with a grunt.

Cautiously approaching the couch, nausea crept up

Rachael's throat as the pungent odor grew stronger. Ms. Perez came to her side, a broom held high.

Reaching for the corner of the couch, Rachael tugged the heavy piece of furniture away from the wall, ready to jump the moment an uninvited guest appeared.

"Careful, Ms. Rachael," Ms. Perez said.

Rachael pulled the couch further still, revealing several dirt piles and another hole in the wall similar to the one she had found in her daughter's room.

"They are smart to hide," Ms. Perez said, gripping the broom handle hard enough to turn her knuckles white.

Rachael stepped between the couch and the wall and lowered herself to the ground in order to get a closer look.

Like the hole upstairs, this one was also four inches in circumference and appeared to have been cut with some sort of tool—almost too perfect to have been chewed by rats. Cautiously reaching inside, she felt around until her fingers grazed the stud. Also like upstairs, a series of grooves had been cut into the wood, creating a makeshift ladder of sorts.

"Eww," she heard herself say.

As she turned her head, she realized the odor wasn't coming from the wall but from the couch.

"Help me up," she said.

Ms. Perez helped her to her feet, unwilling to surrender the broom. "The hole is new. I would have found it yesterday."

If that were the case, why no drywall dust or debris? Rachael questioned, keeping the comment to herself.

She turned back to the couch.

"I need you to help me flip this over," she said, studying the couch carefully. "We need to check the bottom."

"You should not move furniture."

"It's not that heavy. I'll be all right," she assured her.

She shook her head. "Mr. Thad would not approve."

"Mr. Thad is not here right now—I won't tell him if you don't," she replied.

The woman positioned herself on the opposite end of the couch.

Ashley and Buster continued to watch them quietly from the doorway.

"On three we roll it, okay?"

Again, Ms. Perez nodded.

Rachael gripped the back and the bottom of the couch and bent her knees.

"One."

"Two."

"Three—"

The couch was far heavier than it appeared and both women grunted as its weight shifted in their hands, sending the piece of furniture tumbling forward. Rachael pulled her hands free before they were pinned underneath, grateful to find Ms. Perez had done the same—jumping to the side as the couch tumbled over and settled on its back.

The smell drifted up in a cloud of foul, dank air and Rachael turned away, unwilling to allow the stench to overcome her.

"Oh my," Ms. Perez said.

Rachael followed her gaze to the underside of the couch, now facing up. Another hole had been cut in the fabric. Just like the others, this one was about four inches in circumference and perfectly round.

Damp earth covered the floor, the same rotten soil they had found throughout the house, piled where the couch had sat.

Whatever had brought the dirt here was clearly building a stockpile inside the couch—the edges of the hole were damp and the stink rose from within. Rachael imagined tiny worms wriggling through the fabric, searching for their next meal. Tiny little worms everywhere she had found the dirt—their yard, in the walls, within furniture, her daughter's room.

"Mommy, they could be in the couch," Ashley breathed. "The rats might be hiding."

Not rats, Rachael thought. *It's something else.*

Ms. Perez poked at the bottom of the couch with the broom, but nothing moved; only more dirt filtered out.

"Ms. Perez, please call an exterminator."

"Yes, ma'am," she said, poking the couch one final time.

"Do we have any traps in the house?"

The housekeeper shook her head. "I have not seen any."

"As soon as the weather breaks, go to the store and pick some up, okay?"

Again, she nodded.

Ashley was standing behind her, her eyes fixed on the

hole in the wall. "They're living in the house, inside the wall, aren't they, Mommy?"

Rachael turned to her daughter and knelt down. "Don't worry, honey. I don't think we have more than one. The furry little guy probably wants to get out of the rain like the rest of us."

"There's more than one," Ashley told her.

Rachael ran her hand through her daughter's hair. "Why don't you go finish your breakfast? Ms. Perez and I will take care of this."

Ashley nodded, then headed back toward the kitchen. Buster eyed the hole suspiciously for a moment longer before following her out of the room.

"Please find something to seal it," she instructed, "at least until the exterminator gets here."

Ms. Perez nodded. "I'll find something in the garage."

CHAPTER TWENTY-SIX

Day 2 – 9:50 a.m.

Ms. PEREZ STEPPED INTO the garage and crinkled her nose. *"¡Esto huele terrible aquí!"* she howled. *"¡Tal suciedad, en todas partes!"*

Noxious odors hit her like a wall.

She fumbled with the light switch, bringing the large fluorescents overhead to life.

Dirt covered the floor, the same foul-smelling dirt they had found inside the house.

Careful not to step in it, Ms. Perez crossed the garage to Mr. Thad's workbench on the far wall. "So unorganized," she said, scanning the cluttered shelves. After shuffling past assorted cans of used paint, she spotted a small canister of plaster and drywall patches and scooped them up. She also found a box of mousetraps and rat poison. She knew Ms. Rachael would not want her to place poison around the house, but sometimes these things needed to be done. If the filthy dog was dumb enough to eat the powder, so be it. She couldn't be expected to clean up after all of them and look out for their mutt, too—not for the little they paid her.

With the arsenal in hand, Ms. Perez headed back into the house, turning off the lights with her elbow.

━━━━━━━

When Rachael's hand fell upon the doorknob to her husband's office, she hesitated.

Was she trespassing?

Of course not. She had been in the room more times than she could count.

With Thad, always with Thad.

He wouldn't care, though, would he? They don't have any secrets.

This is his space. His private place.

Why was her heart racing so? This was ridiculous. If he had been home to ask, he would tell her to go right in; maybe straighten up a little while she was in there, he would joke.

She recalled her dream from the other night, how the door stood open. The journal, left unguarded on his desk.

Drawing a breath deep into her lungs, she twisted the knob and crept over the threshold. The light from the hallway sliced into the dark room and she followed behind it, stepping only in its wake.

His office felt cold, the air stale. She glanced up. The vent was open. The central heat was on.

Reaching across the desk, she turned on the Tiffany reading lamp. Its glow creeped over the dark space, sending the shadows scurrying to the corners.

What am I doing?

Years had passed since he had cheated on her, only the one time.

You were pregnant then. About nine months in, just like now.

They were in such a bad place back then. His failed first novel had brought little income. There were so many bills and the landlord—God, she had almost forgotten Mr. Rainey. His incessant pounding on their door at all hours. Thad, eyes wide, shushing her with a finger to his lips. If she hadn't taken a second shift at the donut shop, they surely would have moved back in with her parents.

She had hated him. Hated how he had plucked her from her life and trapped her, trapped her in an impoverished marriage with a child on the way. She had given up everything for him: school, career, any chance at a successful future.

He secretly blamed her for getting pregnant. He resented her, she knew he did.

And the drinking.

The only thing keeping his drinking in check was their lack of funds.

He had been working around the clock with her, this Alyssa. A twenty-something brunette brought in by his publisher to help edit the second book. He wrote at a maddening pace, scrawling the text in his journal; a reckless hand, unreadable by most. His publisher tasked this girl with putting Thad's words to paper and making sense of his work. They spent days together locked in a small office downtown, huddled over that damn journal. She imagined Thad over her shoulder as she typed frantically at a computer. A whiff of her hair, the scent of perfume, the hint of a breast behind a thin blouse as she bent to turn the page. It was bound to occur, the two of them alone, his home life in ruins.

He had told her that same night, collapsing at her feet in tears. Smelling of bourbon, he had confessed the entire torrid episode. He explained how they had finished the book, how incredible this one was—beyond anything else he had ever done. He told her they had gotten caught up in the celebration, lost in the excitement.

Rachael had been too bitter to care, to feel an ounce of jealousy.

The girl boarded a plane, gone from their lives. Manuscript in hand, she returned to New York.

Rachael planned to leave Thad the next morning, and would have if not for his publisher's phone call just after first light. He had met Alyssa at the airport and read the entire book, unable to put the story down. The girl had raved, and with good reason. Thad had a bestseller on his hands. He had no doubt. And they planned to put every possible resource behind this one.

And they had.

A FedEx envelope had arrived a day later containing a $10,000 advance check and two first-class tickets to the city.

Fewer than six months later, Thad was at the top of the New York Times fiction list.

Talk of a movie followed.

That was the first book he had written in the journal, the first of many.

In the years that followed, Thad still drank but only in moderation. The man she had hated during that dark time faded away along with their problems, replaced by the caring father and husband he was today. All of this seemed a lifetime ago.

He had cheated on her, and while there was no excuse, she had forgiven him. They had moved on.

She learned to trust him again.

You want to trust him.

When was the last time he touched you?

She closed the door and studied the room.

His desk was bare but for his MacBook and a ream of crisp, white paper beside the printer.

She searched each drawer and found the usual clutter: paper clips, old magazines, rubber bands, pens, pencils, the anniversary card she had given him in January. A rose on the cover. She opened it—*My love, may our next year be as happy as the last. Love always, R.*

She stared down at the card.

Once a cheater…

Rachael replaced the card and powered on his laptop.

The familiar Apple logo blinked past and the screen settled on his desktop. No password set.

Clicking through the various icons, she loaded his mail program and scanned his e-mails. Dozens contained spam and advertisements. Four messages were from Del (a waste of time); two jokes forwarded from Facebook, and the third was a picture of a rotten tomato with the caption *We're making a movie! Get your ass to NY!* The fourth contained only his flight itinerary.

The oldest e-mail came from his publisher. The subject read—Proposed Cover Art. She clicked on it, opening the message:

From: Ryan Dermotte
To: Thad McAlister
Date: Thursday, December 03, 2014 8:14 pm
Subject: Proposed Cover Art

Got your text yesterday with proposed cover art. Did you draw those? Didn't know you could draw. The old woman might be a little too creepy for the cover—you want people to pick up the book when they walk past, not run and hide. I like the ones of the girl, though. Maybe go with something like that? We can talk when you get back from NY. Give the manuscript to Del like we discussed. I'll get the book from him. Can't wait to read it!

Safe trip!
Ryan D

Thad couldn't draw, he never could. And since when did he text? He had an iPhone, but only because the flip phone he had carried for years died after taking a header off the kitchen table a few months back. At last check, he hadn't installed a single app.

She, however, used hers religiously, and as an avid member of the Cult of Apple, she was well versed in all the various intricacies of their ecosystem—in particular, iMessage's ability to sync across platforms. Most people don't realize this, but if you own an iPhone and a Mac both systems will stay in constant sync. If you bought a song or movie on your MacBook, the purchase immediately appeared on your iPhone. If you took a picture with your phone, you can go to the photo stream on your Mac and the image is there. Users can seamlessly jump from one device to the other and pick up right where they left off. The same holds true of iMessage, the iPhone's built-in texting application. Conversations on one instantly appear on the other. The system has a quirky side effect, though—if you delete a text conversation on one device, the messages remain on the other until the system needs the space. Text messages rarely got lost.

Rachael clicked on LaunchPad, bringing up a list of Thad's available programs. She located iMessage and opened the program.

Only one conversation in the queue: two days ago, with Ryan and his publisher.

Thad: Ryan? Are you there?

Ryan: Thad? When did you join the 21st century?

Thad: Ha

Thad: Smart ass

Ryan: What's up?

Thad: Heading to NY to meet up with Del. Want me to give him the manuscript? He said he's meeting with you too.

Ryan: Can't you email it?

Thad: Um. Some of it's in longhand. Also has some sketches and drawings. Not sure how to get them into my Mac. Best to give you a printout with photocopies.

Ryan: Seriously? You haven't gone old school with longhand since your second one.

Thad: Hopefully this one will do as well.

Ryan: K. Give the manuscript to Del then

Thad: I've got some ideas for the cover, I'll send them to you in a second.

Ryan: No problem

Thad: Ok, bye.

Ryan: People don't say 'bye' in texts, Thad. You're not hanging up. You crack me up :)

Thad: Ok. Signing off.

Thad: Bye.

Thad: Seems weird to not say bye.

Ryan: Ok. Bye, Thad.

He followed the conversation with two photographs of sketches. Rachael's eyes widened as she double-clicked on the first image, enlarging it to see a profile of an old woman in tattered clothing. The hood of the woman's cloak pulled over her head cast a shadow across worn, wrinkled skin. Her eyes stared out from the page and bore into Rachael. The woman's hand was raised, her twisted fingers ending in long fingernails scratching at the air.

The woman from her nightmare. The one who claimed rights to her child.

Rachael knew the image had been drawn in Thad's journal; she could see the metal binding gripping the paper's edge.

How?

A single word scribbled beneath the woman.

Her.

Rachael scrolled down to the second image and opened it.

A young girl. The most beautiful girl she had ever seen. Radiant dark hair, flowing past her shoulders. Flawless skin. And her eyes...although the sketch was black and white, Thad shaded the eyes with blue, the only color to appear on the page.

Four words scrawled below the image, this stunning girl.

Her?

Then beneath that—

Anything for Her.

CHAPTER TWENTY-SEVEN

1692
The Journal of Clayton Stone

*T*HICK AND COLD, THE *air caused me to wake suddenly. A fog of chilly night lit by the moon inched across the floor, chasing the shadows. I glanced around in search of her, but she was gone—for how long, I could not be sure. My throat was dry and my bones ached. I wiped my weary eyes and slid my feet to the cold, wooden planks.*

It was then that I saw the footprints.

Muddy tracks leading to the door.

I will not attempt to explain my reasoning. I do not understand myself. My actions were not sound, not that of a God-fearing man.

I reached for my coat and boots, and followed the tracks into the night.

—Thad McAlister,
Rise of the Witch

CHAPTER TWENTY-EIGHT

Day 2 – 9:45 a.m.

DEL THOMAS STEPPED INTO his apartment and quickly went to his desk. Carefully, he opened his briefcase, removed the manuscript, and set the pages down before him, his fingertips feeling the warmth rising from the stack.

He had finished the manuscript on the plane and didn't have the words to describe what he read. The story both disturbed him and inspired him, it brought fear and excitement—more so than anything else he had ever read. Her life brought chills to his tired bones.

He couldn't get her out of his mind.

Outside, lightning filled the morning sky followed by a thick roll of thunder, which shook his building like the angry hands of a giant on a toy.

Del didn't waste any time.

Running to his kitchen, he tore open the cabinets and began gathering all the bowls he could find—large and small, plastic and glass. As a bachelor, he quickly realized more of the objects he sought were in the sink rather than the cabinets, freeing three more from a mess of unwashed dishes. He found eight in all and stacked them in his arms, then went to his balcony.

Again, lightning filled the sky. He grew anxious. The balcony wasn't large, but it would do. Carefully, he began placing the bowls on the floor before him, setting down the last as the first drops of rain fell.

Del stood and admired his work.

Within moments, the heavens opened up and rain began to fall in thick sheets. He watched as the bowls began catching drop after drop.

Del knew he had much more to do today. The book was very specific.

Her needs were very specific.

Grabbing his coat and an umbrella, Del headed out into the dismal morning. The next item on his list might prove to be more elusive.

━━━━━━━

Thad retrieved his cell phone from the corner of the room.

He had thrown the iPhone hard enough to shut it down, but at least he didn't crack the display. He pressed the power button, hoping he hadn't damaged it. When the Apple logo appeared, he breathed.

When the main menu filled the screen, Thad clicked through to the call log.

Blank.

E-mails and texts were gone as well.

Why did he have to throw the phone?

Part of him needed to find her call in the log—something to confirm last night had really happened.

But if she's real, then what she's asking is real. You have to find the Rumina Box.

Better that she's not real. Better that he imagined everything—the park, the call this morning. That would mean his family was safe, not held by…by whom? This group? Followers of the witch in his book? How was that even possible? Maybe some cult would pop up after publication. The world was filled with crazies. But how could such a group exist before the book's publication?

She told the truth, Thad. You know she did. The witch is real. She planted the book in your head. She made you write it. She made you put the entire story on paper for them. For Her.

She wants to come back.

And you're going to help.

Thad stared down at the pill bottle still in his hand.

When he took them, he couldn't write. They shut down the creativity, the desire. They silenced the voices of his characters. Would they silence her?

Not if she's real.

═══════════

Thad showered and dressed, then went downstairs.

At this early hour, the bar was closed but he spotted the bartender from last night taking inventory, preparing for the night ahead. The young man looked up when Thad approached. "Sleeping Beauty lives!"

Thad offered a weak smile. "I wanted to apologize for my behavior yesterday. We were celebrating and things got out of hand. I should have stopped when my agent left."

The bartender heaved a case of Coors Light onto the counter and began filling the well. "No worries, Mr. McAlister. If we don't celebrate life's little moments, what else have we got? You most definitely looked like you had a good time. That's for sure."

"Speaking of that, any idea what happened to the girl I was talking to?"

The bartender laughed. "You're going to need to be more specific; you had quite the crowd around you."

Crowd? Thad didn't remember a crowd—only her.

"Long dark hair, blue eyes, dark skirt, white blouse…I…I may have left with her."

He frowned. "Sorry, last night was busy."

"She said she came back and asked you and a friend to help me up to my room."

"I think someone's playing you. I went out for a smoke and found you standing outside, covered in mud.

Smelled like you recycled a meal or two. Didn't see a girl. I got your room number from the front desk. Billy and me took you up to thirty-one in the elevator and dropped you at your suite so you'd sleep it off," he said.

Thad tried to recall what had happened, but nothing came back.

"Hey, we've all been there. That's how I got this tattoo." He rolled up his sleeve, revealing a dolphin with an angry smirk. "One too many tequila shots. Next thing you know, I've got this and some girl I'd never met going through my wallet at three in the morning. Alcohol can lead to many a bad night. You've got to shake it off. Forget. Start the day anew."

"Yeah, you're probably right. Best to turn a blind eye than try to sort out what happened."

"Exactly."

Thad's phone vibrated and he glanced down at the screen.

A single text—

Unknown: You have three days, Thad. You need to get started.

CHAPTER TWENTY-NINE
Day 2 – 9:55 a.m.

FROM THE SAFETY OF Fort Buster—an overstuffed recliner positioned in the far corner of the living room, surrounded by strategically stacked pillows—Ashley and Buster monitored the couch with attentive eyes. Ashley had ordered Buster to take the first guard-duty shift while she had scoured the house in search of weapons and supplies. He obeyed, laying low to the ground, his worried gaze fixed on the couch.

When Ashley returned fifteen minutes later, he had whimpered a soft hello before turning back to the couch, his tail thumping on the hardwood at his back.

"Shhh," Ashley ordered, holding his tail still with her free hand. "I got us lots of good stuff," she told him. "I got my slingshot, Daddy's fishing net, some cheese—hey!"

141

Buster had found the cheese and made quick work of the morsel. His muzzle was now searching the ground for crumbs while his large brown eyes begged forgiveness from his superior officer.

"That was the last of our bait," Ashley frowned. "How are we going to catch anything without bait?"

Buster cocked his head and whimpered.

"It's okay, boy. We'll find something else."

When Buster's ears stood at attention and he fell silent, Ashley knew she was coming back.

The enemy.

She ushered Buster deeper into their alcove and held her breath as Ms. Perez stepped back into the room with an armload of supplies of her own. She dropped them at her feet and said something in Spanish that Ashley could only assume was naughty. She was always saying naughty things.

Lying on her stomach, Ashley peered under the recliner at the housekeeper. Beside her, Buster licked her face and then turned his attention back to Ms. Perez and the strange items she had brought into the room.

She struggled with the couch, wrestling it further away from the wall.

Reaching into her supplies, she pulled out a small piece of drywall, rounded the edges to fit the hole, and forced the patch into place. She then applied tape and drywall mud, sealing the small space.

Ashley and Buster remained still as the housekeeper set a number of mousetraps (without cheese), then spread a black powder on the floor at the baseboard.

Finished, Ms. Perez stood and inspected her handiwork. With a satisfied grunt, she gathered her supplies and left the room.

Ashley and Buster waited a moment before leaving the safety of Fort Buster and making their way to the newly patched hole, remaining clear of the smelly couch. Buster guarded the door as Ashley knelt down to get a better look at the hole, avoiding the traps and dark powder.

She could hear them on the other side.

At first, the slight scratching was barely audible, but the sound grew louder.

Ashley imagined not two tiny hands clawing at the new plaster but four, then six, then eight, their numbers growing as they attempted to break through before the patch dried. Buster was standing beside her now, also eyeing the hole, a subtle whimper growing in his throat.

When a little fist poked through, Ashley tried to scream but her voice had left her.

———————

Thad watched the driver load his luggage into the back of the cab, then climbed inside.

"Where to, buddy?"

"JFK Airport, please."

With a blast of the horn, they wedged out into traffic.

Thad pulled out his phone and glanced down at the screen.

As before, everything had reset. All the logs were empty, including text messages.

He must have broken the phone when he threw it.

Or she never really texted you; you imagined it.

He dialed home, unsure of what he would get. The line rang several times, then went to a fast busy signal.

No voice mail.

Thad hung up and felt another surge of guilt.

You didn't cheat on your wife, he told himself. *You wouldn't do that. In your drunken haze, you dreamt the whole mess. Had to be a dream.*

It was natural to dream of a sexual encounter with a stranger, particularly when you're away from the woman you love.

But she's not a stranger, is she?

His phone rang and he quickly pressed the ANSWER button. "Rachael?"

"I thought I set the rules, Thad. Wasn't I clear? You are to have no contact with your family until this is over."

Christina.

"I need to know they're all right," he told her.

"Your only concern should be the box," she said.

"I have to speak to them," he insisted.

"You need to keep them alive," she replied, "long enough to find the box."

"How do I know you won't hurt them?"

"You will not be permitted to speak to them. You will not be permitted to see them. You will not be permitted to return home until you have the box," she said. "Those are the rules. Do I make myself clear?"

"Yes," Thad replied, disconnecting the call.

He checked the call log.

UNKNOWN – 5 seconds ago

She was real.

She had to be real. This proved it, didn't it?

This girl had his family. He had no idea how many other people were involved, but he assumed she wasn't working alone. In fact, something told him she had eyes and ears everywhere, possibly even here.

He looked up at the driver, then turned away when their gazes met in the rearview mirror.

CHAPTER THIRTY

1692

The Journal of Clayton Stone

A **THICK FOG WRAPPED** around me as I found myself deep within the forest, the town lost behind me, now sleeping at this late hour. I had considered turning around a number of times. I had no business in these woods, of this I was certain. My curiosity led me forward, though; it would be the death of me someday, I thought. Always silencing my better judgement, tempting the fate laid out for me by my Lord.

I had been to this place only once prior, long ago as a child on the dare of Jude Olsen. For even then our parents had told us it was an unholy place, one to which we were never to go. On that night, I hadn't traveled as far as I had tonight. Instead, I had turned back with the first hoot of an owl—an owl that became a bear when I retold the story. I hadn't found the witch's house on that night, but like the others in our town, I knew where it was.

Tonight I heard many animals, most of which watched me cautiously from behind a blanket of shadows as I pressed deeper into the woods.

When the cabin came into view my heart raced within my chest, my breath caught before me in a misty haze. I crouched low among the brush and peered across the clearing.

A single candle burned at the window, the only light on this darkest of nights, the moon and stars cast out by a thick veil of clouds.

I recalled the stories of childhood.

The witch of the woods. The old woman clad in rags with fingernails long and sharp, clicking and clacking as she anxiously awaited the souls of children to venture within her realm.

Childhood tales and nothing more. Bumps in the night spun by our parents, meant to raise the gooseflesh and keep us from wandering alone in this vast forest, away from our homes, away from the safety of the town.

Yet there was something about this place.

Something…wrong.

Within the cabin, a shadow stirred.

A cry filled the night.

The mournful wail pierced the silence, sending birds fluttering from the trees as they found flight.

I turned to flee only to find an old woman standing mere inches behind me, her eyes wide, her lips peeled back over yellowed teeth in an unholy smile. "I knew your father, Clayton of Stone," she hissed. "Will your blood be as sweet as his?"

I pushed past her and raced back toward town without so much as a backward glance, my skin crawling, her rancid scent lingering as I fled, her nails snapping against one another—

Clickity, click.

—Thad McAlister,
Rise of the Witch

CHAPTER THIRTY-ONE
Day 2 – 10:30 a.m.

"**I NEED TO EXCHANGE** this ticket for one to Boston, Massachusetts. Can I do that?"

The girl behind the North Eastern Airlines counter eyed Thad wearily, then took the ticket from his hand and began typing away at her terminal.

Although dressed in an airline uniform, the counter girl wasn't quite what she seemed. A streak of bright pink hair poked out from under her regulation cap and when she turned to fetch something off the printer. Thad glimpsed the top of a red thong beneath her tight slacks. Her perfume was familiar to him, but he couldn't quite place it.

She returned to the counter with the printout in hand. "I've got a three fifteen into Boston but nothing earlier. I'm sorry."

Glancing at the clock behind her, Thad noted the time. It was almost ten thirty in the morning. "That will have to do," he told her.

"Can I see your driver's license, please?"

Reaching into his wallet, Thad removed his driver's license and handed it to her.

She glanced at the name and smiled back at him. "You're that writer, aren't you?"

Thad nodded. "That's me. Which one is your favorite?"

"Dunno, I don't read that trash," she said with a grin, returning his driver's license. "I've never been into fiction much."

"Really, what do you read?"

She shrugged her shoulders. "Between my class schedule and work I don't have the time for recreational reading anymore, just textbooks. This week I'm buried in algebra and European history. Not what I would call fun."

"That's a shame."

"Yeah, it is," she replied. "Do you like it?"

"Like what?"

"You know, writing."

"Most of the time I do," he told her.

"But not now?"

Thad shrugged his shoulders. "Sometimes it takes me in directions I really don't want to go."

"Like Boston?"

"Yeah right, like Boston."

"So why go?"

I have to.

"Sometimes choices aren't always your own to make," Thad said.

"Aren't you Captain Mystery," she joked. "Is that an occupational hazard?"

"Something like that," he said. "Are we about done here?"

Her face flushed and she returned to her computer. "Sorry, I didn't mean to pry."

Thad shook his head. "That's not what I meant, I'm sorry. You're not prying. I guess I'm just a little tired. I had a long night."

"Here you go, Mr. McAlister," she said, handing him his updated ticket. "You're all set to fly out of Gate 24 at three fifteen arriving in Boston at four twenty. Would you like me to arrange a rental car for you?"

Thad shook his head.

"Thank you for flying North Eastern Airlines," she said. "Can I help the next person in line, please?"

Thad smiled, scooped up his belongings, and made his way across the terminal to the waiting area where he found a seat in the corner. He settled in for a long wait.

Running his hand across his stubbly chin, he sighed, then clicked open his briefcase.

His journal sat inside, open to the sketch of the box.

The Rumina Box.

"Carved of oak and lined with lead, it forever holds the souls of the dead," he said softly.

The simple phrase had come to him as easily as did the name of the box, the story itself.

Was he to believe the line had been placed in his mind? Just dropped into his head, where it waited patiently to be told? To be written in the journal? To be shared with the world? Not a work of fiction but a roadmap, one he followed now?

The witch in his story had been capable of such a task. Of that, he had no doubt.

But She's not real.

Last night seemed real enough.

Her.

He shook his head. What the hell was he doing? He should go home, just go home.

Thad's rational side told him there was no box; there never had been a box. Yet, the rest of him was convinced it would be right where his mind's eye had left it at the end of his novel—beneath an old oak tree, sleeping under a blanket of rotten earth.

He wouldn't be able to get Her out of his mind until he held the box in his hands.

The story wasn't over yet—the ending yet to be written. Perhaps this was an epilogue, writing itself as he went. An epilogue to the book he had handed Del.

He had to follow through.

If the Rumina Box did exist, if Her story was real, he had to find the box before someone else did—before it fell into the hands of someone unaware of its true power. Or worse still, before it fell into the hands of someone who did.

There is no box. There is no girl. Your mind is breaking,

buddy. You're slipping fast. You're jumping on a plane to follow a delusion.

Thad thought about the pills in his bag. He wanted to take another. Make all of this go away.

But he needed to know if it was true.

So go.

CHAPTER THIRTY-TWO

Day 2 – 10:30 a.m.

DEL THOMAS FISHED TWENTY dollars from his wallet, paid the cab driver, then darted from the car into the pouring rain with his jacket held above his head like a makeshift umbrella. Careful not to slide on the wet pavement, he hurried onto the sidewalk and pushed through the thick crowd hunched below the awnings of the various storefronts of downtown Boston.

Searching the signs, he spotted Rosemarie's Flowers about three doors down and stepped inside, leaving the weather at his back.

The aroma hit him at once and Del thought his allergies would quickly surface, but they did not. Instead, he found himself taking in the pleasant scents of the hundreds of flowers lining the shelves and tables—his eyes lost in a sea of color as they took in every bloom, every leaf. Until today, he had never thought of himself as much of a flower person. In fact, for the most part, he despised them. He wasn't home enough to care for a plant and didn't see the point in keeping something around only to watch it meet an untimely demise, particularly at his hand.

"You seem lost," the shopkeeper said from behind the far counter, eyeing him with the suspicion of a bank teller watching a customer wearing a hooded jacket in July. "Are you looking for something in particular? No wedding band, so I doubt you're picking up flowers for the missus, and today is certainly not the day to start a garden."

Del shook the water from his jacket and crossed the store, forcing a smile. "Well, you've got me pegged, don't you!"

The shopkeeper grinned. "Let's just say you don't look like one of my regulars."

"Fair enough," Del replied. "I'm trying to find a very special plant, one not usually found in this part of the country. A bougainvillea."

"Mmm, that is going to be tough. They typically only grow in the southern states and out west in the desert. They're not real fond of rain, so they're not hardy out here. They'll grow, but you won't see any blooms. What do you plan to do with it?"

Del hesitated for a moment, choosing his words with care. "It's actually for a friend. She said she wants one, and I'm not about to question her motives. Her wish is my command, right?" he said with a wink.

The shopkeeper frowned. "There's not a whole lot you can do with these. Sure, they're pretty, but they're covered in nasty thorns—prickly little things—they'll take a good bite out of you if you're not careful. And see these blooms—" He pulled a photo off the wall behind him and handed it to Del. "Those gorgeous blooms are deadly poisonous. Your friend, she doesn't have any pets, does she?"

Del shook his head.

"That's good. I'd hate for a dog or cat to chow down and get sick. Let me make a few phone calls and I'll find out how quickly I can get them delivered," he said.

Del frowned. "You don't carry them here?"

"Something like this? Naw. I'll have to get them from out west somewhere or maybe even Florida. Give me a minute," he said, disappearing into the back room.

Del swore under his breath. He didn't have that kind of time. He glanced down at the photo in his hand and flipped it over. "I'll be damned." There was an address written in the top left corner.

CHAPTER THIRTY-THREE

1692
The Journal of Clayton Stone

"**MERCY SHORT IS DEAD!** *Murdered as she slept!*"
I glanced up from my writings to find Carol Bender's plump frame standing in the doorway.

She was pale, clearly frightened.

"What is this?" the magistrate bellowed.

"We were to meet today, and when she did not appear by midmorning I went to her home. The door was open and she did not answer my calls, so I went inside," she dropped her head into her hands. "It was the smell that I noticed first. Then I saw her." She began to weep. "...so much blood," she breathed.

The magistrate went for the door, led closely by the other elders. "Come, boy," he ordered as he passed me. "This should be documented."

—Thad McAlister,
Rise of the Witch

CHAPTER THIRTY-FOUR

Day 2 – 10:30 a.m.

ASHLEY WATCHED IN HORROR as the tiny little hand poked through the fresh plaster and wiggled before her, grasping at the air. Like her own, the hand had four fingers and a thumb, but the similarities stopped there. Its nails were long and sharp, its skin a dark gray—almost black. The hand was bony, yet strong. It seemed to reach for her, held back only by the thinly repaired wall which cracked away at a fast clip.

Buster had backed up, growling, his angry throat working itself up to a bark.

Ashley remembered the red eyes from the night before, eyes which clearly belonged to the owner of this hand. She also remembered how the monster had bitten Buster, how it had wanted to bite her.

A small piece of plaster broke away and the arm reached closer, its tiny shoulder poking through the hole. Ashley frantically looked around her, eyes settling on the various mousetraps Ms. Perez had left behind. Fighting back tears, she picked up one of the traps and eased it toward the flailing hand. When its fingers brushed the wood, the creature paused for a moment, no doubt attempting to determine what it had found, then snatched the edge, pulling the trap away from Ashley and slamming it into the plaster. Like a battering ram, the monster continued to pull the trap back hard against the wall, chipping away at the plaster with each hit. Unsure of what to do, Ashley gripped the trap with both hands and tried to take it away. From behind the wall came a frustrated grunt. Then another hand appeared and reached for the wood. Tiny fingers brushed the trap's trigger and the metal spring released, sending the bar crashing back onto the little hands, severing them above the wrists. The creature squealed in pain and disappeared back into the hole. Ashley fell back, the mousetrap still in her hand.

In all the commotion, Ashley hadn't heard Buster barking, nor did she notice her mother rush in from the other room. Both were standing over her now, staring at the mousetrap in her hand.

"What did you do?" her mother asked. "Are you hurt?"

Ashley couldn't take her eyes off the trap.

"What's wrong?"

Ashley shook her head. The hands were gone, replaced with small piles of foul-smelling dirt.

"Show me your fingers. Did they get caught in the trap?"

Ashley dropped the trap and held her hands up to her mother.

Satisfied that Ashley had not hurt herself, her mother let go and frowned. "Those things can break your bones. I don't want you anywhere near them, and God knows what that powder is. Go wash yourself and promise me you'll stay away from here."

Ashley could only nod her head.

She wanted to tell her mother what she saw, but she didn't have the words. She wouldn't believe her anyway—no more than she did last night when the creature bit Buster. She needed proof. She needed to show her mommy they were real.

Pouting, she stood and left the room with Buster following at her side—her only soldier. She couldn't help but wonder how many the enemy had, but she was sure it was a lot.

CHAPTER THIRTY-FIVE

Day 2 – 10:32 a.m.

RACHAEL WATCHED AS HER daughter sulked away before turning her attention back to the small hole in the wall. Ms. Perez had obviously sealed it as she had asked, but then why did Ashley try to reopen it? Did she think the rats were pets like the furry little creatures in some of her cartoons? Perhaps she wanted to rescue them? She wasn't in the mood to try to get into her daughter's thoughts right now. She only wanted to solve this problem and possibly get some rest.

Quickly searching the room, she found a stack of books on the end table and braced them against the hole like she did upstairs. She then repositioned the mouse-traps around the books in case they were able to get through.

The stench in this room had grown stronger and was making her nauseated. She hoped Ms. Perez had reached the exterminator. The couch had to go, too. They couldn't keep it—not after what they had found inside.

Thunder crackled in the sky.

Just what we need, she thought, *more rain.*

She pulled her cell phone from her pocket and dialed Thad.

Voice mail.

"Dammit." Should she try Del?

Not yet. He'll call. She had to give him space, had to trust him.

As she returned to the kitchen, she switched to iMessage and opened the two images she had forwarded from Thad's MacBook: the girl and the old woman. Both faces looked up at her from the phone's tiny screen, eyes so lifelike they seemed to follow her gaze. The old woman, haunted, horrifying. The young girl, longing and lustful.

She had so many questions.

How could Thad possibly have drawn the woman from *her* dreams? Her nightmares? Not once had she mentioned the old woman to him, not once.

"Ms. Rachael?"

Rachael jumped, nearly dropping the phone.

"I'm sorry, Ms. Rachael. I did not mean to frighten you."

Ms. Perez was at the kitchen door, a dust cloth in her hand.

Rachael forced a smile. "I'm a little jumpy."

"Mr. Thad will call," Ms. Perez said. "I am sure he is just busy. He has much love for you."

Rachael nodded. "Thank you, Carmen."

"The exterminator will be here Friday before lunch. I called a friend of mine. He is very nice. He will do a very good job."

"He can't come sooner?"

"No. Friday is the earliest. I called two others, but none are able to come until next week. My friend is the soonest and the best. He said no problem to wait until Friday."

"Please try to find someone who can come sooner," Rachael said.

The woman nodded. "I will try."

Rachael glanced down at her phone, then back at her housekeeper. "Ms. Perez?"

"Yes, Ms. Rachael?"

"Have you ever seen my husband draw a picture?"

The woman appeared puzzled.

"When you clean his office? Have you ever spotted any sketches?"

"I would never snoop through Mr. Thad's work."

"I know that," Rachael said reassuringly. "But maybe while you were cleaning, maybe you saw something?"

Ms. Perez's eyes turned to the floor. "In his old book, the one on his desk, there are many drawings. I did not open the book, though; it was already open."

"I'm sure you didn't," Rachael said. "And if the journal happened to be open on his desk, there is nothing wrong with taking a peek."

Perez said nothing.

"What did you see, Carmen? What kind of drawings are in his journal?"

"Mr. Thad would not be angry?"

"Of course not. If he left the book open on his desk, I think he'd want you to look."

"I see many drawings," she told her.

"Drawings of what?"

"There was an old tree. And a picture of a box," she recalled. "Both were very good drawings. Mr. Thad is a talented man."

"Any pictures of women?"

Perez hesitated. She tugged at her left thumb with her right hand and shuffled her feet.

"Carmen?"

She spoke softly, "There were women."

Rachael held the phone out to her. "Did you see these two?"

Perez glanced at the screen and nodded. "Many of both."

"Do you know who they are?"

She shook her head.

"Are they characters from his book, or do you think they're real?"

"I do not know."

"Has he ever mentioned them to you? Maybe he saw you looking through his journal?"

The woman grew quiet. "Your marriage is happy, yes?"

"Of course," Rachael said without hesitation. "Why do you ask?"

Perez fidgeted, unsure if she should continue.

"Why do you ask, Carmen?"

Her housekeeper pointed to the picture of the young girl. "In many of the pictures, this one is naked. He draws her many times naked."

CHAPTER THIRTY-SIX

1692
The Journal of Clayton Stone

I DIDN'T WANT TO GO—*let me make that perfectly clear. The magistrate insisted, however, leaving me with little choice but to follow him back to the church and down the dark, narrow staircase at the back.*

I carried a candle, but the flame neither fought back the shadows, nor intimidated the cold, which grew stronger with each step as we descended the stairs into the damp basement. The earthen floor was muddy with last night's rain. Tugging at my every step, muck seeped into my boots.

"It's just ahead," the magistrate told me.

We came to a large oak door and he pulled a key from around his neck. The lock turned with a clunk that echoed in the narrow hallway. He pulled at the large door and it slowly opened, revealing another hallway. This one was lined with black metal bars on either side. Cells. At least four of them beneath the church, my church.

"When were these built? Who authorized such a thing?" I couldn't help but ask.

The magistrate silenced me with a glare.

Our breath formed a fog trailing at our backs as we stepped into the chamber. The magistrate tensed as he neared the cell on the far left. With his candle he lit the lantern hanging on the corridor wall, sending an eerie glow dancing across the stone.

I didn't spot her at first. It wasn't until I approached the bars that I saw her small frame curled tight on the floor beside the wooden bed. She was shrouded in a frilled blanket. I could feel her eyes on me, but her face was lost to the shadows.

"Get up, you wench!" the magistrate ordered, his voice bellowing off the stone walls.

Her tiny frame remained still.

He picked up a bucket of water from beside the wall and flung it at the bars, soaking the girl and her wooden bed. Her head jerked up from beneath the blanket and she hissed at him, her eyes dark as coal.

"Enough!" the magistrate shouted. "Mercy Short and her husband were murdered in their bed. What do you know of this?" Although his voice was strong and sure, I couldn't help but hear a sliver of fear in his words. I refused to look at her directly, knowing if she truly was a witch, only a direct glance would be enough for her spell to grip me.

I found it hard not to gaze at her, particularly after the visit of her sister—a visit of which I had failed to tell anyone.

She glanced up at me and a smile filled her lips. "Finally, you have brought a witness to view the conditions in which I've been kept. Perhaps his heart isn't as dark as yours."

The magistrate raised the bucket, ready to soak her again. I reached up and grabbed his arm mid-swing.

"How dare you?" he breathed.

"Angering her will not bring us answers," I told him. "Perhaps if she agrees to tell us what we need to know, there will be no need for further punishment."

The magistrate held the bucket with quaking hands, then set it down at his feet. "You shouldn't find pity for such a foul creature. She is less than a dog."

It was not her I pitied, but I dared not speak my true feelings.

"What part did you take in their deaths?"

She smiled back at him. "What would you like me to say? That witchcraft allowed me to leave this cage and dispose of that liar and her wretched man, then return unnoticed? Would that satisfy you?" She rolled her eyes. "Perhaps I stopped at the local tavern for a drink and nourishment as well. I have told you, I am not a witch. I'm not capable of such things."

The magistrate kicked the bucket of water at her. "You lie! You had a hand in this!"

She stood, and the blanket fell from her petite frame, her long dark hair cascading over her shoulders. She approached the bars. Her dark blue eyes burned through the shadows, so much so that I had to look away.

"If I were capable of taking a life while locked in this terrible place, don't you think it would be yours?" she said to the magistrate, her finger gently brushing against his on the cold metal.

The magistrate pulled away. "You sicken me."

"I don't think it was you," I told her.

She smiled. "Finally, a man with sensibilities."

"Where can we find your mother and sisters?" I asked, my eyes locked with hers.

She turned away, ever so quickly, and walked toward the back of her cell. "I have no sisters, and my mother is long dead," she replied.

"I don't believe you."

She leaned against the back wall and ran her hand through her long dark hair. "And why should you? After all, I am but a witch and a whore, am I not? Not someone to be trusted or believed. I was wrong about you. You're no different than the rest, no better than him," she nodded toward the magistrate.

"This is a waste of time," he spat. "The trials will decide your fate soon enough. If there truly is blood on your hands, you will pay for your sins."

Her glare found his, her eyes black and cold. "As will you," she concurred. "As will you."

—Thad McAlister,
Rise of the Witch

CHAPTER THIRTY-SEVEN
Day 2 – 3:15 p.m.

THAD SETTLED INTO HIS seat in first class with his briefcase on his lap. He watched in silence as the passengers of Flight 931 boarded the plane, filling it from front to back.

He needed a drink.

He knew after the previous night that the last thing he should do was hit the bottle, but his nerves were on edge and if he didn't do something to calm down soon he wouldn't be able to focus on his task. He wouldn't be able to find the box.

The box.

Did they have Rachael and Ashley?

Just because they weren't answering the phone didn't mean they were in danger. They might be out shopping or visiting neighbors, or even—

They have them. They have them for sure.

"Excuse me, miss?" The flight attendant paused in the aisle, turned, and smiled. "Yes, sir?"

Thad did his best to smile back. "Would it be possible to get a drink?"

"I'm sorry, sir, but we're not permitted to serve alcohol until after takeoff," she replied, pressing against his arm in order to allow a passenger to pass down the aisle. "Sorry," she blushed.

Thad smiled. "No problem. Listen, normally I wouldn't ask but I'm a real nervous flyer. I usually take a sleeping pill, but I didn't have a chance to pick some up. I could really use a drink before we take off."

She sighed, then nodded her head. "Let me see what I can do."

"Thanks."

Thad watched as she made her way to the flight attendant station behind the cockpit and disappeared around the corner. She returned a moment later with a can of 7 Up and a plastic cup filled with ice and soda. She winked and handed it to him. "Don't let the appearance fool you; it's Grey Goose."

Thad took the cup and raised it to his lips, putting it down in one gulp. He shook as the cool liquid burned his throat.

"Wow! You did need that!" She chuckled, taking the empty cup away. "My name is Francine; let me know if I can get you anything else."

"Will do."

171

A woman one row up on the left side stared at him. She turned away when he spotted her. Thad spied one of his books in her hand. *Among Us*, he believed. It was hard to tell from the dust jacket. He recognized his photo staring back at him.

"Wonderful," he muttered.

Turning, he found another woman sitting three rows back with another of his books in her hand. Behind her was a man in his mid-fifties. He held one of his books too. Unlike most, when their eyes met he didn't turn away. Instead, he met Thad's gaze.

We're watching you, Thad, Christina had said.

Is this what she meant?

Am I being paranoid?

Thad sunk low in his seat, his fingers clutching his briefcase so tight they had turned white. He thumbed the locks, rolling the dials to random numbers (not that anyone with a screwdriver and a little determination would be denied access for very long). Reaching up, he twisted the small air conditioner vent until he felt the trickle of recycled air streaming down on his face. Thad closed his eyes and hoped this was nothing more than a very bad dream.

The plane roared to life and began down the runway.

CHAPTER THIRTY-EIGHT
Day 2 – 7:30 p.m.

THE SCREAM WAS LOUD and echoed through the old house.

At the kitchen sink, Rachael froze as the cry cut through the otherwise silent house, riding the still air until reaching her with a slap, causing her to drop the apple she had been rinsing under the warm water.

The scream was followed by a mix of English and Spanish obscenities, each louder than the previous, nailed haphazardly together by the deep sobs which fell between them.

It had come from upstairs.

"Ms. Perez?" Rachael called out. "Carmen?"

If the woman had heard her, she was not inclined to answer. Only her cries drifted down from the second floor.

Where is Ashley?

———

Leaving the water running, Rachael raced to the staircase as fast as any woman in her third trimester possibly could, the pains in her abdomen growing stronger with each step. The baby kicked as she reached the second-floor landing. She rubbed her stomach, her touch reaching for the child within her, fingers soothing it until it stilled.

She found Ms. Perez standing at Ashley's door, her hand over her mouth, her tear-filled eyes wide, her cries now nothing more than a faded whimper.

God, my baby. . . Please let Ashley be safe.

The housekeeper stepped aside as Rachael drew close, her eyes dropping to the floor. "Ms. Rachael, I have no idea how this has happened," she murmured. "I leave her alone for just a minute, only a minute."

Drawing a deep breath, Rachael looked into her daughter's room.

The odor wrapped around her, choked her, and she almost fell back as her breakfast threatened to rise up her throat.

Ashley stood at the center of the room, her clothing piled at her feet. Her eyes were glazed over, staring blindly at the ceiling. A muddled gurgle rose from her lips, increased to a growl, then fell silent. She repeated the noise seconds later, and again after that.

The walls were covered in dirt, scrawled across the

bright pink surface Rachael had painted last summer when her daughter had insisted she was too big for the clown-covered wallpaper that had adorned her walls from birth.

The vile substance had been spread with no rhyme or reason except to cover every square inch.

"Dirty child," Ms. Perez snarled.

Yet she wasn't, Rachael noted. Her daughter was perfectly clean. She stood in the dead center of this disgusting mess, yet down to her fingertips she was free of the foulness that surrounded her.

Her daughter's shelves were bare, too; all the toys which had filled them as recently as an hour ago were stacked to the ceiling in the far left corner, a freestanding structure inches from the walls and nearly eight feet in height.

Her daughter couldn't have possibly done this.

"Mommy?"

Her voice seemed distant, and at first Rachael wasn't sure she had spoken at all. She watched in awe as her daughter lowered her head, meeting her gaze. She reached for her and Ashley snapped to life, her eyes flooding with tears—in one instant shifting from a comatose state to one of fear as she stared in horror at her room.

"Come here, sweetie," Rachael said, her arms outstretched. "It's all right."

The little girl came to her, her feet padding across the damp carpet until she found her mother's fold. "I told him not to do it, Mommy, but he wouldn't listen. I told him over and over but he wouldn't stop, he wouldn't!"

175

"Who?"

"Zeke," her daughter whimpered between sobs. "It was Zeke."

"Her make-believe friend did this?" Ms. Perez frowned. "I am to believe this?"

Rachael silenced the woman with her glare and stroked her daughter's long blonde hair. "Don't worry, honey. We'll clean this up. Why don't you run a nice warm bath, okay? I'll be there in a minute."

Ashley nodded. "I think he's still in my room, Mommy."

"Please, honey, go start a bath," Rachael told her.

Her daughter stared up at her with shame gathered behind her wide eyes, then turned and waddled to the bathroom. The sound of running water came a moment later.

Buster poked his head out from his hiding spot behind the master bedroom door, gave Rachael and the housekeeper a quick glance, then trotted into the bathroom behind Ashley.

Rachael sighed. "I know this goes way beyond your job description, Ms. Perez, but I don't think I can go in that room. The smell is making me nauseated and with the baby so close. . . I can't go in there."

The housekeeper swore under her breath in Spanish. "I'll clean this time, but you must speak with your daughter. There is no excuse for this. So much mess, and to blame a make-believe friend? The child must be punished for this or she'll do it again," the woman said.

"I think with her father leaving town and me focused so much on this baby, she's feeling neglected. I'll talk to her later about it, when we've all had a little time to calm down," Rachael said. "I promise I will."

"Something is wrong with a child who can do this," Ms. Perez pointed out.

"I'll talk to her."

Behind them, the stack of books and toys tumbled to the ground with the rumble of a bomb and both women jumped. The tower collapsed into the center of the room, sending toys sliding across the floor.

Ms. Perez shook her head. "I'll get the carpet cleaner from the garage."

"Thank you," Rachael said, her mind racing as she tried to figure out what could drive her daughter to do something like this.

CHAPTER THIRTY-NINE
1692
The Journal of Clayton Stone

*F*ROM THE OUTSIDE, THE Short home appeared eerily normal. The small structure sat quietly at the edge of town with the thick forest at its back. Mercy had planted various flowers in the beds near the door and along the path that reached around the side of the home.

The front door stood open, revealing nothing but darkness beyond its frame.

"Where is her husband?" the magistrate asked of no one in particular.

Carol Bender stood beside me, no longer able to speak. Instead, she raised her hand and pointed at the open doorway.

"Wait here," Constable Metcalf ordered.

"I will do no such thing," the magistrate replied, pushing his way past and through the door.

As he entered the small home, his gasp was audible even from where I stood. The constable followed quickly behind him. When I started toward them, Carol Bender reached out and took my arm. "You don't want to."

She was right; I did not want to go inside. However, I felt a duty to do so. The magistrate felt this was related to the trial; as such, it was my obligation to document our findings just as he had asked.

I carefully pulled away from Carol Bender's grip and slowly approached the door, fighting the knot growing within my chest.

The smell hit me first. The thick scent of copper wormed through the air and landed upon me with bony fingers, sending a chill across my spine which only grew worse as I stepped over the threshold.

The constable and magistrate both stood at the back of the room, their wide eyes fixed on what could only be the bedroom in such a small structure, their skin pale and damp with sweat. Neither man spoke, only stared inside.

Nothing could have readied me for what we found inside.

Mercy's naked body was spread across the top of the crimson sheets, her eyes and mouth still open wide in a silent, fearful cry. Her chest had been cut open with haste and her organs removed, then placed around her on the bed. Her heart in one hand, her liver in the other.

I felt bile rise in my throat and forced it back by telling myself this was all just a terrible dream from which I would wake very soon.

The magistrate pointed to the side of the bed; it was then that I saw her husband lying in a pool of blood. His hands were wrapped around a large knife embedded deep within his chest. A fatal wound, one which it appeared he had inflicted upon himself.

"It ends," the constable murmured.

"What?" The magistrate replied, his eyes locked on the scene before him.

The constable pointed at the far wall, still lost beneath morning shadows. He pointed at the words scrawled on the wall in blood.

It Ends.

—Thad McAlister,
Rise of the Witch

CHAPTER FORTY
Day 2 – 8:00 p.m.

THAD WASN'T SURE WHEN he had dozed off, but when he woke he found Christina sitting next to him. The plane was dark and quiet; the flight attendants had retired to their cramped quarters at the front.

"What are you doing here?"

Christina smiled up at him and brought a single finger to her lips.

She had draped a blanket over the two of them while he slept. She had also lifted the small arm between their seats; her warm body now pressed up against him.

Christina took his hand in hers, wrapping her fingers around his wrist. She placed his palm against her thigh and guided him until his fingers found the soft, moist hair between her legs.

"Are you naked?" he asked.

With her free hand, she slowly pulled down the blanket, revealing her bare breasts.

Thad jerked it back up.

Christina giggled.

Glancing around, he realized they were alone. The flight attendants had pulled the curtains separating first class from the rest of the plane. The passengers were gone; nobody else was in sight.

"Where is everyone?"

"Shhh," she breathed.

Reaching under the blanket, she found his belt and began to pull it free. Thad reached down and stopped her. "We're not doing this."

Her dark eyes grew wide. "I think we are, Thad. I think you really want to."

Thad felt his arms move to his sides, pinned against the seat. He tried to move them but couldn't; they were held still by unseen hands. Somehow, she controlled them.

Her hands returned to his belt. A moment later, she unsnapped his pants and pulled down the zipper. When she reached inside, he was unable to stop her.

"You're so tense, Thad. You need to learn to relax," she teased. "Would you like me to help you relax, Thad?"

He tried to respond but found only silence as her fingers wrapped around him.

"Haven't you ever wanted to do this, Thad? Share a private moment with someone special on a plane? I've often fantasized about it, but until now I just couldn't work up the courage. Will you help me, Thad? Will you help me overcome my fear?"

With her free hand, she pulled off the blanket and dropped it on the floor, exposing herself in the dim light of the cabin. She then ran a finger down her chest, over her breasts, to her thighs, moaning as her fingers briefly disappeared before continuing down her legs. Christina closed her eyes for a moment, then leaned against him, her warm breath drifting over his ear. "I want to fuck you, right here, Thad, right now."

Sliding over to him, she pulled down his pants and slipped into his lap. Thad's arms wrapped around her, a will all their own. His arms wrapped around her and pulled her close, slipping down to the small of her back. When her lips found his again, he tried to fight, but his body wouldn't obey. His tongue pressed into her welcoming mouth.

Bring me my box, Thad.

Bring me my box and I'll reward you so...

═══════════

"Sir?"

Thad looked to his left and found the flight attendant watching him, her hands on her hips.

Christina was gone. The blanket was bunched around his waist, covering the briefcase still resting in his lap.

"We're going to be landing soon. Please fasten your safety belt and place that beneath the seat in front of you."

Thad nodded and she moved on to the next row.

Christina's perfume filled the air; he could still taste her breath.

On the seat beside him lay a small pile of dirt, much like the ones he had seen in his yard yesterday morning.

It smelled dead, moist with rot.

Reaching into his pocket, he pulled out his Risperidone. Without hesitation, he took one more.

CHAPTER FORTY-ONE
Day 2 – 8:30 p.m.

RACHAEL WORKED THE SHAMPOO through her daughter's thick blonde hair, careful not to get any in her eyes. Ashley hadn't spoken since they had found her in her room, and she was getting worried. She had tried calling Thad's cell again but as expected, only reached his voice mail. She left a rather harsh message that she now regretted and tried to put it out of her mind.

"Honey, it's okay. I'm not mad at you."

Ashley continued to stare down at the water, her hands brushing across the top of the bubbles. Buster sat at the side of the bathtub, his tail thumping against the tile. He appeared to be worried about Ashley, too.

Just beyond the door, Ms. Perez banged around the hallway, going out of her way to make as much noise as possible as she cleaned up the mess in Ashley's room. "Ashley, baby, you need to talk to me," Rachael pleaded.

She glanced up, but didn't make eye contact. Instead she looked at the door, then returned her gaze to the bubbles. "I want Daddy to come home," she finally blurted out.

Rachael sighed. "Me too, honey. He should be home soon."

"He'd believe me; he'd know it was Zeke who messed up my room. He knows I wouldn't do that."

Rachael frowned. "Let's not talk about that right now."

"You don't believe me," Ashley sulked. "You don't think Zeke is real."

Now it was Rachael's turn to fall silent. She wouldn't fall into her daughter's delusion. Having an imaginary friend was one thing, but it wasn't healthy to blame him for her own mistakes.

"Zeke is very angry about something. He wants us to leave."

Enough, Rachael thought.

Behind her, Buster's tail thumped twice.

Rachael reached for the handheld faucet and rinsed out her daughter's hair. "Do you want to sleep with me tonight?"

"Can Buster sleep with us, too?"

Rachael forced a smile. "Sure, Buster can stay with us, too. We'll have one big sleepover."

"Maybe Zeke will stay out if we're all there," Ashley hoped.

"We can only hope," Rachael agreed. "Are you ready to rinse?"

Ashley nodded, stood up, and pressed her eyes shut tight.

With the handheld faucet, Rachael rinsed away the bubbles and soap. She then lifted Ashley from the bathtub, wrapped her in a large bath towel, and dried her off. "Do you want some hot chocolate before bed?"

Ashley smiled for the first time in hours. "Yeah!"

Rachael grinned. "Okay. I set some clothes out on my bed for you—go get dressed and I'll meet you down in the kitchen; I just want to clean this up."

Ashley rushed out of the bathroom with Buster chasing behind her while Rachael released the tub drain and mopped up the water from the floor.

She was exhausted.

Sleep had been eluding her, and tonight's little episode would only add to the problem. If not for the baby, she would take a sleeping pill or two, something to knock her out.

Down the hall, Ms. Perez started the carpet shampooer.

She felt bad about asking her to clean up her daughter's mess, but she didn't really have a choice. In her condition, she wasn't able. She couldn't expect her daughter to scrub that mess off the walls. How had she gotten the dirt so high? If Thad were home...

But he's not home, is he?

Who knows when he'll be home again.

CHAPTER FORTY-TWO

1692
The Journal of Clayton Stone

*V*ERY FEW SPENT TIME with her—that is to say, with the exception of William Hobbs. A husband, he was not. Perhaps a close friend at best. One of the few she allowed inside her small home, one of the few with insight into her life. By association, many considered him to be a witch, although little evidence exists—certainly not enough for a trial, most definitely not a conviction. Those who know him speak of a quiet man, an outcast. Those who do not know him fear him, if for no reason other than his association with her.

William Hobbs entered the church cautiously, scanning the faces of the gallery. Most turned away, unwilling to meet his gaze. The magistrate guided him to the pulpit and allowed him time to seat himself before beginning the morning's questioning.

"Please state your name for the record," he ordered.

"William David Hobbs," he replied in a deep, raspy voice. One that belonged to a much older man.

"Do you fear testifying today, here, in this house of the Lord?"

Hobbs shook his head. "I can speak in the presence of God safely, as I must look to give account another day," he declared, "that I am clear as a newborn babe."

"Have you never hurt these?" inquired Tauber, indicating those in attendance. They winced at Hobbs's every glance.

"The children claim to have seen your spirit moving throughout the town on many occasions: at the home of Mercy Lewis, Mercy Short, Mary Walcott... How can you explain this?"

"It is nothing more than the imagination of a child."

"This is not a skill taught to you by her?"

He shook his head. "I have no such skill. I have hurt none of them. I will deny it to my dying day," he insisted.

"You have not attended services in some time. What of that?"

"I have been ill."

"Yet you and your spirit have been seen around town," Tauber pointed out. "You have been seen with her."

"Her roof was in need of repairs. She paid me for my services, nothing more," he told them.

Whispers washed across the crowd.

Tauber cleared his throat. "Did she make you sign her book?"

"I know of no such book."

Tauber scoffed at him in disbelief, but he left the subject unanswered. "What can you tell us about her sisters and her mother?"

Hobbs returned a puzzled gaze. "I have never met a sister, nor her mother. I know nothing of her family."

"What of her name? Do you know her true name?"

"I do not."

"So you are nothing to her? Just a roofer, a handyman at best?"

Hobbs paused for a moment, taking in his words. "Yes," he finally said. "Nothing more."

His lie was clear even to my untrained ear, but Tauber didn't press him further. He dismissed the man with the knowledge that he was being watched, that he could be called back at any time.

I couldn't help but wonder if this man was intimate with her. I understood his reluctance to speak of this, for I hadn't told anyone of her visit to me the previous night. I held no plans to ever speak of this.

—Thad McAlister,
Rise of the Witch

CHAPTER FORTY-THREE
Day 2 – 9:30 p.m.

DEL GLANCED DOWN AT the directions he had printed from Mapquest, slowing his car as he neared the next intersection.

"Bridleway Road, bingo!" he said aloud, turning right.

The rain had slowed to a steady drizzle as night crept across the sky. He dropped the printout on the passenger seat and began scanning the house numbers for 5375. When he found it, he drove past about one hundred feet, then pulled the car to the side of the road and placed it in park.

He killed the engine and surveyed his surroundings.

The tree-lined road represented picture-perfect America, the type of place Del avoided at all costs. He

191

may have sold his goods to this demographic, but he never had a need to live among them. He would make this fast.

Scooping up a brown paper sack from the floor and a pair of scissors from the passenger seat, Del stepped from the car into the evening air. The thin rain found him and goose bumps crawled over his arms. He started down the road at a brisk pace, heading back in the direction he had come.

5375 was a large two-story English Tudor-style home probably built in the late twenties, early thirties. The dwelling was set back from the road about fifty feet and surrounded by a tall stone wall topped with wrought iron spikes pointing at the heavens. A cobblestone driveway began at a gate and wove through large oaks to the front of the house. There was a small metal box (presumably an intercom) as well as a camera mounted atop the gate, glaring down the drive.

None of this concerned Del, though; he had spotted the bougainvillea bushes flanking the driveway at the gate, only a few feet from the road. He approached them with caution, monitoring the road for the prying eyes of strangers. It wasn't every day an overweight man in a black trench coat wandered their streets during a rainstorm. A conscientious neighbor may consider him a threat and call in the cavalry while others may spy from their windows, curious to see what would develop from such an intrusion into their private little world.

As he stepped off the road, the muddied earth sank beneath his feet.

Not quite the work his nine hundred-dollar shoes were made for, he thought.

Jumping a small drainage ditch, Del found himself facing one of the tall bushes—his breath caught in his throat as he realized how beautiful they were. The plants' long, thin branches seemed to twist and turn together as if caught in a timeless waltz, dressed in the most elaborate of violet blooms, glistening as the rain dripped over them and fell at their feet, creating a shimmering dance floor on the ground below, one which reflected back the thick purple mass with a hint of jealousy, knowing it would never know its touch.

It's just a plant.

They hold power—the book had told him so. She had told him so.

While the long, sharp thorns would have frightened away most, Del was drawn to them. Like the teeth of a vampire, they drew the blood of the unsuspecting, providing the nourishment this beautiful flower required to survive. They also protected the branches against those who wished harm.

The perfect plant. Gorgeous.

Del reached for the bougainvillea with trembling hands. He only needed one branch, two at the most.

The blades of the scissors crunched down on the first branch with a hungry jaw, severing it from the rest, sending the piece falling toward the ground. Del caught the sampling midair, grimacing as the thorns dug into his palm, as the plant fed on the drawn blood.

Hurriedly, he dropped the branch in the paper sack, then cut another, then finally cut a third in case the first two proved insufficient.

He traced his footsteps back across the ditch to the road and shuffled back to the car.

Once inside, he placed the bougainvillea samples on the passenger seat and wrapped his injured hand in a handkerchief before starting the car and heading back toward the city. Behind him, the moon began its slow journey across the night sky.

CHAPTER FORTY-FOUR
Day 2 – 11:30 p.m.

THUNDER CRASHED WILDLY, STIRRING the dark clouds swirling ominously above the McAlister home, dropping a thick veil of rain on the remains of their lawn, now nothing more than a muddied furrow, brown and dead. Carver knelt, ran his hand through the soil, and smelled. "Ahh, settled like a fine wine," he crooned. The frigid rain drifted across his skin and quickly soaked him. Carver didn't care, though; he welcomed the rain.

His eyes never left the house, nor did he disregard the varied movements just beyond the curtained windows. He was very much aware of his surroundings, particularly the actions of the McAlister family.

"You're never that far from my thoughts, Mrs. McAlister. Don't you worry your little head about that, no ma'am."

The muffled moon provided little light, but it was enough. Carver reached into his leather bag and pulled out a small canvas sack. Carefully, he placed the bag on the ground at his feet and closed his eyes.

"Be ye far from us, O ye profane, for we are about to invoke the descent of the power of Her. Enter Her temple with clean hands and mind, lest we serve the source of life. Learn now the secret of the web that is woven between the light and the darkness, whose warp is life evolving in time and space, whose weft is spun of the lives born upon this earth. Behold Her sanctuary; arise with the dawn, from the grey and the mist and the dusk. Behold life; arise for Her."

Thunder bellowed through the night, defiant and angry.

"Evocatio Spiritualis de Septendecim Valcyriis Mortiferis."

The wind and rain grew with an unnatural anticipation, swirling around him in a mist of life, lapping at his old bones, craving the contents of the bag.

Removing the twine twisted at the top of the sack, Carver held it over his head and tilted the mouth toward the McAlisters' home. The black seeds were whisked away, thrown across the yard by the gentle hands of the livid wind, scattered within the rotten dirt. Carver held the bag high until there were no more, then crumpled the empty sack in his pocket.

With a tip of his hat, he bid farewell to the McAlisters and made his way back to the truck which he had parked down the road, taking a moment to inspect the large tree that had fallen in the center of the yard. "Sleep, my child," he breathed, stroking its bark. "All will be well soon."

CHAPTER FORTY-FIVE

1692

The Journal of Clayton Stone

I **WOKE IN THE FOREST.**

On the lives of my family, I have no idea how I ventured to this place. My last memory was of lying in my bed, overcome by sleep. Then I was here, standing among the brush and trees in the black of night, wearing nothing more than my night clothes, my bare feet sinking in the damp earth.

The moon drifted across the sky, and soon my eyes adjusted to the dim light. When I spotted the small cabin centered in a clearing to the north, I knew exactly where I was and I knew She had brought me here.

These grounds had been forbidden by the magistrate the moment She was arrested. I was breaking the law just by being here; how I arrived would be of no concern to anyone.

I knew at that moment I should have returned to my home, but I did not; instead I found myself drawn closer to the small cabin, toward a flickering candle in its single window.

The door opened just moments before I reached for the handle, creaking inward like the mouth of a beast welcoming its prey. Although I should, I felt no fear as I stepped inside, not even when it closed behind me. I simply held still and waited for my eyes to adjust to the glow cast by that single candle.

When a hand found mine, I knew it was her; how she could be here I did not know.

She led me inside, toward the glowing embers of a fire that had died some time earlier, and gestured for me to sit at its hearth.

"I knew you would come," she said, finding a seat at my side. "You are a good man; you can see how my family has been wronged."

"I have not come of my own free will," I told her, "but you know that already."

"I cannot make you do anything you do not wish to do. Your heart led you here, not I."

I turned to her for the first time, ready to argue this point further, but when I saw the sadness in her face, I could not bring myself to hurt her.

"Please tell me I am not wrong about you."

"If you are not a witch, how do you explain this? You are locked in a cell beneath the church, yet you are here, too. How is that possible?"

"Because I can do such things, does it make me evil?" she asked. "Does it make me deserving of death?"

"Witchcraft in all forms is against God's law."

"For generations we have cared for the sick. Your own father came to us when you fell ill as a child and again when your mother suffered the red fever—"

"Stop—"

"We have never harmed anyone."

"There are many dead, two this week alone."

"Not by my hand," she countered.

"Then who?"

"There are those who wish us dead."

"At such cost?"

"Yes."

"Who would be willing to do such a thing?"

"The very same in which you place your trust."

"The magistrate? Tauber? They are men of God! To speak such an accusation is blasphemy!"

"Let me open your eyes so you may see them for what they really are. I can show you the truth."

"More witchcraft?"

Her hand reached out and gripped mine, her fingers entwining with mine before I could pull away. My vision filled with light, then quickly went black. An energy the likes of which I cannot describe flowed through my every fiber, chilling my bones as if I'd fallen in an icy lake. Then I heard her voice. I heard her weeping softly as my sight returned.

I was in the cell beneath the church and she was in the far corner, cowering on the floor, her eyes filled with tears.

"Please, don't!" I heard her shout.

How could this be? How was I here?

"I have done nothing wrong!"

"Silence yourself before I do it for you!" a male voice shouted back—Tauber's voice.

It was then that I saw him, standing just inside the cell. Another man I did not recognize guarded the door from the other side. Tauber held a large knife.

Neither man could see me; I was just a voyeur intruding upon this moment. If she could see me she gave me no sign. She remained in the corner, shivering with fear.

"Stand!" Tauber commanded.

A moment passed before she complied. I felt her fear as it mingled with my own, watching her stand, her arms wrapped around her chest in defense.

"Please, don't," she pleaded.

Tauber sneered back at her. "There are many tests to expose witchcraft. Unfortunately, the most effective can also be quite painful. I take no pleasure in what I am about to do, but I think you agree that it must be done—for your own safety as well as that of every person in this village. Sometimes we must all suffer for the greater good, don't you agree?"

A tear streamed down her cheek. I wanted to go to her, stand between them, even disarm Tauber if I could, but I knew such action simply wasn't possible. I was no more in their moment than they were in mine.

He stepped closer to her, candlelight glistening on the blade. "Turn around."

She shook her head and backed further into the corner until she could go no more.

"Turn around!"

With a soft whimper, she did as she was told. Her eyes were lost to the shadows but I knew they were filled with tears, with fear. Surely as a witch she could harm him, make him stop, but she did no such thing.

"Now remove your garments," Tauber breathed.

Behind him, the other man finally spoke. "Sir! Our instructions were clear. There is no need—"

"Our instructions were to find the mark. How do you suppose we do that while she is fully clothed?"

"But to force her to—"

"You may leave anytime you wish; I do not need your help here. Frankly, I should have known I could not depend on you."

The other man fell silent and returned to the door. He knew better than to cross Tauber.

Tauber turned back to the girl and pressed the edge of the knife to the back of her neck. "I will not ask again."

She flinched. "I won't," she finally murmured.

Tauber twisted his fingers into the cloth of her dress and pulled it apart, snapping the buttons and tearing the thin material. She tried to catch it as it fell, but Tauber slapped her hands away. "Don't."

It fell at her feet and she remained still.

Tauber ran the knife down her arm, the pressure just enough to leave a mark without drawing blood.

"Well, Tobias, do you see anything?" Tauber said, his voice low but unwavering.

"There is nothing to find," she countered.

Tauber raised his hand and slapped the side of her head.

"Not a word from you!"

"I asked you a question, Tobias! What do you see?" Tauber pushed.

Tobias took a step forward, clearly uncomfortable. His eyes combed over every inch of her; she shied away, looking to the floor. "There, on her leg," he finally said, pointing at her right thigh. "There is some kind of mark."

Tauber took a step back, eyed her cautiously, then knelt on the filthy ground. At first he didn't see it in the dim light, then a thin smile crossed his lips. "My good Lord," he breathed. "How is this even possible if you are not a witch?"

Her hands moved to cover it, but he was quick with the knife, leaving a one-inch cut in her palm. She cried out, then cradled her injured hand in her other. "It is nothing but a birthmark," she told him in a thin voice.

"It is the mark of the devil himself."

No more than two inches tall, he traced the mark with the tip of the knife. He had never seen such a thing. It was an upside-down cross, perfectly symmetrical with exquisite detail, as if drawn by the finest of artists.

Tobias had backed away; he now stood against the door, his face pale in the dim light.

"Perhaps we can exorcise the devil from this child simply by removing his mark," Tauber said under his breath. Without hesitation, he plunged the knife deep into her thigh. She let out the most agonized of screams.

I pulled my hand away from her and found myself standing in the cabin. She had fallen to the floor at my side, her pale skin covered in perspiration.

"How did you..." My voice trailed off as I fought the urge to pass out. I felt drained of all energy, my legs weak. I couldn't help but sit on the floor beside her.

She buried her head in my shoulder and began to cry. "I couldn't bear to show you more, what they did to me...the other ways in which they hurt me. You have to help me. Nobody else will."

I remained still, able to do nothing but hold her in my arms.

—Thad McAlister,
Rise of the Witch

DAY 3

CHAPTER FORTY-SIX
Day 3 – 03:10 a.m.

RACHAEL WOKE SUDDENLY TO the sound of thunder crashing outside her bedroom window; if there had been lightning, she hadn't seen it. She had been dreaming but didn't remember about what. Her mind was cluttered with cobwebs, muddled with thoughts of worry.

Beside her, Ashley slept, lost in a motionless slumber.

A sickly sweet scent drifted across the room, and she knew they weren't alone; the old woman was close. Her warm, stagnant breath crept through the air, betraying her presence.

Rachael tried to sit up but found that she was unable to move, held still by unseen hands.

"I know you're here," she said, her voice far quieter than she would have wished.

From the corner of the room came the slight shuffle of feet on the wooden floor. Rachael heard the soft click of the old woman's fingernails as she tried to hold them still but simply could not.

Rachael wanted to turn her head, but motion betrayed her; she remained still as the old woman's breath grew warmer, nearer.

"You're almost out of time, Raaachael," she hissed, her voice like a serpent nearing its prey. The steady sound of those nails drifted closer, her feet shuffling across the floor.

Rachael closed her eyes and began to count, a feeble attempt at distraction.

"It's mine!" the old woman shrilled.

Rachael opened her eyes to find the old woman bending over her, her decrepit mouth only inches from her own. As she spoke, hot saliva dropped from her jaw and landed on Rachael's cheek, burning her.

The old woman grinned. Her rotten teeth were filled with gaping holes and filed to sharp points.

She reached down and pulled away the covers. Rachael wore only a thin nightgown and panties—she shivered against the cold night air. The old woman looked down upon her with a yellow, toothy smile. Her warm, rancid breath licked at her.

"Stop," Rachael breathed.

The old woman reached for her, brushing her long, sharp fingernails across her swollen belly. "I will take the child if I have to cut the unborn vessel out of you, my sweet Rachael. It's mine; the baby has always been mine. Why don't you understand that?" Her sharp nails sliced the thin fabric of the nightgown with little effort, cutting from waist to neck—Rachael cringed as she passed over her breasts, the nails tearing at her skin. Her gown fell to the floor, lost from her field of vision. "This could so easily be your skin and muscle peeling away, layer by layer." Her panties went next, gone with just two swift cuts. Rachael lay beneath her, trembling with cold, with fear, as the old woman pressed her nails into her. "I could kill it right now if I wanted to, you do know that, don't you? You understand, my Raaachael?"

Rachael tried to nod, but could not. She couldn't move at all. The old woman's clothing was nothing but rags, and they brushed against her skin as she leaned into her.

"One day, my sweet Rachael," she hissed in a dark rasp. "If I can't have this one, I will surely take the other," she said, glancing at Ashley as she slept. "She is nearly as tender as the babe."

Rachael felt the nails drive deep within her belly but couldn't scream. She couldn't make a sound at all; she was only able to stare in silence as the old woman raised a bloodied hand to her lips and licked the crimson liquid from her fingertips, a garbled laugh climbing in her throat.

When Rachael woke for the second time, the old woman was gone. Perhaps a dream, perhaps something else. She ran her hands over her belly only to discover she had not been harmed. She found no sign of the cuts, which had seemed so real only moments earlier. Turning to her side, she discovered Ashley was gone.

"Ashley!" she shouted, her voice much louder than she expected.

"What, Mommy?"

Her daughter was standing at the bathroom door, a glass of water in her tiny hands.

Relief washed over her and she reached out to her. "Come back to bed, sweetie."

Ashley remained still, though, her face growing pale.

"What is it?"

"The sheets," her little voice trembled. "They're all bloody. Mommy, are you hurt?"

Rachael looked down at the sheets; her daughter was right. For the first time since waking, she also realized she was naked. Her clothing had been cut away. She had missed the tiny hand which reached out from under the bed and grabbed the remains of her nightgown from the tattered pile on the floor. Not Ashley, though—she dropped the glass of water and let out the loudest of screams.

CHAPTER FORTY-SEVEN

Day 3 – 03:30 a.m.

"**M**OMMY! UNDER THE BED!" Ashley shrieked. "It's under the bed!"

Buster saw too—he raced in from the hallway and slid across the floor, burying his nose under the bed frame.

"Buster, no!" Ashley chased after him. "It's gonna bite you again!"

Rachael pulled her legs back up on the mattress and wrapped the bloody quilt around her. "Ms. Perez!" she shouted. "Ashley, get away from there!"

Ashley tugged on Buster's collar, but he wouldn't come out; he scampered deeper under the bed. "Buster, no! Out!"

His tail thumped against the hardwood floor and his torso twitched as a low growl rumbled from his throat, followed by an angry bark. He scurried deeper.

Rachael reached across the nightstand and turned on the lights. Beneath her, a scuffle ensued—the tiny patter of little feet followed by Buster squirming behind them, all heading toward the wall. Buster growled, then slammed into the bed frame. Rachael heard an ungodly squeal as the dog sunk his teeth into his prey.

Then silence.

A moment later, Buster began gagging and backed out from under the bed, a brown oily foam dripping from his mouth. He backed up so fast he ran into the dresser on the other side of the room. Ignoring the pain, he shook his head wildly, expelling the foam in all directions as he whimpered.

"Mommy, it hurt Buster!" Ashley cried.

Buster backed into the corner and spat the foam from his mouth. The brown liquid hit the floor and began to steam, dissolving into the air. He wiped at his snout with his paws, eyes pinched shut.

"Ms. Perez!" Rachael shouted again as she reached for her robe and rolled off the bed, avoiding the blood-stained sheets.

When Ms. Perez rushed through the door, Buster took one glance before darting out of the room and down the stairs, no doubt heading for his water dish.

"Oh my!" Ms. Perez exclaimed, noticing the bloody sheets. "The baby?" She went to Rachael and placed her hands on her belly. Rachael stroked her arm. "It's not the baby, the baby is fine," she reassured her, although not entirely sure herself. She wasn't in pain, though, and after a quick examination the source of the blood eluded her. In Rachael's dream, the old woman had pierced her belly with those knifelike nails, but she found no wounds.

Rachael told Perez what had happened.

A sour scent filled the room, and they both knew it came from whatever Buster had attacked under the bed.

They had to move it.

"Ashley, go downstairs and check on your dog. Make sure he has plenty of water," Rachael told her.

"But I want to see," her daughter pouted.

"Please, baby, I don't want to argue right now," she said. "Please go check on Buster."

Ashley opened her mouth, ready to argue, then changed her mind. With an exasperated sigh, she went out the door after the dog.

Rachael reached for the corner of the bed, but Ms. Perez hesitated. "What if it is still alive?" she asked.

She was right; they didn't know how badly Buster had hurt the creature. It might be cowering under the bed, injured and angry.

Rachael went to the closet and pulled a nine-iron from Thad's golf bag and dropped it on the mattress. She then grabbed the corner of the bed frame. "Okay, pull on three, ready?"

Ms. Perez nodded and wrapped her fingers tightly around the nearest bedpost.

At three, both women pulled and the bed scraped across the floor, away from the wall. The stench grew stronger, coming from behind. Vomit crept up Rachael's throat; she forced it back and reached for the golf club.

Circling the bed, the two woman peered into the shadows behind it. Both noticed the hole in the wall at the same time. "It's like the others," Rachael pointed out.

Ms. Perez crinkled her nose, pointing toward something on the floor.

At first Rachael thought it was a doll, maybe one of her daughter's.

The dark, empty eyes staring back at her weren't those of a doll, though. They were unlike anything she had ever come across.

Not a doll nor a rat.

Something else.

Both women knelt closer.

No more than a foot tall, with two legs, one remaining arm, and a small head, a creature stared back at them from behind dead eyes. Eyes that were large and out of proportion with its head. Its ears were pointy, much like those of a mouse. Its face didn't resemble a rodent at all; the face looked human.

Tiny pointed teeth protruded from an oversize mouth. Its hairless chest, arm, and legs were made up of thick, well-defined muscles, its skin a glossy black. A tail appeared to be poking out from behind its back.

"What is it?" she gasped.

Ms. Perez must have felt a similar connection to the spiritual world, for she crossed herself before saying something in Spanish. It sounded like "El Diablo," the Devil.

Small trails of smoke rose from the creature's tiny form like thin little ribbons, a foul scent spreading through the air.

With the tip of the golf club, Rachael rolled the creature over, exposing its back. When she saw worms wiggling within a long gash, she couldn't hold back the vomit any longer; she turned her head and coughed up at her side. Ms. Perez gasped as the worms tried to escape but were engulfed by the smoke rising from the creature as if attacked by the air itself. The smoke intensified, crackling and popping, sizzling before coming to an abrupt end. The creature was gone; only a small brown pile remained.

Nothing more than a pile of dirt.

Then something moved from within the hole in the wall, something with beady little eyes.

CHAPTER FORTY-EIGHT

1692

The Journal of Clayton Stone

"**SILENCE!**" **THE MAGISTRATE SLAMMED** his gav-el. "I will have quiet!"

The number of afflicted had grown overnight—so much so that not an empty seat was to be found; almost a dozen stood along the walls with even more outside. The complaints were abundant, everything from aches and pains to nightmares and specters visible throughout the night. George Jacobs Sr. was by far the most vocal; he was nearly removed when he began swinging his cane wildly toward the magistrate.

"She came to me last night with her book in hand and brought a pain upon me unlike any I have ever experienced. My legs buckled beneath me and I fell to the floor. I cried out for my wife, but not a sound escaped my throat. Then she came at me with her book, her bare feet inches above the floor, as if riding the air itself. I heard this strange clicking, much like she produced in court yesterday and her eyes..." he paused and shook his head. "Her eyes were red with blood. It streamed down her cheeks and dripped to the floor where the drops burned at the oak, filling the room with the scent of sulfur."

I listened to this in silence.

How could it be true? I was with her last night, was I not?

But she had already proven she could be in more than one place at a time. Is it possible that she visited Jacobs while still in my presence? While still locked in her cell? Was this just a trick of sisters? Was she even capable of that which he accuses? It was difficult to believe she was, yet he went on with such conviction.

"I felt a needle prick my finger and my arm unwillingly reached out to her, to her book. It opened hungrily before me and she smiled before speaking in a tongue unknown to me, a witch's tongue." The old man paused for a moment.

Those present in the courtroom were silent; one's heart-beat could nearly be heard.

"I tried to stop it, I truly did, but my hand reached for her book and I signed it; with the blood on my fingertip, I signed it. Then she was gone and all went black. My wife found me moments later and woke me from this unearthly slumber only to show me this..."

He raised his arm to the court and tore back his sleeve, revealing a fresh mark on his forearm. Although I was across the room, I could make it out. It was the same mark I had seen on

Her, the mark of Satan himself—a reversed cross clear as day. The magistrate recognized it, too. Although he didn't say as much, his glance at Tobias Longstrum told me so.

Jacobs fell back into his seat and began to weep, his head held in his large hands. Nobody attempted to comfort him; instead, those closest moved away in fear, knowing that such an admission could easily place him in a cell of his own.

—Thad McAlister,
Rise of the Witch

CHAPTER FORTY-NINE
Day 3 – 03:30 a.m.

THUNDER CRACKED WILDLY OUTSIDE as Thad sat at the small table in his room at the Torrington Motel just outside of Boston. His head throbbing and in dire need of rest, he was afraid to close his eyes, afraid She would return if he so much as blinked.

You're chasing ghosts, he thought.

You've abandoned your family to chase a ghost.

Thad rested his head in his hands and sighed. The sooner he completed this, the sooner he would get home to them.

Reaching into his briefcase, he removed the journal and flipped to a page near the center, one that contained a map he had sketched more than a year earlier. At least, he thought he had sketched it; in reality, he didn't recall drawing the map at all. Like much of the journal, something else seemed to guide him as he created the rolling hills, large forest, and worn roads—the sketch had been completed before he even realized he had started.

Her.

Was it really possible?

Could She have somehow placed the entire story in his head? Could She have somehow driven him to write it?

Thad recalled how he had feverishly worked on the book, drafting page after page in such a short amount of time. The words flowed without effort—as if the story itself was a memory rather than a creative work.

He'd known something was wrong; the words, the phrasing, they weren't his own.

You knew someone was in your head, Thad. Acknowledgement, though; that's another story. Hell, you were never that good a writer, were you?

Thad returned his attention to the journal, to the map.

He had always imagined the small town was on the coast about fifty miles south of Boston. Wedged between rocky cliffs on the ocean side and protected by a dense forest to the west, it was more than secluded: The town was forgotten.

Reaching across the table, Thad unfolded the Massachusetts map he had purchased at the airport and spread it out before him. He then began searching the coastline for something, anything, that resembled his drawing.

When his fingers brushed across a thick forest at the far corner of the map, something seemed oddly familiar.

He reached for the drawing and placed it beside the map, then placed the thin paper directly over, lining up the forest and the penciled-in roads—they were nearly a perfect match.

"How is this possible?" he said aloud.

Highway 80 was identical with the exception of the far east end. On the printed map, the road ended nearly ten miles from the coastline, but in Thad's drawing it continued through the forest to the water, to a place that until now had existed only in his mind.

The small town of Shadow Cove.

Her final resting place.

CHAPTER FIFTY
Day 3 – 03:31 a.m.

RACHAEL GRIPPED THE GOLF club with both hands and shoved the driver into the hole with enough force that she thought the club might poke through the drywall of the opposite wall. She expected to feel it squish through the soft flesh of another one of the creatures but had no such luck. She pulled the driver back and shoved again, this time twisting around the inside. If she hit the creature, she couldn't tell. She assumed they got away, moving through the walls of the home as effortlessly as she moved through its halls.

Are they intelligent?

Are they gathering somewhere right now, plotting revenge for their fallen brother?

What the hell are they?

"El Diablo," Ms. Perez answered. "Servants of the Devil."

Rachael pulled the golf club out of the hole. Her torn nightshirt was stuck to it, covered in blood. Blood She had drawn from her in her sleep.

They work for Her, she thought. *All of them, they work for Her.*

Rachael didn't want to believe the woman was anything but a creation of her own mind, yet the bloody clothing and sheets told her otherwise; what she had just witnessed told her otherwise.

"We need to get out of this house," she said.

Ms. Perez nodded in agreement, then stood and glanced toward the hallway. "Where is Ms. Ashley?"

CHAPTER FIFTY-ONE

1692
The Journal of Clayton Stone

*A*FTER THE OUTBURST OF *George Jacobs, the magistrate ordered that she be brought to us. The gallery had grown eerily quiet. Some had even left, unwilling to risk an association with her—even if that simply meant being in the same room.*

I too was worried. After all, I had spent time with her. She had come to me; I had even gone to her. Such an admission would surely put me on trial at her side.

She had not asked me to sign her book, though; that made it different. The reason was unknown to me. Did her book even exist? Also, when she appeared to me it wasn't the ghoulish fiend described in various testimonies, it was but a scared young girl, a lost soul in need of help, nothing more. In fact, to think her a witch seemed outlandish, a farce. I thought of the pain inflicted upon her by the magistrate and Tobias Longstrum—the indig-

nity, to be imprisoned in such a way. She had no choice but to seek out someone who may be willing to offer help using whatever means were known to her. Most would not hesitate to do the same if given no other choice. What right did I have to persecute her? What right did any of us have? She could be put to death based solely on the testimony of drunkards and lonesome housewives with no one willing to side with her.

I'm no better, writing such thoughts but lacking the courage to act upon them. What kind of man does that make me?

If she dies, her blood will be on my hands no less than the others.

She arrived a moment later, her hands and feet bound in thick chains, led to the pulpit by two members of the congregation, each carrying thick crosses anointed in holy water. She was thin and frail, her tattered gown hung loose. She held her arms close to her chest in an attempt at modesty. He dark hair hung down her back and shoulders, concealing her face. I caught a glimpse of her tear-filled eyes, and my heart tightened in my chest.

When she glanced back at me, I could not help but look away.

Who was I to her?
Who was she to me?
Was there something there at all?
How could I allow it?

—Thad McAlister,
Rise of the Witch

CHAPTER FIFTY-TWO
Day 3 – 03:40 A.M.

D EL THOMAS'S HEART POUNDED in his chest as he fumbled with the key to his apartment door with his injured hand while holding the bougainvillea branches in the other. The lock gave and he pushed his way in, kicking the door shut behind him. The air felt damp and musty as the day's storm reached inside from the open balcony door, fingers of rainwater creeping across the hardwood floor from the body of the storm. The chilly waft of night had also taken up residence, moaning as it drifted through the open door and caressing the pages of the manuscript, still open upon his desk.

All these years, Thad!

Why keep such a story to yourself for all these years?

Her story needed to be told, cried out to be heard,

yearning for so much as a whisper from the few that kept her tale captive in the darkest recesses of their minds.

Unforgivable, Thad…you've known for so long and didn't tell your old friend Del?

He would have a long talk with him, a long talk indeed.

Some secrets just shouldn't be kept.

Del ran his fingers over the pages. He wanted to read the story again, but there simply wasn't enough time. He had been gone for hours and the gathered rainwater was growing stale. Soon it would be of no use at all. He had marked the appropriate page earlier and he turned there now, carefully reviewing the ritual that had played over and over again in his mind since the first moment he took in the words. He glanced at the clock—

Nearly four in the morning.

There was very little time; light would come soon.

He carefully set the bougainvillea branches down on the desk and began the tedious task of carrying the various bowls and pots of rainwater from the balcony to his large master bathroom where he poured them into the bathtub, wary to not waste a single drop along the way. When he was through, he lit a candle and placed it on the floor in the center of the room. He then returned to his desk for the bougainvillea branches and the manuscript. Del was outside the bathroom door when he froze in his tracks.

A knife.

How could I forget a knife?

Silly boy.

CHAPTER FIFTY-THREE
Day 3 – 03:41 a.m.

THE STAIRS SEEMED PARTICULARLY dark as Ashley descended to the first floor in search of Buster. She had tried the switch. Broken. Daddy would have to replace the lightbulb when he got home.

Buster lapped up water in the kitchen, still whining softly.

From the bottom of the steps, the blue glow of the kitchen nightlight poured into the hallway from around the corner. She found Buster sitting beside his water bowl, panting. "Poor Buster," she said, patting him on the head. "You killed the monster, though. That's a good boy!"

He whined in acknowledgment and stared up at her with sad eyes. His mouth was stained brown and he had small scratches all over his nose. Ashley picked up his bowl and carried it to the sink. Standing on her toes, she pushed back the faucet, rinsed and added cool water, then placed the bowl back on the floor. Buster didn't seem to want more water, though; instead, he stood perfectly still, his eyes fixed on the hallway.

"Buster?"

The dog ignored her; he stiffened and a low rumble started in his throat.

Ashley crossed the kitchen to the back door and fumbled with the light switch, flooding the room with florescent light. Buster remained still, tense.

When she first saw it, she thought someone had stood one of her dolls in the doorway. Then it moved.

Eyes of fiery red first glanced at her, then swept to Buster. Ashley spotted another one standing under the end table in the living room. She tried to call out to her mommy, but her voice had escaped her; all she could produce was a faint gasp.

Buster's whine had turned to a deep growl, and now he let out an angry bark.

The first creature flinched at the noise but otherwise didn't move. The second came out from under the table and approached the other. There was something in its hand—a sharpened pencil, but thinner. A spear? Together, they started toward her dog.

Buster barked again, this time louder and with more force than the first.

Everything happened so fast.

Ashley heard the rush of footsteps on the stairs as her mother and Ms. Perez came running down; both creatures turned toward the steps. Buster seized the opportunity to lunge at them, his teeth bared in a ferocious scowl. The first creature ran to the left while the other fell to its knees and threw the makeshift weapon with unbelievable force, catching Buster in the leg. He lost his balance and tumbled to the wood floor, scrambling to get back up.

The creature started toward him. Her mother was mid-swing before the little black monster spotted the golf club arching down. The monster ducked, but wasn't fast enough. The driver hit the creature with such force its tiny frame split in two. Both halves turned into piles of dirt before hitting the ground, leaving a sickly sour odor in their wake.

"Mommy, there's another one!" Ashley screamed. "Under the table, see?!"

Her mother swung around, ready to hit the other, but the monster was gone, disappearing somewhere in the shadows of the dark room.

Ashley ran to her and wrapped her tiny arms around her mother. "What are they, Mommy? What do they want?"

Rachael tried to respond but words escaped her. All she wanted to do was hold her daughter and get them both to safety.

CHAPTER FIFTY-FOUR
Day 3 – 03:48 a.m.

THE CANDLE SMELLED LIKE vanilla, but it was all he had. Not that there was anything wrong with scented candles, but somehow, Del thought, they didn't quit fit the bill for what he was about to do.

He had retrieved a Shun Premier butcher knife from the kitchen. Exceptional craftsmanship, its eight-inch blade had cut through countless meats and other culinary delights over the years without fail. Del wasn't about to do this with a dull blade or some cheap utensil; no sir, that would be crazy. He placed the blade on the edge of the bathtub, where it would wait patiently until needed.

Although Thad's manuscript described the ritual in extraordinary detail, the pentagram was another story altogether. Del had made a mental note to ensure the published version would include diagrams whenever necessary so others wouldn't experience the same difficulties. The manuscript did say the pentagram should be at least three feet in diameter and no more than two feet from the water. That in mind, Del did his best to draw one on the bathroom floor with the thick black marker he had found in the junk drawer of his desk. When finished, he stood and admired his work before returning to the manuscript to read the ritual one last time. When he was sure he had committed every detail to memory, he set down the tome and took in a deep breath.

Time to begin.

Reaching for the candle, Del dripped a small amount of wax on each of the pentagram's corners, then placed the candle in the center. The flame danced briefly before straightening up, sending a thin ribbon of black smoke to the ceiling, where it spread across the white coffers. Even though the storm raged outside, the room seemed unnaturally still. So quiet, in fact, Del could hear his own heart beating within his chest as he reached for the manuscript and read the first lines of the spell.

"Bagahi laca bachahe. Lamc cahi achabahe," his voice echoed off the harsh marble of the walls and floor as he repeated the phrase. *"Bagahi laca bachahe. Lamc cahi achabahe."*

He had left the bougainvillea branches on the vanity and he reached for them now, careful not to prick himself on the long, sharp thorns. Although hours had passed since he picked them, they seemed to have found

life rather than death in their freedom. The red and purple blossoms seemed to glow in the dim candlelight,
their sweet aroma drifting through the air. One by one
he began picking off the blossoms and dropping them in
the rainwater, watching as they floated upon the surface,
drifting into one another like tiny skaters on a pond.
Strange how they seemed to move; fluttering in the water
with life, growing stronger as they absorbed the rain.
Their colors became more vibrant, the scent growing
more intense with each passing second.

"Karrelyhos. Lamac lamec bachalyos."

The storm's wind seemed to seep into the room,
drifting around the corner and through the door with a
voracious delight. The temperature dropped at least ten
degrees within a few short minutes and goose bumps
covered his skin.

Del hastened his pace. When he finished the first
branch, he set it aside and moved on to the next. Soon
the entire surface was awash in red and purple.

*"Cabahagi sabalyos, baryolas. Lagozatha cabyolas,
baryolas."*

At first, they drifted in no particular pattern. Then
the tiny leaves began to turn in unison, carried on the
growing current. Del watched in amazement as they began to rotate clockwise around the outer edges of the
bathtub, moving even faster at the center. Reaching for
the last branch, he stripped away the leaves, watching as
they joined the others, dancing atop the water's surface.
The room had grown colder too, the wind rising enough

to send his towels fluttering against the walls. Del's white breath drifted through the air as he spoke the next phrase.

"Lagozatha cabyolas, samahac et famyolas."

He reached for the bare bougainvillea branches, bunched them together in the palm of his left hand, and closed his fingers. When the thorns tore into his palm, he squeezed even harder. Then Del took a deep breath and squeezed harder still, stifling a scream as blood began to trickle from between his fingers, dripping into the rain water. As the drops hit, they fizzled and popped, smoldering like gasoline to a flame. With his right hand, Del reached for the knife and raised it to his head.

In one swift motion, he cut a tuft of hair and threw the lock into the candle. The flame erupted into a ball of fire, which burst toward the ceiling and filled the room with odorous sulfur, burning so brightly that Del had to look away. He dropped the branches into the water and felt a rush of cold air. When he uttered the next word, the final word, it escaped his lips with eager anticipation. He spoke the one word Thad's book cautioned never to speak aloud.

Del spoke her name, *Her true name,* in a single hushed breath.

CHAPTER FIFTY-FIVE

1692

The Journal of Clayton Stone

T *HE STORM HAD RETURNED* with the night. It offered me shelter as I cautiously moved through town from my small home to the church. Most had sealed their homes for fear of the evil creeping across the air. I spotted not a single soul as I walked the desolate streets with only a small lantern to light my way.

She was crying when I emerged in the church cellar and approached her cold, dark cell. The single candle left by her guards earlier in the night had long gone out, allowing a shroud of darkness to engulf the small space.

"I know George Jacobs lied today," I began. "I was with you last night; you couldn't have gone to him." I hesitated before going on. "I would have said something if I thought—"

"No!" she shouted between sobs. "You mustn't say anything! It will do nothing but put you in a cell of your very own. I cannot be responsible for the harm they would bring to you."

"I must ask you something and you may hate me for it, but I must know the truth," I blurted out.

She dried her eyes and faced me, embraced in shadows, lit only by my lantern. She nodded and approached the bars.

I cleared my throat, but the lump which had formed there seemed only to grow larger. "Is there a book? One like that of which they speak?"

There was no turning back now—not for me, not for her. If she lied, and I feared she would, I would have my answer. I would understand how to proceed. I hadn't considered what we would do if the truth was revealed, but we would do it together, of that I was certain.

She looked to the ground, her eyes glistening in the lantern light. She reached for my hand through the bars and I entwined my fingers with hers.

"Not all witchcraft is evil, and certainly not all witches are akin with the devil," she began. "Most are healers, utilizing methods passed down from each generation to the next. Herbs and spells, remedies known only to a few but meant to help the many…this is what true witchcraft is borne of."

I felt her fingers tense within mine, her grip hesitant, yet firm. "There is a book, but it is not what you believe it to be."

—Thad McAlister,
Rise of the Witch

CHAPTER FIFTY-SIX
Day 3 – 03:50 a.m.

"**MS. PEREZ, GET ASHLEY UPSTAIRS** and lock yourselves in my room!"

Ms. Perez stood frozen in her tracks, her wide eyes locked on the coffee table, the shadow of the evil little creature etched in her mind.

"Ms. Perez!" Rachael shouted. "Now!"

"Mommy, I want to stay with you!" Ashley pleaded. She had her arms wrapped around Buster, holding him so tight Rachael wasn't sure he could breathe.

"I'll be right there. Please, Ashley," she said. "Ms. Perez, now. Take her."

Ms. Perez nodded and took the little girl by the hand, leading her up the stairs. Buster hesitated, unsure if he should leave Rachael alone. Then he turned and went after them.

Rachael searched the room but found no sign of the tiny little creatures. They were close, though; she felt their eyes on her. They watched from the thick shadows in the corners of the room, under the furniture, at the windows. She wasn't sure how many in total, but there were many, far more than the two they had already encountered.

With slow steps, she crossed the hallway to the kitchen and grabbed a butcher knife from the drawer beside the sink. She then slid a small stepladder beside the refrigerator and climbed up.

They kept the small metal box in the corner of the cabinet above the refrigerator, far from Ashley's reach. Rachael entered the combination on the lock and the lid snapped open, much louder than she would have hoped. Again, she scanned the room for prying eyes. Although she didn't see them, she knew they were still close.

She reached inside and removed her husband's .38. The steel was cold and oily to the touch. Although they had not shot the gun in years, Thad kept the weapon clean and ready to fire. She didn't have to check the chamber to know it was loaded. Rachael dropped the .38 into the right pocket of her robe and grabbed both boxes of spare ammunition, placing them in the left.

Climbing down, she took the telephone receiver from the wall and pressed it to her ear—dead.

"Dammit," she cursed, replacing the phone.

As she started back toward the stairs, something scurried across the floor in the darkness. She spun toward the sound, her fingers clenching the gun in her pocket, the knife held high. "Show yourself, you little shit." She scanned the darkness for its watchful eyes but found nothing.

Rachael backed out of the room and ran up the stairs at the fastest pace her large, pregnant body would allow. When she reached her bedroom door, it was locked. "Open up. It's me," she breathed. She heard someone fumble with the lock from the other side. Then Ms. Perez cracked the door, peeking out. Rachael pushed past her and pressed the lock on the knob as she slammed the door shut. For a moment, she forgot the large knife in her hand. When she caught her daughter staring, she placed the weapon on the dresser at her side. "I don't want you to touch that, sweetie," she told her.

"Knives won't help, anyway," Ashley told her. "Zeke said they can't die since they're not really alive."

"Zeke said that, huh?"

"She has been talking to herself since we got in here," Ms. Perez said with disgust. "Crazy little child."

"Ms. Perez!" Rachael's gaze burned with anger. "You shall never say such things, or you can find employment elsewhere."

"Maybe someplace without monsters and crazy little children," Ms. Perez shot back.

Rachael wasn't in the mood for an argument. Right now she only wanted to get herself and her daughter to safety. She glanced at the window. "It will be light out soon. We'll stay here until the sun comes up. At first light, we'll get to the car and get the hell out. I don't think we should try at night. We don't know what those things are or how many—"

"El Diablo," Ms. Perez said under her breath.

"Zeke says they work for the scary lady with the long fingernails. He called them minn... mun... munyens..."

"Minions?" Rachael asked.

Ashley nodded. "They work for her."

Rachael swallowed. "The lady with the long fingernails?"

"I...I don't know," she stammered. "I've never seen her, but Zeke says she's a bad person. A really bad person. She won't let us leave, never ever."

Ms. Perez uttered something in Spanish and went to the window. Outside, the rain was falling in sheets so thick she couldn't make out the streetlights, visibility limited to only a few feet. She did notice the dirt piled along the window sill, both inside and out.

CHAPTER FIFTY-SEVEN
Day 3 – 03:51 a.m.

THAD WOKE TO THE RAIN. Not a soothing shower like those that sing you to sleep with the steady patter of raindrops, but instead an angry downpour—dark clouds unleashing their fury and might on the murky twilight. The rumble of thunder still rattled through his bones, no doubt responsible for waking him. He didn't know how long he had slept, nor did he recall falling asleep—exhaustion had simply overtaken him and dragged him into slumber. The maps were still spread out before him on the table beside his journal.

He had drifted off in the wooden chair and his body ached for it. He leaned back and stretched, fighting back the pain caused by sleeping in such a position.

It would be light in about two hours. He hoped the

weather would break but somehow knew better.

The rain wouldn't stop until this was over.

Reaching for his coffee, he swallowed the last of it in a single gulp, cringing as the cold, bitter liquid rushed down his throat and settled in his empty stomach.

Thad fell still for a moment, listening to the storm.

Was she also listening?

From some dark place was her face turned to the sky, feeling the tiny droplets against her skin for the first time in centuries, eagerly awaiting him, knowing he drew close?

Standing, he went to the window and pulled back the dusty curtain.

Could he will her to come?

He imagined her standing out there, in the middle of the deserted parking lot. Not the old woman, but Her in her younger form—the one who had invaded his dreams of late, the one who had started him on this journey.

The one he knew as Christina. This character that had somehow jumped from the pages of his manuscript into real life.

He imagined her smiling face as she looked up at the swollen clouds and spread her arms wide, soaking in each drop. The unwavering wind caught in her clothing, providing quick glimpses of her beautiful legs and thighs. She would giggle when she noticed him watching, not out of shyness but satisfaction, knowing she held his gaze once again. She would reach for the buttons of her blouse and release them one at a time until the experienced hands of the wind opened the faded cloth ever so briefly, exposing only a moment's glance at her perfect breasts.

Such images of her drove him to write the book in the first place. Her touch gave him the strength and determination to continue, and her will helped him finish it.

The young witch of Shadow Cove.

His desire to bring her life to paper was stronger than any he had ever known.

A married man shouldn't long after another with such desperation, not even a fictional character; he found shame and guilt in it. Yet he couldn't allow himself to forget her. Those feelings made her so real, made her jump from the paper.

This Christina.

It's a spell, Thad. She has you under a spell, his mind warned him. *You've become her puppet. No more in control than a train racing down tracks. Her grip tightens with each moment. You need to walk away, deny her—say no to this fool's quest and get home to your wife and daughter while you still can.*

He smelled her sweet scent. How close was she?

Could he deny her?

Silly Thad. Wondering such things, her voice sang softly at her ear. Thad turned but found no one there, yet her breath still warmed his neck.

After all I have done for you? All I want to do to you?

Then he saw her, standing in the rain as he imagined only moments earlier. Her brilliant blue eyes glowed like sapphires from beneath her locks of long brown hair.

Her smile, ever so subtle, seductive, a mouth longing for the touch of another.

Was she real or another dream? Thad didn't know anymore. He was so tired. He wanted her, yet his mind cried out in protest. He longed to stop but only drew closer. His will was no longer his own.

No! Don't you see? It's her! She's doing this to you! His mind fought back. *Don't let her take you! You must fight!*

His feet inched toward the door; he didn't have the willpower to stop.

She'll kill you and your family! Don't you realize that? Once she has what she wants? This seduction, this game— it's all a lie! She's just breaking you down. She's toying with you.

But Thad had no fight left.

He glanced at his pills on the table, left them. Instead, he scooped up the large knife he found in the kitchenette when he arrived. He scooped it up and placed the blade beneath the waistband of his jeans at the small of his back.

Unlatching the lock, Thad opened the door and stepped out into the rain. He knew it should be cold, but instead he found the drops warm as they soaked his clothing. She stopped her dance as he approached, her tongue playing over red lips. When she reached out to him, he had little choice but to take her hand and wrap his fingers tightly around hers. He couldn't help but pull her close and stare into those eyes as she looked up at him with a lust and hunger trapped beneath a veil of innocence.

This isn't real, he told himself. *It's just another dream. Somehow she's in my head, she's making me do this. Her game—it's all just part of her game.*

"Who are you? Christina or the witch? Or are you both one and the same?" he asked.

"I'm whoever you want me to be," came her reply.

"Are you really here?"

"I don't know, Thad. Am I?"

This is her fantasy, not yours. You're just a puppet to her. How easily she controls you.

She massaged his back and leaned into him. "I can be whatever you want me to be. Whoever you want me to be. I'm yours until the end of time," she said. "As long as you bring me the box."

Thad glanced around the parking lot at the various motel windows, each with their drapes pulled tight as the occupants slept safely behind closed doors. No doubt holding their loved ones tight as thunder crackled though the night.

He tried to back away but he had no control over his movements, his words. Thad felt as if he were watching a movie, just a spectator.

The sharp blade of the knife chewed at his back and he welcomed the pain, welcomed the clarity it brought. "I love my wife," he forced out. "*You* mean nothing to me."

Her eyes glistened with a touch of anger.

Rainwater pooled around them.

She took a step back from him and ran a hand through her thick dark hair, then slowly down her neck to her breasts. One by one she unsnapped the buttons, then peeled the wet blouse from her shoulders and dropped it to the ground at her feet. Her skirt followed as she eased her fingers under the waistband and pushed it down over her hips, revealing the creamy pale skin beneath. She wore nothing else. For a moment, she remained still. Then she raised her face to the sky, closing her eyes as she licked the rainwater from her lips. Thad watched the rain cover every inch of her perfect form, he watched the rise and fall of her chest as she took in each excited breath, he watched until he had no choice but to close the distance between them.

"You are mine," she told him. "My little toy to do with as I please, nothing more. You must never forget that."

No!

Thad went to her, his movements no longer his own. His lips found her open mouth and she welcomed him. He then fell to his knees and pressed his face into her, into the warmth burning between her legs. She moaned with pleasure as his tongue found her, and she pushed against him firmer still as the muscles of her legs began to quake.

"I...do not...love you..." He forced out the words. "This...you...means nothing to me."

With his right hand, he reached to his back and retrieved the knife. With his left, he grabbed at her—

But found only air.

When he opened his eyes, he stood alone in the parking lot under the unforgiving storm. For the first time since wandering out into the night, the rain chilled him.

She was gone.

The knife clattered to the blacktop, and he wept.

CHAPTER FIFTY-EIGHT
Day 3 – 04:01 a.m.

THE BATHROOM EXHALED; ALL the air left at once, stifling the candle and plunging the room into total darkness.

The silence grew overwhelming.

Del gasped.

Everything changed in an instant.

With an ungodly roar, the water rushed from the bathtub toward the ceiling in a blood-red geyser before raining back down on the pentagram—a wall of water so thick it appeared solid. The scent of sulfur filled the room, burning at his eyes. Del scrambled backward, pushing away until his back pressed against the wall and he could move no more. Then all fell silent and the room plunged into darkness. Water covered the floor, cold to the touch. Del wanted to stand. He wanted to escape the room and somehow reverse whatever he had done, but he knew it was too late.

His eyes adjusting to the lack of light, she came into view as her quiet voice broke the silence. A young girl of no more than eighteen or nineteen crouched low in the center of the pentagram, the rainwater glistening on her naked body.

"Why have you summoned me?" she said in a voice so soft it was barely heard, yet loud enough to claw at his mind like a screamed thought.

Del stared at her, unable to turn away. He found her to be as beautiful as the manuscript described—more so—a beauty that can't be found in words alone.

Del knew the spell would work. When he read Thad's book, he understood the story was far older than either of them could dare to comprehend. An ancient secret concealed by generations of believers and nonbelievers alike until almost forgotten, until a writer gave the tale life by placing pen to paper.

As it was written, so it shall become.

"Why have you summoned me?" she repeated, this time with far more force and a tinge of anger.

Del watched as she stood, brushing long dark hair from her face. Her blue eyes seemed to glow in the dim light as she took in her surroundings before settling her gaze upon him.

He rose to his feet. Reaching for the bathrobe hanging beside him, he draped it over her bare shoulders, unable to keep from taking in her seductive scent as he did so. "I can't believe you're real," he said as his fingers found her skin.

She shrugged off his touch. "The simple minds of men. Is that all you want? To know the feel of my warmth against your own? The taste of my lips? My touch?"

Del fell silent.

Her eyes landed on the manuscript and she crossed the room, the open robe trailing behind her. Her fingers brushed the pages and she let out a soft sigh. "How did you come into possession of this?"

"It was given to me by a friend," Del told her.

"Liar!" Her voice echoed off the marble and shrieked through the apartment. The wind outside seemed to howl in unison, excited by the outburst.

Del took a step back. "Thad McAlister gave it to me. I'm his agent. It's my job to help him get published so others can read your story." He hesitated, then added, "So others can learn about you. So the world will learn who you are."

This answer seemed to satisfy her. She rested her hands on the manuscript and closed her eyes.

"Why have you summoned me?" she repeated for the third time.

Del crossed the room and placed his hands on her shoulders and then kissed her neck. "Your story was… is…incredible. After reading it, I wanted desperately to know you. I wanted to be close to you, help you in any way I was able."

He watched as her slender hand found the knife. She drew her finger across the blade, back and forth. Then she traced the handle before returning to the blade. She didn't draw blood; instead, her perfect fingertips glistened as the rainwater danced in the blade's reflection. Her nails were long, frighteningly so. To Del, they appeared as sharp as the blade itself.

She looked to the floor and Del followed her gaze. Most of the water was gone, he realized. Only where she stood did some remain. Dried bougainvillea blossoms littered the ground, shriveled with rot, as if dead for weeks. Still looking down, she spoke. "I haven't much time; there never seems to be enough."

"What can I do?" Del asked her.

She lowered her head and reached for his hands, wrapping them around her. "Hold me," she breathed. "Just hold me."

Across the room, the candle flickered to life; its tiny flame began to dance across the walls. The girl's hands guided Del skillfully over her before coming to rest around his own neck. He glanced at the mirror across the room, at the flickering image of them as they stood in the candlelight and gasped.

The reflection wasn't that of the young girl but instead a very old woman in tattered clothing. Her blue eyes had become dark pits, her skin wrinkled to that of death. He tried to pull away from her, but somehow she held him close. When a laugh escaped her throat, he smelled breath of rot and decay. She tapped her fingernails together at his ears in a rhythmic *clickity, click, click* before plunging them into his neck with a twist. He grabbed at her wrists, his fingers finding cold dead skin. He tried to pull her off, but she was the stronger; her nails only dug deeper.

Glancing at the floor, he realized the water had receded even further. Little remained, pooled under her feet. Without hesitation, he kicked at the counter and pushed back with all his strength. Together they tumbled backward. Del's head came down hard against the side of the bathtub and consciousness slipped away, but not before he realized he was alone again—her hold on this world vanished when she lost touch with the rainwater.

Del felt warm for a brief moment before the world went black. He felt the warmth of his own blood as it spilled around his head from the deep slashes in his neck.

CHAPTER FIFTY-NINE

1692
The Journal of Clayton Stone

"**W**ERE YOU PRIVY TO the testimony of George Jacobs yesterday?" Tauber asked of her.

She shook her head. "I was not, but it has been told to me."

Tauber glanced down at his notes. "Then you are aware he has accused you of soliciting his signature for your book? He is one of nearly a dozen now—what should we make of this?"

"I have no book but the Lord's book," she insisted.

I knew the truth now, but said nothing. There was more to learn before I could consider sharing such things.

"The Lord seems to feel differently. Why else would he send so many witnesses?"

"They are all liars!" she shouted. "And God will stop the mouths of liars!"

"*You will not speak in this manner in this court,*" the magistrate scolded.

"*I will speak the truth as long as I live!*" she retorted.

The crowd grew restless, and Mary Walcott stood. "*This is the very woman I saw afflict Timothy Swan!*" *she declared.* "*And she afflicted me several times. She came at us with a long barbed spear dripping in the blood of her victims—the very one she probably used on Mercy Short!*" *She then fell to the floor and seized—pumping, contorting, and twisting in pain.*

John Henry and Timothy Swan lifted her from the floor and began to carry her toward the door, their eyes fixed on the girl at the stand.

"*Is it true, Timothy?*" *the magistrate asked of him.*

Swan hesitated for a moment, then nodded before continuing out the door.

"*Liars! All of you!*" *she cried.*

Tauber turned back to her. "*Are you responsible for that which just befell that woman?*"

"*I am responsible for no such thing!*"

Tauber paced, returning to the afflicted. "*I know it's difficult for you to speak out, knowing she is capable of punishing you in such a way, but it must be done if we are to expose her for what she is—an unbaptized child of the Devil. She is a danger to all of us.*"

She glared at him from the stand but said nothing.

"*She needs to burn,*" *a stranger's voice sounded from across the room.*

I hadn't seen this man enter the church, nor was he familiar to me. Although the sun burned high in the afternoon sky, I could not clearly see his face beneath the shadow of his brimmed hat. His long coat reached nearly to the floor. Such attire was not common to Massachusetts; it was typically found in New York or such faraway places as London. If he had an accent, I could not make it out.

"She must die or all your lives are in danger," he stepped into the room with a pronounced limp of the right leg and a pained effort which could be heard in his voice.

Worried voices flooded the church and the magistrate slammed his gavel repeatedly until the crowd fell silent. He then turned to the stranger. "Who are you and what business do you have here?"

The man did not immediately respond. His eyes were locked with hers; it was clear she knew of him as he did her. When he spoke to the Magistrate he did not look away; instead, his intense gaze held her still. "Did you really think you could hide in such a place?"

"Keep him away from me," she growled, her hands clenching into fists. "He knows not of what he speaks. It is he who brings danger, danger and death by his very hands!"

The strange man stepped closer, fixating on her with dark eyes, reaching toward her with a gloved hand.

She shrank back in her seat. "Keep him away from me!"

When the floor began to shake and the walls trembled it felt as if a sudden storm had found us, yet the sun was still bright and no rain fell from the sky. My papers left the desk and fluttered through the air, riding a wind that could not possibly exist within the confines of the nave, yet it surrounded us all, howling angrily as it grew in strength.

The afflicted cried out and tried to reach the door but it slammed shut before them, sealing us all inside.

—Thad McAlister,
Rise of the Witch

CHAPTER SIXTY
Day 3 – 05:00 a.m.

THAD WAS LOSING HIS mind.

There was no other explanation for the things he had seen and experienced; nothing else could explain her. She was nothing more than a character in a simple story, one born of his own thoughts and imagination, no more, no less. He wanted so desperately to believe that, yet even as he spoke the words aloud, he found the fraud in them, the manufactured comfort they provided, no more real than the tooth fairy or the Easter Bunny.

He didn't know how long he had been out in the rain, but the headlights of a large truck entering the parking lot woke him from his reverie. He was kneeling on the asphalt, surrounded by the gathering rainwater, his clothing soaked straight through. He still felt her in his arms; smelled her sweet scent on the air. Thad didn't want to leave that spot, fearful she might return and he'd miss a final opportunity to end her. Then the cold brought him back, and the fear of being seen by someone overcame all others.

He scooped up the knife and walked back to his room, sat once again at the table, and emptied four of the small bottles of scotch he had found in the room's minibar. When finally numb to his surroundings, he found true sleep. A sleep free of dreams.

Thad woke before dawn to the sound of thunder cracking with vengeance outside, striking so close the ground shook beneath him. Originally he had hoped he could wait until the storm broke before moving on, but he realized that simply wasn't going to happen. The rain was as much part of the story as the witch. Thad knew as he neared Shadow Cove, her final resting place, the rain would accompany him as it had on the night they had placed her there, nearly four hundred years earlier.

Reaching into his bag, he grabbed a bottle of aspirin and took two. He then tried calling home, hanging up as soon as he heard the busy signal he had halfheartedly expected. When the phone rang in his hand, he nearly dropped it. He cursed himself and pressed the ANSWER button, muttering a brief hello.

"You're running out of time, Thad. She's growing restless, and I have to admit, I am too."

Thad brushed a hand through his thick hair. "Was that you out in the rain?"

Christina fell silent, only her breath on the line exposing her presence. "Does it matter?"

"I need to know I'm not going crazy."

He fumbled with the bottle of Risperidone, his fingers popping the cap, then replacing it. Pop and replace, the pills rattling inside.

"I'm flattered that you're having trouble telling us apart, I really am."

"You look so much like Her, but it's not possible."

"Don't you think we're past the point of denial, Thad?"

"I can't tell what's real and what's not anymore," Thad breathed. "How do I even know you're on the phone? What if I'm imagining this call? What if you're making me imagine this call?"

She giggled. "Like our little adventure on the plane?"

He looked down at the knife. "I could end this right now—take my life."

"Then what becomes of your family?"

"If you're not real, then you don't have my family. It's all in my head," he told her. "It ends with me."

"I assure you, we have them," she replied.

"Prove it. Let me speak to my wife."

Silence, save for the sound of her breathing.

"Christina?"

She cleared her throat. "The clock is ticking, Thad. You have your map; you shouldn't waste any more time on such thoughts."

"In the book, they put her away for a reason. She's dangerous. She hurt a lot of people," Thad insisted.

"You need to focus, Thad, for your family's sake. They're running out of time. Their blood will be on your hands if you fail us, if you fail Her."

"When I saw her story, as I put her story to paper, I saw only death behind her and a fierce hatred in her eyes. She has no love in her heart, no compassion, only this deep, dark hatred. If you see anything else, it's only because she's blinding you—using you to get what she wants."

Christina disconnected.

Thad dropped the phone into his pocket.

Outside, thunder crackled wildly. The storm filled with excitement as he gathered up his things and pushed out through the door to his awaiting rental car, the map crumpled in his hand.

Only a few more hours now.

The car roared to life and he disappeared down the dark back roads of Massachusetts, his mind swimming with thoughts of Her.

━━━━━━

Christina dropped her cell phone on the passenger seat of her black Lexus. In her other hand, she still grasped the lock of Thad McAlister's hair. She closed her eyes and reached out to him.

"Coreveo, Balta di mothresta," she breathed.

Her mind transporting—the sensation of floating, flying, racing through blackness. Then her eyes were one with his, seeing what he saw.

Thad back in the rental car. Shadow Cove and Her playing at his thoughts.

He was so fragile, this man. His mind, once complex and sure, broken in only a few short days.

She had no regrets; this had to be done.

For *Her*.

All for Her.

Thad McAlister and his family were nothing more than pawns. Necessary pieces to complete a puzzle.

As a little girl, when she had first heard the stories of Her, she had been fascinated. Her mother, her grandmother, and their mothers before her, they all knew the tales; they passed them down from generation to generation for hundreds of years. Stories of this witch of centuries old, one so powerful dozens had died in Salem to protect her secret, many others in the world beyond. They offered their lives as false witches simply to protect Her, the one true witch. Their willing sacrifice necessary to guard Her through the ages, to keep Her safe until her time of rebirth, until now.

Magic has long since been forgotten. Now nothing more than fodder for film and literature. Witchcraft, thought of as nothing but a minor religion. Spells lost to the ages. Her return would usher in a new era, one in which She would rule. As a direct descendant, Christina would be at her side.

Her eyes popped open and she dropped the hair into the cupholder. She would check on Thad again shortly.

A woman walked past with a toy poodle on a leash, plastic bag in her hand.

Cars raced up and down the road.

A fat jogger leaned against a light post, catching his breath.

They were all oblivious.

They knew nothing.

This world was over; a new one would come with the next dawn.

Lowering her window, she stared up at the large brownstone across the street, her mind reaching out to this man, this Del Thomas. The first to read Her story. The first to cast Her spell. He would awaken soon from his slumber, awaken only to serve Her.

Christina would be there to welcome him. The first to join their order in over a century. He had gotten a copy of the book from Thad. She couldn't help but wonder what would happen when her story was published, when millions read of her and cast the spell for themselves.

Their small family was growing.

It was growing indeed.

Soon she would welcome many new brothers and sisters on this first dawn of dawns.

CHAPTER SIXTY-ONE
Day 3 – 05:05 a.m.

RACHAEL DIDN'T REMEMBER FALLING asleep, but somehow she had. When her eyes fluttered open, gray light from the lamp on the street corner crept in through the bedroom window. Her daughter was asleep at her side and Buster was lying on the floor beside them, his eyes half-closed as he fought slumber. She found Ms. Perez sitting in the chair at her dressing table, her gaze locked on the window and her fingers wrapped around the golf club she had used earlier. She offered a soft nod and wiped the sleep from her eyes.

"They're right outside, Ms. Rachael. In the hallway and also outside the window. I saw one cross the ledge not even an hour ago," Ms. Perez told her in a hushed tone.

She had hoped this was a dream, just another nightmare

bounding forth from one of her husband's tales, but her housekeeper's words erased such thoughts.

"What do you think they want?"

Ms. Perez fell silent, choosing her words with care. "Your daughter, she spoke of the woman with the long fingernails. This woman—"

She held up Rachael's cell phone. The image of Thad's sketch filled the tiny screen.

"Since I saw this drawing last week, she has come to me in my dreams. Terrible dreams filled with death and pain. She is a frightful woman, evil. I've never believed in such things, but now I feel we must. I do not know what she wants and I do not know what they want but if they wished us dead, I think they would have already killed us."

"Give me the phone. I'll call for help."

Perez tossed it to her. "It does not work. No calls out. No calls in. I tried. Somehow, they block it."

"Thad's latest book, I think it's about witchcraft. Old witches and spells."

"*Bruja,*" Perez confirmed. "Evil *bruja.*"

Rachael rose from the bed, careful not to wake Ashley, and went to the window.

Ms. Perez had told her about the dirt last night, but she couldn't see it clearly until now.

Not only did dirt cake the window sills, but the edges of the window jam were packed tight, too. She didn't bother attempting to open the window; she knew it wouldn't budge. She also didn't need to inspect them to know every other window in the house suffered from the same fate.

As lightning struck, Rachael caught a glimpse of her yard.

At first she wasn't sure what she had seen, but when lighting once again filled the sky, her first thoughts were confirmed. "Ms. Perez, come here. Look at this."

The woman glanced warily at the bedroom door, at first unwilling to give up her post, then she crossed the room with the golf club in tow. She leaned into the window, pressing her forehead on the glass. "How could such a thing be?"

Rachael shook her head. "They look like tiny rose bushes."

"Bougainvillea," Ms. Perez corrected her. "They are bougainvillea, many of them."

"They cover the entire lawn," Rachael agreed.

"We had many in Mexico, but they are tropical plants. They don't belong here."

But they were here, Rachael thought. And they were flourishing. As her eyes fought to pierce the predawn veil of darkness, she realized they covered every inch of their lawn, replacing the grass with what appeared to be a solid thorny mass covered in the most beautiful red and purple blooms. *How had they grown so fast?* She didn't know the answer to that question any more than the others. They were simply there now, something else she accepted.

"There is no walking through them," Ms. Perez explained. "Their thorns are like tiny little daggers. I've never seen them grow so thick, so quickly. They must have done it, those tiny little devils."

"Minions," Rachael corrected her.

"Minions," Ms. Perez agreed, nodding her head.

Rachael saw dozens of them running beneath the bushes. Were they carrying something? Rachael couldn't be sure from this distance. "We need to get to the car," she said.

Once again, Ms. Perez nodded, her grip tightening on the club.

As if in response, Rachael heard a loud thud. The bang hadn't come from outside but instead from above, something in the attic.

"Maybe one of the neighbors will see all this and help," Rachael offered.

"The *bruja* has blocked the phone, killed so much in your yard, and now grows all this overnight. Her spells are strong. I fear the neighbors see nothing at all. They only see what she wants them to see," said Perez. "No one comes to help us."

CHAPTER SIXTY-TWO

Day 3 – 05:35 a.m.

RACHAEL GLANCED DOWN AT her daughter's little hand in her own and took a deep breath. She held her husband's gun in her other hand while Ms. Perez stood at her side with the club. Buster sniffed and pawed at the bottom of the door, whining between breaths.

"We'll stay close together; nobody wanders away from the group, agreed?" Rachael said, waiting for everyone to nod in acceptance before reaching for the doorknob and turning it.

She opened the door only enough to peer into the dark hallway. When satisfied that none of the minions were guarding the door, she opened it enough to pass through. With the gun held high, she stepped out of the room and gestured for the others to follow. She felt their eyes all around her, but she couldn't see them. She imagined them crouching low in the corners and beneath the furniture, lurking in the murky shadows just beyond sight. If she listened close enough, she thought she could even hear them breathing—tiny little breaths drawn out of necessity, drawn as quietly as possible, unwilling to give up their position. Ms. Perez spoke softly under her own revealing breath. Rachael recognized the Lord's Prayer.

When Ashley screamed and pointed at the stairs, Rachael didn't hesitate; she lowered the gun and fired off a round at the top step. She caught a glimpse of one of them ducking out of the way, a soft thud followed as the minion jumped to the first floor and scampered off. Rachael didn't think she had hit the creature. Even when a loud, shrill cry pierced the silence, she knew it was out of frustration rather than pain. She wasn't so sure these things even experienced pain.

Behind them, the bedroom door slammed shut, the lock engaged, and dirt poured out from beneath, sealing the space between the door and floor. There was no turning back now.

Rachael felt the baby kick and rubbed her belly, realizing she was doing so with the butt of the gun.

Ms. Perez reached for the light switch on the wall, then pulled her hand away—the plate was slick with damp mud. Rachael glanced up at the light fixture. "Crap." The bulbs had been shattered and the receptacles were filled with dirt.

"They're everywhere," Ashley said.

Buster whined in agreement.

"Come on," Rachael said, walking toward the steps.

With the wall as a guide, they made their way down the steps, one at a time, pausing at the middle landing as at least five or six of the tiny creatures darted across the room below them. They looked up with dark eyes, their tiny teeth gleaming in the shadows. Rachael wanted to shoot them but they moved too fast, disappearing before she even raised the gun. They weren't far, though; they weren't far at all.

Rachael glanced at the front door and realized they had somehow piled furniture in front of it. The minions had managed to slide the couch from the living room to the door and stacked two recliners on top. She couldn't imagine them lifting such heavy items, but they had. The creatures had then packed mud into all the crevices, fortifying their makeshift dam. Eyes glared at them from behind, tiny little hungry eyes. Rachael fired the gun once more—one of the cushions jumped off the couch and landed on the floor at its base and the creatures scattered around the room, letting out a shrill so loud Ashley covered her ears.

Rachael tugged at her and pulled her into the kitchen with Ms. Perez following close behind. Buster had entered the room first. The dog sniffed at the baseboards before looking up at the cabinets lining the walls above the counter. He whimpered and backed up.

"It's all right, boy. I know they're in there. But I don't think—"

When one of the creatures jumped from above the upper cabinets onto the dog's back, he tried to buck it off but the minion held tight, rammed its head down, and buried its teeth into his fur. Buster cried out in pain and backed into the cabinet, trying to jar the monster loose.

Ms. Perez swung the golf club hard, like a baseball player going after a low pitch, and hit the minion's torso. The creature didn't fly across the room as one would expect; instead, the club passed through the tiny monster and the minion fell to the ground in pieces, crumbling into nothing more than a pile of foul-smelling earth. Buster reached around and licked at the spot where he had been bitten and growled up at the cabinets.

Rachael looked down at the pile of dirt in amazement. *What the hell are these things?*

Ashley had watched enough movies to be unfazed by such things. In her world, monsters had always been real, and for them to turn into dirt upon death was as natural as talking animals and large green ogres that marry princesses.

Rachael thought about the piles of dirt that had covered their yard yesterday morning—hundreds of them— was that the birth of these creatures?

At her feet, a small pile of dirt begin to move, morph, take the shape of one of the creatures. It stirred and red eyes snapped open—the newly-formed minion darted away, leaving nothing but a trail of muddy footprints behind.

"Esa loca," Ms. Perez blurted. "I killed it and it came back." Digging through the drawer beside her, she located a flashlight. Perez flicked the switch, sending a thin beam of light across the room and nodded in satisfaction.

Ashley wrapped her arms around her mother's legs.

"Let's keep moving," Rachael told them, already starting toward the garage door. The others fell in line behind her, with Ms. Perez and Buster taking the rear. Ashley stayed close, unwilling to release her grip on her mother.

Although she had the gun, Rachael feared the weapon wouldn't do much good. If these creatures, these minions, could be destroyed by a golf club and reassemble with little effort, a bullet would more than likely pass right through with little or no damage. Yet she held the gun high, finding some comfort in holding the weapon.

The door leading to the garage was unlocked, but mud had been packed tightly around all its edges. Working together, she and Ms. Perez were able to force it open on the third try. The door swung into the dark garage with a creak.

Sweeping the room with the flashlight revealed dark patches of mud on every surface. The garage stunk of feces and urine.

"Phew," Ashley said, pinching her nose.

This familiar scent brought Buster to the forefront. He stood at the door's threshold, sniffing at the air. He sneezed and shook his head before stepping into the garage. Rachael followed closely behind, careful not to step in the mud any more than necessary.

"Look, Ms. Rachael," Ms. Perez said, pointing at the hood of the car. "It's open."

She was right, although only a few inches, probably the result of pulling the hood release. Just enough room for those things to get inside, Rachael thought. Her heart sank.

"Mommy, they're up there," Ashley said. Rachael followed her daughter's pointed finger toward the storage cabinets mounted along the walls. She caught a glimpse of one of the creatures as it darted behind a paint can, its eyes shining bright.

"Just stay close, honey," she told her.

Rachael eased her fingers beneath the hood of the car, pressed the release latch, and raised the hood, ready to fire the weapon at the first sign of movement. Nothing did move, though; the minions had finished their work on the engine some time ago.

What remained of the belts was nothing more than frayed rubber, chewed apart in numerous places. The wiring had fared no better—each had been plucked from the harness or chewed clean through, leaving nothing but exposed, frayed copper. The remainder of the engine had been covered in the same mud they had found everywhere else, packed into every opening, every crevice. Rachael swore under her breath; the smell was making her nauseated again. *Hold it together for Ashley,* she told herself.

"Ms. Rachael, you must see this."

Ms. Perez was standing at the side door, looking out the window at their front yard. Holding Ashley close, she made her way over and peered out through the muddied glass panes.

The bougainvilleas had grown thick, their thorny branches lacing together into a thick, impenetrable fabric.

They rose at least six feet, maybe more. Rachael doubted the door would open even if they tried. It didn't matter; they would never get through that tangled mess. "This isn't possible."

Ms. Perez glanced at her and turned back to the window. "Do you see them? Down near the ground?"

Rachael leaned in closer, pressing her forehead against the glass. She hadn't noticed them at first; there were so many they blended with the ground. Not until one turned and glanced up at her, until the minion flashed shiny little teeth, did she realize there were hundreds—if not thousands—of creatures maneuvering through the bushes. "Oh, my God," she said.

"What is it, Mommy?" Ashley asked, her wide eyes looking up at Rachael.

"We can't go this way," was all she could think to say. "We need to find another way out."

"The driveway is concrete," Ms. Perez pointed out. "The bushes can't grow on concrete, can they?"

Rachael turned toward the large garage door. "They probably cut the power; we'll have to pull the manual release. Can you reach it? That red handle up there?"

Ms. Perez frowned. "If I stand on the car, maybe I can reach."

Rachael couldn't ask her to do it, for an old woman to climb up on a car…

…but she was already kneeling on the trunk with one leg, pulling herself up. The metal creaked under her weight. When she stood, she reached for the red release handle.

Rachael saw the small spear flying through the air seconds before it buried itself in the woman's hand. Perez screamed and pulled away. Another spear came from nowhere and embedded itself in her leg. She lost her balance and almost fell, but Rachael reached up and righted her. Ms. Perez climbed down off the car's hood as two more spears flew past her head with a soft buzz.

"Back in the house!" Rachael screamed as paint cans and assorted other objects began flying toward them from the shelves above.

CHAPTER SIXTY-THREE
1692
The Journal of Clayton Stone

SCREAMS ERUPTED FROM THE afflicted as the windows slammed shut. They rushed the door. It would not budge.

"Where is it?" the man shouted at her. "Where is your book?!"

Wind howled with the voice of death, and I clutched my remaining papers against my breast. I held my pen so tight my fingers ached and my knuckles turned white. The magistrate ducked behind his desk while Tauber stood his ground, staring at the strange figure while shielding his eyes from airborne debris.

"Where is your book!"

The girl twisted in her bonds but was unable to break free. "I have no book!" she screamed over the wind.

"*You cannot lie to me, child! I am not like them; I am not fooled by your guise!*"

He took another step toward her, and the wind fought back angrily; I gripped the edge of the table as my chair fell back behind me.

His coat fluttered at his back and he held his hat with his free hand, still reaching toward her with the other, just inches from her now.

She opened her mouth and a sound escaped unlike any I've ever heard—the screams of a thousand souls at a pitch that burned at my ears. I dropped everything to cover them; however, it did little good. The sound ripped through my mind, turning all to red, then black. Then, finally, silence.

—Thad McAlister,
Rise of the Witch

CHAPTER SIXTY-FOUR
Day 3 – 05:40 a.m.

IT HAD BEEN NEARLY two hours since Thad left the motel in his rearview mirror and started down Highway 80 toward the small town of Shadow Cove. The rain was stubborn, refusing to let up, flooding the early morning sky in cascading sheets.

Around him, few motorists dared to drive. Most had pulled to the side of the road and turned on their hazard lights, content to wait out the storm in the safety of their vehicle.

Not Thad, though. He took advantage of the open road by forcing his rental car to speed up until he was moving at almost twenty miles per hour over the posted limit. He wasn't worried about wrecking the car; he wasn't even worried about getting a speeding ticket. She would ensure he arrived in Shadow Cove without incident. About an hour earlier, he saw her for a brief second sitting in the passenger seat—still naked and damp with rain as he remembered her from the parking lot of the motel. She smiled and ran her hand down his leg, her long nails scarring the fabric of his pants. Then she was gone, her scent lingering. Her scent and the sound of her fingernails, the *clickity, click, click* he had learned to dread.

Thad knew this wouldn't be over until he placed the box in Christina's hands.

He shivered at the thought, the idea of her in possession of such an object.

Bring the box to me, Thad, Christina breathed.

Bring Her to me. Over and over. *Bring Her to me, my Thad.*

He wanted her voice out of his head. Anything to get her out of his head.

Thad wanted to scream.

Would she release Her? If she had the box? Did she know how to bring Her back?

A sign marking one mile to Exit 17 flew by, and Thad began to slow the car.

This is it, he told himself.

Aside from a faded green highway marker, there was little to identify Exit 17. So little, Thad almost missed the turnoff. His tires cried out, fighting the slick pavement as he turned a hard right onto the exit ramp.

The road narrowed to two lanes and he was forced to slow further; the pavement deteriorated from the well-maintained blacktop of the highway to a road long forgotten by city planners and maintenance workers alike. Cracked and muddled with potholes, Thad imagined days, if not months, passing between cars on this lonesome stretch of road. A road somehow familiar to him.

It didn't exist in his book but he knew every curve, every turn—he even recognized the thick branches of the ancient oaks towering overhead, swaying under the storm's heavy breath.

When he reached a battered stop sign, he slid to a quick halt and turned left, followed by a quick right into the first sign of civilization since leaving the highway: a small single-pump gas station and garage under a faded sign which read Grady's. Thad didn't need gas, but something inside him longed for the comfort of seeing another human being before he continued on his mission.

He pulled in front of the lone pump and shut down the engine, glancing at the empty passenger seat before climbing out of the car under the safety of the small tin roof above the pump.

Inside the station, a light burned bright. Thad thought he caught movement behind the curtains. The entire place looked run down and deserted, left to rot away as the rest of the world went about its business.

"We don't get many visitors out here no more," came a gravelly voice. "Forgive me for not noticing you pull up, but this storm damn near drowns out everything if you ain't listening close."

Thad turned to find an old man standing beside the pump, watching him from behind thick glasses and a bushy gray beard. He hadn't heard him approach and wasn't quite sure where he had come from. Aside from the station and garage, there were no other buildings, and Thad had been looking directly at them. Any other approach would have taken him through the rain, yet he was dry as a bone.

"You startled me," was all Thad mustered as a sudden chill raced through his bones. He shivered.

The old man smiled. "Sorry 'bout that. Didn't intend to sneak up on ya." He nodded to the pump. "What's it gonna be, regular or premium?"

Thad shrugged off the cold. "Regular is fine. Just top it off."

He watched as the old man turned a crank on the antique pump and slipped the nozzle into the rental car. A bell rang somewhere and the numbers began to tick away as the gasoline started flowing. "Name's Grady," he said. "I'd offer to shake your hand, but I'm a mess; been working in the garage most of the night. Got a crankshaft on an old Buick that's turned into quite a pisser. Seems sometimes cars just grow old and want to die. No matter how many times we fix 'em, once they reach that point you might as well send them off to the auto graveyard and wish 'em well 'cause they ain't coming back without a fight."

Unsure of what to say, Thad only nodded, his eyes catching movement just inside the garage again.

"That's my boy, Lenny," Grady told him. "He ain't much when it comes to tooling a car, but it's nice to have the company. It can get a little lonely out here—ever since they built that highway you just came from, folks don't have much use for old State Road 27," Grady said, nodding toward the road in front of his station. "Been hell on business, that's for damn sure."

"I'm heading to a place called Shadow Cove. Have you heard of it?" Thad asked, peering down the dark road through the thick rain.

The old man gave him a peculiar frown and replaced the pump's nozzle. "You were only down about two gallons, nearly full." He read the total from the pump and waited in silence as Thad fished cash from his wallet.

"Am I close?" Thad asked.

Grady thumbed the bills, folded them, and pushed them into his pocket.

"To Shadow Cove. Am I close?" Thad asked again.

"It's down the road a piece," Grady finally said. "I don't know if I'd drive out in this kind of weather, though. It tends to wash out with much less than we've had these past few days. This car ain't exactly equipped for offroadin'."

Thad shrugged. "I don't have much of a choice; my schedule is a little tight."

"Is that the case," Grady said with suspicion. "Not a whole lot of business to be had in a place like Shadow Cove. Hardly none at all. Mind if I ask why you're headin' out to that place?"

Thad felt the man sizing him up. He had tensed, grown defensive. "I'm picking something up, then I need to get home, back to my family."

Grady fell silent, mulling over his words in his mind before saying something he might regret soon after. Then he seemed to resign himself from the conversation and turned back toward the garage. "I suggest you hurry, before you lose the road altogether in this rain. I'd hate for you to get stuck out there; could be days before help got to you. Your family shouldn't be kept waiting, not on account of weather."

He disappeared into the garage and Thad found himself standing alone beside his rental car, his eyes drawn toward the road he was about to take—a road which seemed to disappear into the thick forest of oaks surrounding it, swallowed by the rain and dismal morning sky.

CHAPTER SIXTY-FIVE
Day 3 – 05:50 a.m.

RACHAEL LED THE GROUP through the kitchen and into the living room and was about to tell Ms. Perez to find something to block the door from the hallway when a sharp pain coursed through her belly, causing her to double over and drop the gun at her feet.

"Mommy!" Ashley screamed, wrapping her arms around her mother.

The pain seemed to come in quick waves, and Rachael allowed Ms. Perez to lead her to a chair and help her sit.

A full minute passed before Rachael drew in a deep breath and spoke. "I think that was a contraction," she said.

"What's a traction?" Ashley asked.

Ms. Perez looked at her with worried eyes. "We can't get out," she explained. "We can't get to a hospital."

Rachael nodded. "Maybe if I rest for a minute, maybe they'll stop."

The stench of rotten dirt filled the room. Rachael realized the floor was covered in it. In most places, the hardwood was lost beneath the dark mud. Not just the floor—they had smeared dirt on the walls and furniture—layered so thick on the windows not a ray of light shone through, although it was surely morning by now. She saw the creatures, the minions, darting among the shadows. She even thought she heard them, mumbling in some language unknown to her, plotting out the remainder of their plan.

She couldn't have this baby here, not now, not like this.

"Mommy, there are people out there."

Rachael turned to find her daughter at the window. She had wiped away some of the dirt and was peering through the opening.

"Out by the street, there's a whole bunch of them," she added, her voice filled with nervous excitement.

"Help me up," Rachael breathed.

Ms. Perez gripped her arm and helped her out of the chair; together they went to the window, careful not to slip on the muddy floor. Around them the minions stirred but remained hidden, mumbling in that strange language.

"Let Mommy see, baby," Rachael said, kneeling beside her daughter.

Ashley stepped aside and pointed. "There, over by where the tree used to be."

Rachael pressed against the glass and peered outside. She spotted four strangers, not quite at the street but about ten feet into their property, where the large tree had fallen.

"How did they get past the bushes?" Ms. Perez asked beside her. She had cleared her own section of the window and was watching them intently.

Rachael wondered that, too. They were surrounded by the bushes, somehow standing in the middle of them. As impossible as it seemed, she got the impression that the thorny plants had somehow allowed them to enter the yard, then sealed up the path behind them. They also had a clear path to the house, one she was sure hadn't been there when she had looked down from the bedroom window.

"Who are they, Mommy?"

Rachael shook her head. Of the four, two were men and two were women. The tallest of the men wore only black. He read to the others from a small book. The other three held hands and appeared to have their eyes closed, oblivious to the heavy rain falling around them.

Dozens of minions wandered in clear sight around their feet, busy with something, although Rachael couldn't tell just what.

"They're part of this," she said. "Whoever they are."

When a minion jumped up on the window ledge, Rachael screamed. She fell backward, shuffling away before she even realized it was on the outside. The little creature scooped some mud from the side of the window and smeared the glass, obscuring their view. Another jumped up and helped. Within moments, they had the entire window blacked out from the outside. Buster, who had been watching from a safe distance, let out a growl, then grunted when the minions continued their work without so much as a glance in his direction.

A second contraction rolled over Rachael and she fell to the floor, slipping in the mud. She felt a rush of warm liquid on her legs. Ms. Perez gasped.

Her water had broken.

CHAPTER SIXTY-SIX

Day 3 – 05:55 a.m.

DEL THOMAS WOKE WITH a start.

The bright light burned at his eyes, forcing him to squint. It took a moment to realize the light came from the single candle burning at the center of his bathroom, and he lay on the floor in a rather large pool of his own blood.

Oddly, he didn't feel pain.

He should be in tremendous pain.

He remembered how she had appeared after he read the spell, the wonderful explosion of life that brought her here. He remembered her beautiful smooth skin and rose red lips. He remembered her fingernails as they dug into his neck and caused him more pain than he had ever experienced. He remembered the look in her eyes as he died, and make no mistake about it, he did die.

As did she.

She consumed the rainwater with a ferocious hunger, an insatiable thirst, until none remained. Then the life left her, too. She was gone as quickly as she had appeared.

The clicking of the grandfather clock in the other room grew profoundly loud, as did the traffic outside. The breathing of his neighbors—he heard that, too. There was very little Del could not hear.

He raised his hand to his neck and felt the wounds she'd left behind. They had scarred over, healed.

He died, must still be... All this blood...

Yet his lungs drew breath.

He forced his eyes to open, fighting the blinding light of the candle, and took in his surroundings. The sounds around him were deafening, taking all his will to block them out and focus just on those in the room, in his apartment. He couldn't begin to explain how he felt; his body seemed reborn—unaffected by years of use and neglect. Rejuvenated. He seemed stronger. His senses were...

Incredible.

He smelled the cars passing outside. He smelled the rain, the sweet rain.

What had she done to him?

When he saw his eyes in the mirror, when he saw the deep blue they'd become, a blue of bright sapphire, he knew he had been transformed forever.

Reborn by Her.

Del hurried to his bedroom, where he changed clothes, leaving his soiled, bloodied suit in a pile at his feet.

There was someplace he needed to be.

Someplace She wanted him to be.

Downstairs, Christina started the car. It was time to go.

CHAPTER SIXTY-SEVEN

1692

The Journal of Clayton Stone

I **WOKE TO A** dull throb behind the eyes, my body limp on the floor.

Around me are the aches and moans of others as they are released from slumber, each returning to consciousness in their own time.

"She is gone!" a voice shouted.

The table looms above me and I reach for it, pulling myself to a stand before collapsing back into my chair. My strength is all but gone; I crave rest and nothing more.

"Seal the room!" Tauber cried. "She must not be allowed to leave the building!"

But she was already gone; I knew this in my heart. As I struggled to regain my wits, my eyes found the bench.

Her tattered clothing lay in a heap under the chains and

ropes which had held her still only moments (or was it hours?) ago.

Time escaped me.

A glance at the window told me night had befallen us.

I remember nothing of its passage.

Tauber struggled to his feet, aided by one of the guards. Behind him, the magistrate looked out upon us, his eyes wide with fear, his hands moving in the sign of the cross.

I had forgotten the man in the long black coat, the stranger who had arrived only moments before we were overwhelmed by her magic—for that was what it was. There could be no other explanation. He seemed to know my thoughts with his words.

"She used your energy to escape," the strange man explained. "Clearly the work of the devil. Do you still doubt this? She stole your life force with her witchcraft and traveled from this place."

The magistrate glowered at him. "What do you know of her? You arrive here without warning and she is gone. How do we know you are not responsible? Maybe you are as much a witch as she!"

Murmurs escaped the crowd, which had settled back upon the benches. Unlike before, the doors opened freely, but those who had tried to escape no longer wished to leave. I suspected they felt as I; there was a safety in numbers. I took comfort in this even though I also knew it was a falsehood; we knew not how to protect ourselves from whatever was happening this very night.

The stranger approached the magistrate. His dark eyes peered from a face lined with wisdom. "I have hunted that girl, that evil, for all my days. I have followed her across this globe as she left behind a path of death and misery beyond words. To call her a witch doesn't fully describe her evil. Those who harbor her are worse still," he told them. "Her so-called sisters—more disciples than anything else."

At the mention of sisters, my breath caught. I quickly looked around, but nobody had noticed.

The stranger went on. "She is both old and young and able to appear at the age of her choice." He turned to study the faces of the gallery. "Has she appeared to any of you while captive? Perhaps as an old woman or a child even younger than she? You would still recognize it as her. She can only deceive your eyes; your hearts remain pure."

Those in the gallery remained silent, none admitting to such a visit. Surely I wasn't alone in this, was I? When she had first appeared to me the night before last and said she was her sister, I had known the truth, even if I wasn't willing to admit it. Especially after confirming she was still captive in her cell.

I couldn't bring myself to speak of this aloud; not to this man, not to any of them.

"Her book is real; it contains countless souls. Their energy, their very life force given to her by a promise made with a single drop of blood—a signature stronger than any scripted word. Each signature, each name, contributes to her power. It is for this very reason that so many find themselves sickly after such an encounter; they are left with little life force of their own. And she just grows stronger."

He paused for a moment, his eyes drifting to her clothing.

"We need to find her. There is little time. Someone take me to where she lives."

My heart pounded within my chest. I feared for her. But most of all I feared for him and any of those who followed him to that dark place in the woods.

—Thad McAlister,
Rise of the Witch

CHAPTER SIXTY-EIGHT
Day 3 – 06:15 a.m.

THE LARGE, TOWERING OAKS seemed to wrap around the road, engulfing the two lanes with intertwined fingers of bare branches that scratched at the sky and pavement alike. They sealed out the early morning light, growing darker and denser with each passing mile. Thad knew he was pushing his luck driving at such speeds, but he was running out of time.

You're so very close, she breathed in his ear.

When he turned, the passenger seat was empty. He found himself alone. Yet her perfume lingered, the sweet smell of bougainvilleas mixed with spring showers.

"Get out of my head," he murmured.

Silly boy.

Thunder cracked wildly outside, sending a streak of

lightning across the sky. The trees seemed to reach for it, their branches outstretched toward the heavens. Thad swore they moved not with the sway of the wind, but with deliberate motion.

You've been driving too long, he told himself. *You've gone days without any real rest. It's your mind, just your mind.*

He glanced in the rearview mirror in time to see them twist together behind him, sealing the road further still.

Is the forest trying to keep me here?

All the rain on the glass changed perspective—that's all. His car was the only thing moving down this lonely stretch of forgotten road.

The rain fell so hard that he didn't notice the wooden tunnel until he was nearly on top of it. Pumping the brakes, he slid to a stop a few feet before its dark opening.

It was exactly the way he had imagined it.

Hundreds of years old, the wooden tunnel bridged the road over a fast moving creek nearly overflowing with the heavy rains of the past few days. Even within the car, he could hear its rushing waters lapping at the bottom of the petrified planks. The one in his book sat upon a large, motorized gimbal capable of turning 360 degrees on its axis. He had no doubt this was the same. Even when writing the story he had speculated the reason for this—boats didn't travel this creek; its only purpose seemed to be to keep visitors from passing and entering the town.

Or to keep those in the town from getting out, his mind suggested.

Emerging on the Shadow Cove side of the tunnel, Thad brought his car to a stop.

With a deep breath, he shut off the ignition and got out of the car into the thick-falling rain. Thad popped the trunk and retrieved a shovel.

He started off into the forest along the creek's edge, leaving the rental car in the middle of the road, his journal open on the floor—he wouldn't need it anymore.

CHAPTER SIXTY-NINE
Day 3 – 06:20 a.m.

"MOMMY, WHAT HAPPENED?" ASHLEY cried.

"Christ," Rachael moaned, staring at her legs. The warm liquid had flooded the floor around her and soaked her clothing—her water had broken; she was having this baby. Another contraction came, and she grimaced with pain.

"We need a doctor," Ms. Perez said with concern.

Rachael could only nod.

"Help me get your mommy into the chair," Ms. Perez said.

Ashley reached for her mother's cold, shaking hand.

Rachael wished Thad were here.

As Perez and her daughter helped her into a chair, Rachael saw her reflection in the hall mirror. Her skin was pale and shimmered with sweat. Her breathing was shallow and weak.

"What's wrong, Mommy?" Ashley stammered.

Rachael forced a smile and ran her fingers through her daughter's thick hair. "Your little brother or sister is trying to come to us early, honey. Everything will be okay."

Outside, thunder crackled in the distance and the thin light seeping through the muddied windows melted away as dark clouds blotted out the morning sun.

Ashley looked to the window. "It's gonna rain again."

"I'll get you some water," Ms. Perez told her.

Rachael grabbed her arm. "No, stay here. We need to stick together."

The knock at the front door startled them and at first they remained still, unsure of what to do. Ms. Perez moved first, starting for the door.

"Wait," Rachael said.

"They might be able to help us," Ms. Perez said.

"That's not what they want," Ashley breathed.

Her mother looked down at her. "What makes you say that, honey?"

Ashley grew pale, her eyes wide. "Don't let them in, Mommy. Zeke says they're bad."

Another contraction ripped through Rachael, and she gripped the arms of the chair with white fingers. She stifled the cry climbing up her throat. Cold sweat filled her forehead and her vision blurred. Although she didn't time it, she knew only about five minutes had passed since the last one. Ms. Perez was thinking the same thing; her eyes were filled with concern. She took a few deep breaths, her strength slowly returning.

Another knock, much louder than the first, broke them from their reverie.

"What do you want to do?" Ms. Perez asked.

Rachael reached into her pocket and removed her husband's gun. She checked the chamber and noted the five remaining bullets. Looking down at her daughter's frightened face, she took Ashley's hand. "What does Zeke think we should do, honey?"

Behind her, Ms. Perez let out a frustrated sigh. Rachael shot her a silencing glance, then turned back to her daughter. "Has he told you who they are?"

Ashley shook her head.

"You said he told you they were bad. What exactly did he tell you? Why don't you want us to let them in?"

Ashley pouted and shuffled her feet. "You won't believe me. You never believe me."

Rachael forced a smile. "Sometimes Mommy can be foolish, but I should have believed you. I believe you now—we both do."

Rachael shot Ms. Perez another glance, but her housekeeper chose to remain silent.

Ashley turned to the door. "I think Zeke wanted us to leave. That's why he did those terrible things. He wanted us to go before they got here."

"But he hasn't told you who they are?"

Again, Ashley shook her head. "But I know they're bad, Mommy. I don't know how I do, but I do."

Two of the minions appeared in the hallway. First, they glanced at the two women and child in the living room, then to the front door.

Rachael raised her gun and pointed the weapon at them.

With a loud grunt, one of them ran to the front door. The other quickly followed. The two seemed to communicate in a garbled chatter. The first then scrambled onto the shoulders of the other and reached for the deadbolt.

Without hesitation Rachael fired, hitting the bottom minion in the back. The creature crumbled into a pile of dirt, causing the other to fall to the floor with an angry howl. Before Rachael could shoot the other, three more appeared and climbed atop each other until they reached the lock.

When Rachael again raised the gun, Ms. Perez pushed the barrel back down. "There are too many," she told her. "Save the bullets for them." She was referring to the people just outside the door.

Before Rachael could respond, the deadbolt clicked and they watched in silence as the door swung open, their four unwelcome guests standing at the threshold.

Rachael heard the gunshot before she even realized she had pulled the trigger.

CHAPTER SEVENTY
Day 3 – 06:25 a.m.

THE WATERS OF THE creek rushed past him on his left as Thad walked along the bank. The rain had grown relentless, pouring from the sky in frigid sheets that ate at his skin, growing stronger by the minute.

Thad tightened his grip on the shovel and pressed on, careful not to slip in the muddy earth.

He was very much aware of the eyes that peered at him from the opposite side of the creek and did his best to ignore them. But with each step, their numbers seemed to grow. Red eyes poked through the rain and darkness to land upon him with both curiosity and hunger. Thad pretended not to know what they were—or more precisely, who they were—but his mind wouldn't agree to such a plan. He had written about the residents of Shadow Cove too and knew to fear them.

The thick black branches of the oak trees reached for him while the wind danced across his path with a ferocious strength, howling with demented laughter. Thad continued to ignore it all, pressing forward, led by the map he had detailed so clearly in his mind's eye.

For one brief moment he thought he felt the warmth of Christina's hand in his, but when he looked down Thad found nothing. He smelled her perfume, though. She seemed all around him, emanating from the trees, the rain.

She wasn't far. He glanced at the red eyes, then turned away.

Not with them, she couldn't be.

There is so much you don't know, she said softly. *So much you don't understand.*

"About you?" he replied.

Her voice fell silent, lost to the wind.

Thad pressed on.

He was close. The dead trees around him told him so as did the waters of the creek, now moving with a rage that raised whitecaps, phosphorous beneath the stormy sky.

He heard their whispers now, tiny papery whispers escaping their angry lips as they watched from across the creek. They wanted to rip his limbs from his body, to spill his blood on the rain-soaked soil. He tasted their hatred on the air.

Will they kill me, Christina? When they learn why I am here?

Do you honestly believe they'll allow me to leave with the box?

He waited for a response from Christina, but none came. There were only the sounds of the storm, of the forest, of them.

Thad stopped.

The dead forest stood before him.

He had seen the tangled mass so clearly when he had written the story, and now he stood at its edge.

Not a single tree, plant, or weed flourished. Only death remained in the blackened earth where life once thrived, as if a terrible plague had somehow killed everything in its path with such swift vengeance nothing escaped. There was an edge to it, clearly defined—a place where death met life. He sensed it growing—the large circle of death expanding even today, centuries after it began, encroaching upon the living earth, eating the bordering life away with an insatiable appetite.

Thad knew a spell had created this circle of death. A spell cast hundreds of years ago with a dual purpose, to isolate Her and keep others away. It began—

By scattered leaves,
By blood of saints,
Taint this ground,
Earth, air, and place.

To enter seemed foolish, but Thad had no choice if he wanted to retrieve the box. In his book, the box was buried at the center of this place. He had no doubt the real one rested there as well.

Again he sensed Christina at his side, anxious and deeply excited. Although he didn't see her, she no doubt peered into the gloom as he did. He wondered if she feared it as he did. *Did she even understand what this was?*

Of course she did. Perhaps her understanding of this place kept her from making this journey herself. Maybe she knew where the box had been buried all along. Even now, she didn't follow him in the flesh, but with some projection of her mind, her soul.

My dear Thad, she finally spoke. *You only have to realize what this place is, what the death represents, to discern that I, of all people, may never enter. For the same spell that keeps Her trapped here keeps her ancestors out. I'm blood of Her blood, Thad. I dare not enter such a place, or I risk the same fate. You, of all people, should appreciate such is true.*

Thad stood at the edge of the dead forest and peered inside. His eyes sliced through the rain, through the very trees that stood in his way, until his mind's eye found what he sought: the great oak at the center of this place. The mother of this forest, she stood tall and proud over the other trees. Even in death, her trunk and branches were unyielding. Unwilling to crumble and rot, the oak had petrified centuries earlier and was now stronger than stone, marking her final resting place as a monument.

Would he be able to cross the barrier without harm?

He didn't know. He hadn't asked this question while writing the book, nor had it offered an answer. Thad may die the second he stepped in, or the spell may not affect him at all.

You must hurry, Thad. Christina told him. *Your family only has hours remaining.*

Thad had little choice. With a deep breath, he stepped across the boundary between the living and the dead, his feet sinking into the rotted, damp earth below.

Even in her projected state, Christina proved unwilling to follow. He sensed her at his back, standing with anticipation at the dead forest's edge.

The rain grew colder and his skin tingled at its touch. Not a tingle accompanied by goose bumps, but something else—an electricity in the air, the kind that makes the hair on your arms stand on end.

He gripped the shovel with new vigor, holding it close to his chest, ready to swing should he encounter one of the creatures. They were the only other living things likely to enter such a place, the only ones to call this dead forest home.

CHAPTER SEVENTY-ONE

1692

The Journal of Clayton Stone

W*E STARTED OUT AT* nightfall.

For the past four hours, we had listened to the stranger as he shared tales of his journeys, the magistrate prompting him along with much doubt at first, then with a keen interest, then enthrallment. For this man had traveled the world for much of his adult life in search of the woman now hiding among the shadows of our wooded home.

Death followed her too, he explained. Nipping at her heels was always a trail of death and loss. When he had lost her just outside of Paris nearly twenty years earlier, he only had to follow the stories of the locals to learn of the plague eating through the small villages to the north of the grand city. The fallen cattle and missing children; he had seen it all before. The very ground smelled of her as he approached.

The worn, distant looks of the locals simply gazed upon him with vacant stares. Their energy was now Hers.

It would happen here too, he insisted.

It was hard to fathom, of course. For this man insisted that he had chased her for the better part of sixty years, much of his life. Yet she appeared to be no more than sixteen or seventeen years of age.

Stranger still, he went on to tell us that she appeared to be of a different age to each of us—an old woman to some, a little girl to others. She became what we wished to see, he explained. This was confirmed as those around us began to share stories of their encounters with her. All spoke of the same person, of this there was little doubt. But she was different to each of us.

As those around me told their tales, I remained silent, unwilling to share my experiences with her. Instead, I stared intently at my script, documenting each story as it unfolded. For this was my duty, was it not?

Through it all, the stranger did not share his name. When inquired of such, he simply shrugged off the request. It was not important, he had said.

I was unable to determine his age.

His skin was deeply weathered and scarred. It told of a harsh life, as did his eyes—a gray of which I had never seen. His accent could not be placed. After four hours, I felt I knew less of this man than I did at his appearance.

Nearly an hour ago, we had begun to amass in the town proper. Many carried lanterns, knowing this night would be late. Most hefted weapons. There were crosses and holy water taken from the church, soil from the yard at its side.

William Hobbs initially refused to lead the stranger to her home, but his mind was quickly changed when the magistrate reminded him that he had knowingly colluded with a witch—and at this point all had agreed that she was indeed a witch—the penalty for which he did not wish to face.

Reluctantly, Hobbs started down Corning Trail toward the thick oaks, flanking the village with the Stranger at his heels and the remainder of us closely behind.

I carried no weapons.

I would not be willing or able to hurt her should the need arise. To bring a weapon would be nothing more than a falsehood told to myself.

—Thad McAlister,
Rise of the Witch

CHAPTER SEVENTY-TWO
Day 3 – 06:45 a.m.

THE BULLET SEEMED TO travel in slow motion.

Rachael watched as the projectile left the barrel of the gun, a thin trail of smoke following close behind. It raced across the room toward the four strangers standing in the doorway.

The oldest of them, a tall woman wearing a black dress buttoned to the neck, calmly raised her left hand and closed her eyes.

Rachael and the others watched in awe as the bullet stopped in mid flight and fell to the ground with a thump on the mud-covered wood floor.

The four stepped into the foyer together, their cold eyes locked on Rachael. Behind them, three minions scrambled to close the door and secure the deadbolt.

The old woman stepped forward and glared at the gun. "I think we've seen the last of that."

The gun was ripped from Rachael's hand, flew through the air, then slowed and landed in the old woman's outstretched fingers. She passed the weapon to the large, bulky man at her side, who secured it in a large black leather case.

Ashley began to cry and buried her head in her mother's side. Rachael wrapped her arm around her and combed through her hair.

The old woman turned to the two men behind her and passed on instructions, her voice low. With silent nods, they turned and disappeared—one into the kitchen, the other heading upstairs. Minions followed at their feet, tripping over each other to remain close.

The large man set his black bag down at his side and folded his arms. The old woman stepped forward, her cold blue eyes glaring down at them. "My name is Eleanor. You must be Rachael McAlister."

"Get out of my house!" Rachael sneered.

Eleanor smiled. "And this must be your lovely daughter. Ashley, isn't it?"

She reached out to run her hand through the girl's hair, and Rachael slapped her away. "I'll kill you, do you understand? I'll fuckin' kill you!"

When the next contraction hit, Rachael doubled over. She grimaced and squeezed her daughter's hand.

"Mommy, you're hurting me!" Ashley cried.

Again, the old woman grinned. "Yes, Rachael, you're

hurting her. Perhaps you should let go. Perhaps you should let me take her."

Rachael pulled her daughter tight, wrapping her arms around her shivering frame.

"Out of my house...," she growled, fighting back the contraction.

"By my count, it's only been five minutes since the last one, Rachael. Your baby will be here soon, just a few hours at the most. Since you will not be leaving this house, your options are very limited. You can attempt to have the child on your own, lying in all this filth with your daughter and housekeeper standing over you in horror, or you can let me help you. I have substantial experience in such matters; I've been a midwife for more years than I care to remember."

The woman reached for Rachael's wrist, but she pulled away.

"I only wish to check your heart rate, my dear. There is no need to fear me."

When she reached again, Rachael allowed Eleanor to touch her, clutching Ashley tightly against her chest. The woman pressed cold fingers to her wrist while following the hands on her watch. "Your pulse is a little high, but that is to be expected. Aside from the contractions, do you feel any other pain?"

Rachael shook her head.

"That's grand. Now, please relax as we prepare this place for the birth of your child."

"Who are you?"

Eleanor smiled, then turned to the large man at her back, whispering in his ear.

Rachael glanced at Ms. Perez, who remained silent at her side, her face filled with fear.

"Make them go away, Mommy," Ashley breathed.

"Who the hell are you?" Rachael said again, raising her voice.

Eleanor glared at her, eyes dark and cold, her skin as pale as death. Rachael remembered the woman from her dream, the old woman with the long fingernails and gravelly voice. Although this wasn't her, she knew they were connected.

Clickity, click, click, click.

The sound came from nowhere and everywhere, echoing in her mind. She would have written it off as her subconscious if not for Eleanor—for she was grinning again, and Rachael knew she had heard it, too.

CHAPTER SEVENTY-THREE
Day 3 – 07:00 a.m.

THAD STOOD BEFORE THE great oak tree in awe. Its trunk was wider than any he had ever seen, at least five or six feet across. Its crusty old bark appeared both dead and alive, riddled with moss and mold, ravaged by insects, the weather, and time. Yet the oak stood strong—unyielding to the elements, unwilling to surrender, its trunk petrified to that of the hardest stone.

This tree, this place, had only existed in his mind months ago, as the story, as Her story, took shape. *How could this have been here all along?*

Thad knelt down before the tree and closed his eyes, remembering the exact words from his book:

Follow the trunk to the east, to where the bougainvillea once grew thick, its thorns now thirsting for blood. Beneath the blanket of dead moss, you'll find a hollow damp with the waters of the rain. It is here she rests, her box buried deep within this earthen grave. It is here she is to remain, her evil caged for all time by the binding spell of Shadow Cove, by those who protect it, by the Order of the Draper.

Again, Thad remembered how the words had flowed when he wrote the book, materializing in his mind faster than he could put them to paper. He knew now they didn't come from his imagination, but instead came like memories. Not his own memories, though—memories placed within his subconscious by Her, those who worship Her, or both.

If the tree is real, if She is real, that also means the danger is real.

The thought came into his mind, awash in sounds of the forest. Thad looked up—dozens of tiny red eyes watched him from behind the trees. They disappeared into the night, fading into the shadows with his gaze.

He stood and shined his flashlight at the base of the tree. He circled around until he came to a large bougainvillea bush.

"The east side," he muttered to himself. Moss wasn't supposed to grow on the east.

Like the rest of the forest, the bush had died many years ago but somehow remained preserved. Even its dried leaves still held the faintest hint of color, glistening under a coat of rain. The thorns scratched angrily at him, larger than any he had ever seen on such a plant. Thad shied away from it, taking a step back. His grip tightened on the shovel, and with a deep breath, he brought the blade down hard against the plant.

He imagined cries of pain as the stainless steel sliced through the tangled mass of branches, the thorns scratching against the shovel in defense. He pulled the blade back and brought it down again, then again—each blow with more force than the last, until the plant gave way and he exposed the bright green moss underneath.

Ten minutes passed before he had cleared enough away to reach the moss with his hands. Thad set down the shovel and fell to his knees, then pressed his fingers into the thick green carpet, tugging at the earth with all his remaining strength. The moss gave way, spilling warm water upon him. Thad couldn't help but envision blood seeping from an open wound, his fingers piercing skin. Then the wound came to life as thousands of tiny black spiders fled from within, running across his arm, up his legs, prickling at his skin with angry feet. Thad let out a soundless scream and jumped back, brushing them away, stomping them under his shoes. When the last one scurried across the muddied earth to the safety of the creek's edge, Thad shivered.

Once again he knelt down before the tree, shining his flashlight into the hollow behind the moss.

The space was large, much larger than he had imagined.

Large enough.

With the flashlight in hand, Thad clambered into the hole, his fingers digging into the rotten soil. The air rushing forth smelled of death, the earth damp with decay. The walls glistened with the decomposed syrup of rotting moss. The spell filled his mind, joined by the second stance of the spell, now as real as the rain falling from the blackened sky:

By scattered leaves,
By blood of saints,
Taint this ground,
Earth, air, and place.
Of life it's not,
No life shall leave,
Trapped for all time,
In the bowels of this tree.

Thad traced the trail of moss with his eyes, from the dead strands within the tree; they found life as they passed through the opening to the forest, growing greener with each inch, healthier with distance.

Thad realized he had this backward—the moss didn't grow healthy as it left the confines of the tree; life was lost as it entered.

He had to hurry.

With his bare hands he clawed at the earth, digging through a soft layer of mud at the top until he reached the harder packed soil inches below.

The hollow wasn't large enough to use the shovel properly. He angled it and scraped at the ground with the blade, cutting through the rocky soil. Sweat broke out on his brow, and his muscles began to ache. He ignored the pain and continued, unwilling to stop.

It's the curse, the spell! His mind cried as he fought for energy. *The curse on this place. It's stealing your strength, your life.*

Thad dug faster.

Another ten minutes passed before the shovel scraped the top of the box. The wooden box he knew would be here but shouldn't be, his imagination come to life.

With bloodied fingertips, he scratched at the earth; his eyes widened with every racing heartbeat. He scraped away the earth until he could grip the sides of the box and pull it free from its long-forgotten resting place.

The box tingled in his hands; it was far heavier than he had anticipated. Thad stared down at the intricate carvings in awe, amazed that he was holding the box at all.

The Rumina Box.

Fatigue weighed him down. The lead-lined box grew heavier with each passing second. He could not stay any longer.

Backing out of the tree, Thad's breath escaped him as he tried to drag the increasingly heavy box through the thick mud.

Looking down, he noticed his hands ;they no longer seemed his own. The skin had grown pale and loose, riddled with dark age spots. His nails had yellowed, turned brittle, grown much longer than just minutes earlier, appearing as if neglected for years. He drew a breath and felt pain in his lungs as they fought to expand. Again, the spell filled his mind:

By scattered leaves,
By blood of saints,

Taint this ground,
Earth, air, and place.
Of life it's not,
No life shall leave,
Trapped for all time,
In the bowels of this tree.

———————

Without hesitation, Thad began running through the forest back the way in which he had come, leaving the shovel lying in the dirt, the box wrapped in his straining arm. He pressed on, knowing the pain would only get worse if he stopped to rest. He had to get out of the forest. He had to get as far away from this place as possible.

Their eyes were on his back as he ran, their angry cries drifting from the darkness. He dared not look back, knowing that if he saw one he would no longer be able to move. To face them meant death, a death he wouldn't wish upon anyone.

The Draper lived in this miserable place. Only by their grace would he be allowed to leave. He knew them well, for they lived within the pages of his next book, *Keepers of the Rain.* A novel he would ensure never saw the light of day. He would destroy it along with all the others—they would burn in a fire kindled by that damned journal.

Thad ran, the thoughts of his wife and daughter pushing him beyond the pain.

CHAPTER SEVENTY-FOUR
Day 3 – 07:05 a.m.

"**TAKE HER UPSTAIRS,**" **THE** old woman instructed the large man at her side. "Place her in bed and see that she is comfortable."

Rachael inched backward as he nodded his head and bounded toward her in large, awkward strides.

"No, Mommy! No!" Ashley cried at her side, clutching her arm.

"Perez, hold her back," the man said.

"How do you…," Rachael breathed, glaring first at the man, then back at her housekeeper.

Perez turned away, unwilling to meet her gaze. "I'm sorry, Ms. Rachael. I never meant… they help me get this job, get to America—"

Rachael lunged at her, but the large man held her

318

back. "You bitch, how could you? We let you into our home and treated you like family!"

Ashley was sobbing; Perez put her hand on the young girl's shoulder. "It's for the best, Ms. Rachael. You will see this. I do this for you, for you and little Ashley, and the whole world."

"Come on," the large man told her, lifting her to her feet. The blood rushed from her head and she suddenly felt weak, her vision turning to white.

"She's fainting," someone said. "Get her upstairs—pour her a glass of cold water." It was Eleanor. Even through the thick veil of unconsciousness, Rachael knew her voice, her harsh voice, so much like that of the old woman in her dreams.

From her fog, Rachael watched the minions clear a path and follow them up the steps to the second floor. She tried to cry out for her daughter but found herself unable to make a sound.

Ms. Perez spoke with Eleanor, both smiling. Two old friends.

CHAPTER SEVENTY-FIVE
Day 3 – 07:20 a.m.

WHEN THE CAR CAME into view, Thad nearly collapsed in the muddy earth. His legs were numb, his heart and lungs throbbing within his chest. The box grew heavier with each step. Only the rain comforted him now, the thick, cold drops running against his thirsty skin, tingling with energy and life.

This place held more secrets than he could possibly imagine. Thoughts of good and evil did not enter his mind, for he never saw anything in such black and white. The forces living within this forest were different, one of the shades of gray in between. He did not pretend to understand, nor did he believe he ever would. The forest didn't want him to remove the box but nothing stopped him. The creatures, the Draper, they had observed him but did little else, spectators at best.

The Draper were real?

He had to focus. He had to think about Rachael and Ashley.

"They miss you, buddy," a voice said.

At first Thad couldn't tell where the voice had come from. Perhaps another trick of the mind? Then he saw the shadow of a man standing beside his car, a large man, familiar.

"Del?"

Del stepped forward into the gray morning, his clothing soaked. "You were right, Thad. It's one helluva book. Couldn't put it down to save my life. I can't remember the last time I actually read a manuscript straight through, but goddammit if you didn't come up with one crazy story."

Out of breath and exhausted, Thad stumbled to his car, set the heavy box on the hood, and leaned against the door. "What the hell are you doing here?" he finally said, the words scratching at his raw throat.

Del frowned. "Christ, that's not a very warm welcome for an old friend. And to think, I came all this way. Maybe I should head back to the city and let you fend for yourself?"

Thad forced another breath. "How did you find me?" His own voice sounded different to him, ragged, tired.

Del's eyes fixed on the box and he stepped closer, reaching with a cautious hand. "I'll be damned. That's it, isn't it? I pictured something a little larger based on your narrative. We'll need to work on that, but otherwise it's exactly the same. His fingers slipped across the smooth surface, tracing the carvings on the sides. "It must be heavy, right? Lined with lead and all."

Thad stepped between Del and the box, forcing him to take a step back.

"Easy, Hoss. I only want a little look-see, that's all."

"Del, how did you find me?" Thad repeated. Something wrong, something different about him.

Del smirked and took a few steps toward the trees, catching the rain in his hands. "Funny story. Nowhere near as good as yours. Not that I could ever put it on paper, but it's a good one nonetheless, a real page-turner. If I told anyone else, they'd probably lock me up and study this fat head of mine, but you, I think you'd understand. I think you might believe me."

Thad watched as he stopped at the edge of the forest, his gaze peering into the darkness, as if able to see well beyond the trees.

All the way to them. *Could he see the creatures? Their eyes? The Draper?*

"You can tell me, Del. We're friends; you can tell me anything."

Del snorted. "Best of buddies...you'd never tell anyone, right? After all, I kept your secret: the horror writer dancing with antipsychotics. That's just between us buddies," he winked.

Thad grew impatient. He had to get back. "Tell me, Del. I don't have time for this."

"No, I guess you don't, do you...," he agreed, glancing back at the box.

He knew. Somehow he knew. He was part of this.

Thad charged him, but Del raised his hand before he reached him. A force unlike any other threw him back against the car, nearly cracking the glass in the door. "She told me where to find you, Thad. She knew exactly where to find you."

"Who?"

"*She of whom we don't speak*, of course. *Her.* Tell me, Thad, do you know Her real name? 'Cause we need to call Her something. The 'unspeakable name thing' may play out well in a book, but not in real life. That bullshit is for reserved for Harry Potter and his little wizard friends. I thought I had it earlier, but I lost it. So much going on. When the reporters cover the story, they'll want to call Her something, though, don't you think? I know I need to call Her something. I'm guessing if anyone still knows Her true name, it's you, am I right? I had it, right on the tip of my tongue, but now..."

"She's not real, Del. It's just a—"

"Story? Yeah, I get that. But you of all people know it's more, much more. You can't honestly tell me after going into that forest and coming out with the box you don't believe? You know the power of this place, how it craves life, how easily it takes it. Christ, look at yourself! You've got all the proof you need!"

Thad had never seen him like this. He sounded like a madman.

"Look! Look in the mirror!"

Thad knelt down in the mud and turned the mirror on the door toward his face. The image staring back at him was no longer his own.

"See! How long were you in there? A few hours? You lost decades to the forest, to Her! The damn spell that trapped Her in an old gnarly oak robbed you of years. Luck of the draw, I guess. Better you than me and all that…"

"This isn't possible." His fingers ran over his leathery, wrinkled cheeks. He looked like an eighty-year-old man. "The spell…must be…"

Del approached him and knelt down at his side. "I tried one of the spells in your book too, Thad. Something told me it wasn't some made-up mumbo-jumbo and I tried it. I'll be damned if it didn't work!" His voice dropped to a murmur. "She spoke to me, Thad. She honest to God spoke to me! Stood right there in my house! In my bathroom, of all places. She told me everything. No…wait…she didn't tell me. We didn't have time for a conversation. When I saw Her I sorta knew, you know? Everything became so clear. Like a picture coming into focus. And it's amazing! It's so goddamn amazing, I don't know if this world is ready for Her, but it sure as shit needs to be! It's going to be incredible!"

Del glanced up into the cloudy sky and wiped the raindrops from his forehead. "She's about to be reborn, Thad. None of this would have happened without you, none of it. Don't think I'll ever forget. I won't let anyone forget, buddy."

It was getting harder to breathe; Thad's heart pounded within his chest, straining with each beat. Del frowned with concern.

"The aging process hasn't stopped, Thad. I guess you were in that place too long. Doesn't look like you've got much time left. I promise I'll take good care of your wife and daughter. I'll treat them like my own. They won't want for anything; I swear."

"Help me up," Thad breathed, his throat aching with each word.

Del shook his head. "You're too weak. You need to rest. Not much longer now."

"You've got to get me home, back to my family. They need me." Thad stared at his hands; nails long, yellow, and brittle. His skin, riddled with age spots. He dared not look back into the mirror. His mind reached out for Christina, but if she was near she didn't respond.

Del laughed. "Wait until the book's published, Thad! Wait until the world gets a gander at it... They'll embrace Her. I know they will. All because of you!"

Thad watched as Del reached for the box. This time, he couldn't stop him; he had no strength. Del took the box and held it in his large hands. "It's warm, isn't it? Unbelievable, even through all the lead..."

"You've got to help me, Del."

Del smiled and placed a thoughtful hand on Thad's shoulder. "I really should, shouldn't I? It wouldn't be right to leave you out here to die."

Thad looked up at him, his eyes pleading.

With his large arm, Del pulled Thad to his feet and led him to his car. He used his free hand to pop the trunk with his key-fob, then eased the man inside.

Thad gave in to sleep before Del brought the trunk lid down.

Del shook his head. "Too bad you're not going to be around to see all this, buddy. It's going to be a helluva show."

Reaching through the driver's window, he dropped the keys on the seat.

"Adios, Thadios," he sang.

With the box in hand, he started down the muddy path back toward the black Lexus, which he had left at the main road. He didn't need to glance at his watch to know he had little time to get back to Charleston, South Carolina. He wasn't one to obey speed limits anyway.

He reached the car and crammed his large frame into the driver's seat as the sky opened up, releasing another round of thick rain.

"You got it!"

Del smiled and handed the box to Christina before planting a big kiss on her cheek. "You knew I would, sweet thing. I'm not about to let this party end just yet. How much time do we have?"

Christina closed her eyes for a moment. "Not long. Maybe fifteen hours at the most."

"Well then, I guess it's time we find out if watching NASCAR has improved my driving skills any," he said, with a laugh. "You may want to fasten your seat belt. It's Go time."

CHAPTER SEVENTY-SIX
Day 3 – 07:25 a.m.

ELEANOR'S EYES OPENED SLOWLY and she drew a deep breath.

The box was now in their possession, back where it belonged.

She was coming home; after so long, finally coming home.

The woman was about to give birth, all proceeding as scheduled.

Eleanor knew She would be pleased. She could hear it in the rain and thunder outside, feel it in the thickening air. She would be here soon and Eleanor would be her savior.

Eleanor dared to consider how she would be rewarded, the witch's strongest and most knowledgeable ally. Surely she would be taken under her wing, guided in her ways. That was all she wished. As with the others, she dedicated her life to the teachings of the Shadow Cove witch. She was a woman of extraordinary power, whose light was extinguished long before her time by those who did not understand.

She only slumbered. Today would mark the beginning of a new era. One in which She would dominate, with Eleanor at her side.

The old woman smiled, her heart pitter-pattering in her chest.

CHAPTER SEVENTY-SEVEN

1692

The Journal of Clayton Stone

*T*HE NIGHT FELL AROUND *us, choking the sky until its last breath escaped and it silenced in slumber. The air grew still and cold, nipping at my bones. I'm finding it difficult to write, as my hand has taken to shaking under the frigid air. I must, though; these events must be documented. As incredible as they may seem, as unbelievable as they may seem, her story must be told, if only as a warning.*

Just how long we have walked, I am unsure. The large oaks seem to grow thicker with each step, swaying slowly with the heavy wind, dripping with the piercing rain falling from the heavens.

Time was uncertain. Not just to me, but to all. The Stranger said this was a typical ploy of hers. She had the ability to make minutes feel like a lifetime and years feel like seconds. She manipulated time as she desired. No one questioned him of this; it was simply accepted. All he had told us had come to pass, so we held no reason to doubt him.

He went on to say his pocket watch was protected from all witchcraft and with a quick glance exclaimed less than two hours had passed before it disappeared back into the deep pockets of his long coat.

Knowing this, I still found it hard to accept. She and her sisters (if she truly had sisters; for he had told us they were all really just her in different forms) lived such a distance from the town proper, in such isolation. It was unimaginable they would travel so far on such a regular basis, but it was clear they had. Not a day passed without a sighting of the peculiar group. As the moon had grown full of recent, they were spotted frequently—not on horseback but on foot. For they were rarely in possession of the supplies that one would expect to be carried on a journey of such hours. Sometimes they carried nothing at all.

I inquired this of the Stranger but he only shrugged, explaining that little of what was seen was true when it came to her. Much like the way she had escaped from the church and the bindings that held her, she could come and go from town with the same ease. The distance mattered little. She could cross oceans in an instant, appear in numerous places at once. She wasn't bound to this earth as we. She was of the wind and sea, more a flicker in the mind's eye than human—a nightmare born to the living.

His words confused me more than aided my need to understand, but I said nothing more of this.

Hobbs walked wordlessly but with purpose. Leading our small group through the thickets and trees, cutting down the branches that seemed to knot together before our path, attempting to slow our progress. Sweat trickled down his forehead—I believe it derived from fear rather than exertion. He had grown pale, his breathing shallow and fast. More than once he had stopped, and I thought he would turn and head back the way in which we came. But a glance from the Stranger had squelched such thoughts, sending him forward again and closer to her with the rest of us at his heels.

Around us, many eyes glowed in the moonlight, weary and bright as the forest creatures looked on from the safety of darkness. They didn't follow, though, and I couldn't help but wonder if we should take heed from this.

—Thad McAlister,
Rise of the Witch

CHAPTER SEVENTY-EIGHT

Day 3 – 07:30 a.m.

ASHLEY SAT IN SILENCE on the family room floor, her back against the recliner, Buster's head resting in her lap. Both of them eyed the strangers with suspicion and fear, especially Ms. Perez, now that she had exposed whose side she was really on. Ashley was not surprised. She had never liked her.

Buster peered up at her with sad eyes, as if in agreement. She expected them to tie her up like they always did in the movies, but they didn't. In fact, they were so wrapped up in hushed discussions she wasn't sure anyone was even keeping an eye on her at all.

"Zeke?"

She looked around the room for a sign from him, but found none.

"Zeke?" she repeated, this time a little louder.

Buster tilted his head and whimpered.

One of the minions walked up to her, scratching his head with tiny fingers. Another came from behind the couch and stood beside the other. Both eyed her with curiosity. Buster drew closer, pressing against her side, his whine turning to a soft growl.

"Get away from me!" she told them.

Both stepped closer, their teeth bared.

She shuffled backward until her back pressed against the wall. Ashley pulled her knees tight against her chest. "No, stay away!"

Buster barked and lunged at them, sinking his teeth into the closer of the two—it let out a shriek before crumbling into a pile of dirt at his feet. Buster shook his head and whined, his mouth foaming. He fell to the ground and began scratching at his snout with both front paws. A moment later, it was over and he coughed, spewing dirt with a frustrated grunt.

The remaining minion had backed up and was observing from a safer distance, its face expressionless. Ashley wrapped her arms around the dog. "You saved me!" she breathed at his ear, unable to take her eyes off the pile of dirt where the creature had stood. The minion was now studying the dirt, too. It then turned to Buster, then back to Ashley, its eyes cold, lifeless. It held a spear in his hand, not much more than a sharpened toothpick, and Ashley thought for sure it would throw it at her. But it didn't. Instead it continued to glare, occasionally turning back to the pile of dirt.

"You must be careful, child," the old woman, Eleanor, said. Ashley hadn't heard her approach. "They have nasty little tempers. I wouldn't dare irritate them."

"Where's my mommy?" Ashley said, refusing to cry.

The old woman knelt down at her side, her hand sinking into the dirt left behind by the minion. "Your mother is safe, my dear. No need to worry. She is among friends, as are you." She ran her fingers through Ashley's thick golden hair. "Do you know why we're here?"

Ashley tried to pull away from her, but her back was against the wall.

"It's okay, child. Do you know why we're here?" she asked again.

"You want my little sister," she said, looking to the floor.

The old woman smiled. "So you do know it's a girl."

Ashley nodded.

"And how do you suppose that is?"

She shrugged her shoulders.

"You know what I think?" the old woman asked. "I think you can see her. Not only now, as she rests in your mother's belly, but years from now—you can see her playing as a child, you can see her as a teenager, and even an adult. You know all about her, don't you, Ashley?"

Ashley wasn't sure how to respond to that. Somehow, she did know all those things. At first she wondered if Zeke had told her, but it seemed more likely it came to her in dreams. That wasn't right either, though, because she just knew. These thoughts, these memories of things which hadn't happened yet, appeared in her head like a movie.

"It's in your mind's eye, Ashley, your very thoughts," the old woman told her. "It is nothing to be ashamed of, not at all. This proves how special you are; you and your little sister." The woman reached out and touched Ashley's hand, a series of flashes filling her mind.

Olden time.

Witches.

Fire.

The Book.

A large tree.

A beautiful girl.

Death.

Ashley pulled away and held her one hand in the other. "Who is she?"

At first the old woman appeared surprised; then she looked down at her own hand and understood. "Your sight is strong!" she exclaimed. "More so than I dared hope. Your sister's will be stronger still. It's in your blood, your family. That's why She picked your family. That's why She needs her."

"She wants to keep my sister?" Ashley questioned, more to herself than anyone. The old woman didn't have to nod; the truth lived in her dark eyes. Beside her, Buster whined; she reached over and stroked his head.

Eleanor smiled for the first time, her yellowed, rotten teeth causing Ashley to turn away. "Your sister belongs to Her. Through her, She will be reborn."

"You can't take her; she's my mommy's baby, not yours!"

"Keep your voice down," the woman sneered.

But Ashley no longer needed her voice. As the woman leaned close, her thoughts poured out of her mind into Ashley's. Thoughts of her mother, father, and soon-to-be-born sister as well as thoughts of herself...many thoughts of herself. Ashley shivered and took it all in, as much as she could remember.

CHAPTER SEVENTY-NINE

1692

The Journal of Clayton Stone

*T*HE MOON WAS HIGH into the night when we came upon a small clearing with a weathered cabin at its center.

It was much as I remembered from my dream.

Large bougainvillea rambled along the ground and up its walls on all sides, surrounding the structure in a bath of bright colors—pinks, purples, and reds, entwined and flourishing, spreading from the cabin through the open field until they found the forest, then climbed the trees, reaching for the heavens. The night air was scented heavily with the blooms.

A single candle burned in the window.

A trickle of smoke escaped the flue and scratched the night sky, tendrils of white.

I took up behind a massive oak, an arm's breadth from

the edge of the clearing. Hobbs, Tauber, and two others were to my left. The Stranger stood alone, his long coat fluttering behind him on a thick wind.

Reaching into his pocket, he produced a small burlap sack tied with a leather band. Unlashing it, he tipped it to the ground and began walking around the cabin, spreading a chalky substance on the earth at his feet. Within moments, he had lapped the structure, completing a circle.

The sack disappeared within the folds of his jacket.

"Sea salt," the magistrate informed. "Evil is unable to cross such a boundary."

I nodded and quickly added this observation to my writings.

"Come out! I command of you!" the Stranger shouted. His voice echoed off the trees, booming through the clearing. He had produced a small wooden box. It was carved ornately with a large metal clasp at the front. He gently placed it on the ground at his feet.

I heard the clatter of a musket and turned to see Tauber nervously clutching at the weapon.

I thought I saw movement at the window, but I couldn't be sure.

Clickity, click, click.

The odd sound rode in on the wind, approaching from all sides.

My heart pained within my chest at the anticipation. I had heard this before.

Clickity, click.

Behind us, others began to emerge from the trees—

Herrick, Groton, Hobbs, Lawson.

"Hobbs," Tauber said, turning to the man. "She is familiar to you; go to the door. Draw her out."

Hobbs grew pale, his eyes wide. "I will do no such thing!" he replied.

Tauber frowned. "You have an obligation. You are facing charges. This is your opportunity to redeem yourself in the face of the Lord. Prove you are not in league with the witch."

Hobbs shook his head.

Tauber looked around, his face a mix of fear and disgust. "Jacobs, then. You testified that you signed her book. She will bring no ill to you."

George Jacobs was to my left. I heard the breath fill his chest as he gasped. His eyes grew wide.

I still felt his testimony was fraught with lies, but I knew he would never admit to this. To do so would subject him to the magistrate's wrath and the anger of the township. Why he had lied, I held no knowledge, but I knew he would continue the lie even before he stood and faced the cabin. His skin grew a pale white.

"Leave your weapon," the magistrate barked.

Jacobs considered this for a moment, then set his musket down at his feet.

He looked to me, but I couldn't meet his gaze. I turned back to my writing.

The cabin door was no more than fifty paces from where we crouched in the trees, but his journey was slow going. He shuffled his feet, covering less distance with each step. I couldn't help but wonder if this, too, was some manner of spell cast by the witch and her siblings—some unforeseen force holding him back.

His breathing grew labored too, ragged.

"He will not make it," The Stranger told them. "She will not allow it."

He came to a stop just five paces from the door, mere inches within the salt boundary.

"Jacobs!" the magistrate shouted. "You have nothing to fear. God is with you!"

Jacobs began to shake uncontrollably. He stiffened, then fell to the ground. We watched in horror as he seized, then went limp, then seized again and again—the cycle repeating, growing with intensity. Not a sound escaped his lips. He twitched like a fish caught upon the shore, then finally stilled.

"Mercy, my lord," someone blurted at my back.

Clickity, click, click.

I was not alone in hearing this. Puzzlement filled each face I found in the darkness.

Was I alone in knowing its source?

It was then that Jacobs burst into flames, a pyre nearly to the canopy of trees.

Someone screamed.

We watched helplessly as this man grew black, then turned to ash. A gust of wind picked him up and he was gone. Nothing remained but scorched earth where he had lain. A moment later, the bougainvillea took this too, somehow growing over the space in mere seconds.

Three or possibly four people left our group for the trees, fleeing back to the town in utter panic. I would have gone too were it not for the Stranger; he had somehow made it to my side in silence.

"You are familiar to her?" *His voice was rough but steady. He had not been deterred by Jacobs's death.*

I did not respond; I knew not what to say.

"I know she has visited you, scribe," *he continued.* "On more than one night, I imagine. That other man, he lied of this, but you..."

I shook my head.

"Boy, I have followed her to the ends of this earth. I am inside her head as she is inside mine. There are no secrets between us; we moved beyond that game long ago."

He raised my head to meet his. "Your eyes tell the truth, even if you do not. She has revealed herself to you, has she not?"

It was then that I looked down at my paper, at my writings of the past hour. Gone were the words I had committed to paper, the sentences I had formed and scribed. There was only a single phrase; I found it repeated down every page, every inch of paper.

Come to me

Come to me

Come to me

The Stranger saw it too, but he did not appear surprised.

"If you do not go, scribe, more men will die," *he told me.* "Do you want this blood on your hands?"

Again, I shook my head.

"Then you know what you must do."

The crushing within my chest that was my heart harshened, my stomach twisted.

Come to me

This time, I heard the words too. I watched in amazement as my hand scribbled them across the paper, the movement not my own.

It was then I knew I had no other choice.

I rose from concealment and approached the small cabin.

—Thad McAlister,
Rise of the Witch

CHAPTER EIGHTY
Day 3 – 07:45 a.m.

RACHAEL AWOKE ON THE bed. Someone, the large man, was busy tying her feet and hands to the frame. She tried to struggle but was simply too weak.

"No, please…," she breathed.

"We're going to need water," he mumbled. Rachael couldn't see whom he spoke to, but she sensed others in the room. The air smelled of dust and dirt and the foul scent of feces. The walls were covered in it, no doubt the work of the little minions running about the house. The windows had been blocked out entirely, denying whatever light tried to find its way into the room. Outside, thunder rumbled and rain tapped against the roof and windows with a steady fury.

God, where was Thad?

These people came into their lives, into their home... Where was he to stop them? Where was he to protect his family?

The baby kicked and tears began to well up in her eyes. She felt so helpless. They had Ashley downstairs. What did they have planned for her little girl? Her baby?

The large man finished tying her last wrist, then took a step back to admire his work, licking at his lips with a fat tongue. "It's true what they say about pregnant women, you know. The glow and everything. You look absolutely stunning lying there. You should try and relax. This will go so much easier for everyone if you're relaxed."

"What are you going to do to me?"

He stepped closer. Rachael heard the mud at his feet squishing into the carpet. "Something wonderful." He wiped his nose on the sleeve of his jacket before sitting on the edge of the bed, his eyes drifting over her.

"You can't hurt my baby," she pleaded.

"It's coming, you know."

"Promise me you won't hurt my baby or my little girl."

Running his large, rough hands over her dress, he paused at her belly. "She'll want to come out soon, no doubt about that. And when she's ready, ain't nothing gonna stop her. Her destiny is so much more special than mine or yours—anyone's, for that matter. I'm honored to see this in my lifetime—we've waited so long."

"Waited? Waited for what?" Rachael pleaded. "What's going to happen? What are you going to do with my baby?"

"Luther? What are you doing?"

Rachael and the large man turned together. Eleanor was standing in the doorway, her frame a mere shadow against the murky light coming from the candlelit hallway. "Go downstairs and help the others prepare."

"You shouldn't use our names…"

Eleanor scowled. "Now, Luther!"

He leaned to Rachael's ear. "We'll finish our little chat later," he said, winking. Luther rose and left the room, unwilling to make eye contact with the woman planted firmly in the doorway.

"You can't keep me here like this!" Rachael shouted at her. "Where's my daughter? I want to see my daughter!"

Eleanor offered her a cold smile. "You must calm down, Rachael, for the baby's sake. If necessary, we'll give you something to help you relax, but I'd rather not do that." She stepped into the room and stood at the foot of the bed, her dark eyes staring down at her. "Your daughter is safe; Ms. Perez is looking out for her. As long as you cooperate, you have my word: No harm will come to her."

Another contraction wracked her, and Rachael fought back the urge to scream. She held her breath until the pain passed. A defeated breath escaped her lips.

"Oh dear. They are getting close now, aren't they?"

Rachael nodded.

Eleanor reached for a tissue from the nightstand and blotted the sweat from her brow. "I know you think you're losing your baby and I understand how painful that must be for you, but you need to understand that

345

she is about to become part of something larger than all of us—greater than you could possibly imagine."

"Would you give up your own child to this madness?"

Eleanor nodded. "Without hesitation. Madness indeed—such a statement could not be further from the truth. You should be honored."

"You keep saying *she*. What makes you think it's a girl?"

Eleanor smiled down upon her. "Rest, child. The next contraction will be on you soon. You'll need all your strength for what is to come."

"Dormious," she said, placing her hand on Rachael's forehead.

As Eleanor said the word, Rachael felt a veil of sleep drift over her. If only for a few minutes, she lost focus on the terror around her.

"We'll need to move her soon," Luther said from the doorway.

I know, Eleanor thought. *I'll prepare her.*

Luther nodded his head and started down the stairs, her words still echoing in his mind.

CHAPTER EIGHTY-ONE

1692

The Journal of Clayton Stone

·

*T*HE GROUND CRINKLED UNDERFOOT *as I crossed the clearing. I watched bougainvillea thick with thorns twist and turn all around me with the elasticity of a snake. The brush parted as I approached, then weaved together at my back, growing taller with each moment. It wasn't long before the Stranger and the others disappeared from my view and I from theirs.*

I crossed the salt line without incident and stepped to the door; I found it ajar.

With a deep breath, I pushed past the threshold and went inside.

The darkness nearly choked me.

The air was still and silent, yet smelled of the blooms outside.

It took a moment for my eyes to adjust.

I found her alone. Crouched in the corner near the stove, she was draped in a wool blanket.

"You know what they have done to me," she breathed. "The torture, the rape... Yet you stand with them tonight, part of the mob that wishes nothing but death for me."

"I am only here to document the events," I countered.

"We helped these people. We cured their sick, protected them, and now they wish us dead. From fear, from lack of understanding, they wish us dead rather than to comprehend."

"You just killed a man before my eyes!"

"It was not me."

"Then who?"

She glanced around the small room worriedly, then pulled the blanket tight. "You know who it was."

I went to her and knelt at her side.

"That man out there, the one in the black cloak, he told us you are one and the same—that the old woman and you are the same being—nothing more than witchcraft creating this illusion," I said, gesturing to her.

She shook her head in defiance. "I am not Her."

"Then where is she? A man just died simply for approaching this place. I see no one here but you. How am I to believe anyone else responsible?"

Taking my hand, she gently stroked my fingers. "Do you believe I could do such a thing? Does your heart tell you this?"

"I believe what I see."

"Yet you believe I am an old woman, even though you see otherwise," she countered. "You believe I am capable of murder and deceit—that I would just as soon take a life rather than let him through my door."

"You have offered me no other explanation."

She wiped a tear from her eye, then prodded the flames at the stove's hearth. The dry wood crackled as the fire chewed it hungrily. "Then why have I not killed you?"

My stomach tightened at this thought, for I had wondered it myself. I did not know why she entrusted me. Nor did I understand the purpose I served to her. I felt I had to tread carefully.

Was anger her catalyst?

Self preservation?

"Why is that man pursuing you?" I found myself asking. "The man in the black cloak. He says you know him, that he knows you."

She motioned for me to approach, to sit at her side. I did not want to but found myself beside her anyway, the warmth of the stove flushing my face. I sat upon the floor; there were no chairs in the cabin. There was very little in the way of possessions. It occurred to me that this did not appear to be a home; it held no signs of life, no belongings. There was just the stove, the girl, and the blanket in which she was draped. This could not be where she lived, could it? In such beggary?

Outside, rain had begun to fall. With it came an angry thunder. I thought of the men huddled in the trees and bushes watching this place.

How long had I been in here?

I did not know.

I had no sense of time.

Lightning flashed, and for a moment the cabin flooded with light.

It was odd. I thought I saw a table covered in spices, pots, and various cooking utensils. Even the corner of a bed covered in thick linens caught my eye. It was gone then, just a split second later—these things were there with the lightning, gone with the darkness. It wasn't that I could not see them; they simply were no longer there. Where the table had stood, the room was now empty, the floor covered in thick dust.

I felt her hand take mine. It was cold, unnaturally so. I tried to pull away, but she held firm.

When the lightning flashed again, when the light flooded the cabin, I had been looking at her. For that briefest of moments, it was not her; it was an old woman. A hideously scarred old woman with large black eyes, crooked yellow teeth, and thin wisps of gray hair. Her clothing changed, too—gone was the blanket and white dress. She appeared in a long black gown, tattered and threadbare. It smelled of dirt and rot. It smelled of death.

In a blink, I found myself staring at the young girl again, the room lost to pale darkness. She appeared puzzled.

"What is it?"

I gasped and tried to pull away, but she would not release me. I had no words for what I had just seen. I wanted to scream for help, to draw in the others from outside, but my voice failed me. All I heard was my ragged breath and the pounding of my heart.

Clickity, click, click.

I looked down at her free hand. The nails were long; they were tapping at the wood floor.

Clickity, click, click, click.

When thunder struck again followed quickly by another flash of lightning, there was no mistaking what I saw. The old woman leered at me. Then it was the young girl. Her nails dug into my wrist; I felt blood trickle down my fingertips.

"We haven't much time," she breathed.

"For what?"

"For me to tell you my story."

—Thad McAlister,
Rise of the Witch

CHAPTER EIGHTY-TWO
Day 3 – 08:30 a.m.

THAD **WOKE TO THE** smell of mildew and the sound of thunderous rain pounding against his metal coffin. The insidious dark held him like a black tarp wrapped around him. He imagined himself the victim in one of his own books, bound in the trunk of the killer's car, en route to some remote location for a quick (and messy) disposal.

The cobwebs left his mind, and he remembered the conversation with Del. The blackness made way for the dull gray of a stormy night, and he realized where he was.

"That sonofabitch," he muttered under his weak breath. He tried to move his arms, but they ached with arthritis. He couldn't look at his hands, his skin. He wasn't willing to confirm what he hoped had been a nightmare; he had aged. Somehow, he had aged to near death in a matter of minutes.

But how was this possible?

It was in his book, all of it.

Groping the darkness, Thad felt the damp, thin carpet beneath him as well as the metal ceiling inches from his face. He hoped for a tire-iron but found nothing; some other renter had probably removed it. Thad didn't know if they even kept them in rental cars. It didn't matter because he had another way out. All cars built after 1999 have a trunk release button on the inside to ensure children don't accidentally get locked inside. In his haste, Thad doubted Del had disconnected it; he was not convinced Del even wanted to hurt him. He'd had the opportunity to kill him and didn't. Instead, he had picked him up out of the rain and put him in here. Granted, not the best accommodations, but still better than most of the alternatives when alone in the middle of the forest.

His fingers brushed over the button. He retraced their path and pushed at its center. A sharp pain resonated back through his finger from the simple movement as the lock disengaged and the trunk lid popped open.

Rainwater rolled down the trunk and came into the back with the sound of a broken faucet, rushing at him in a wave. Thad sat up as quickly as he could, rising from the damp heat of the trunk to cold, prickling raindrops pouring from the blackened sky. They stung his skin like tiny wasps.

How long had he been unconscious?

He didn't know.

With all his strength, he forced his legs over the edge of the trunk, wincing as pain shot through his spine. His feet found the mud with a thud, sinking into the damp earth, and he forced himself to a stand with the car as his brace. His own weight proved too much and he found himself tumbling to the ground, welcoming the soft earth as he landed in the mud.

Rolling over onto his back, he peered up into the dark clouds, the rain falling all around him, burning at his face and arms. He dug his fingers into the mud, feeling a slight tingle in his palms. He closed his eyes, turned his head toward the sky, and opened his mouth, drinking in the rain. At first, the drops stung. But then, like the mud, they began to tingle as he swallowed, spreading a warmth through his chest and muscles.

The rain is our redemption.

The rain is our life.

He had written the words without truly understanding their meaning. He had written them—*because She wanted me to.*

He began to tingle and surge with energy as the water crept through him, finding every organ and every cell.

As the minutes passed, he found himself able to sit up, finally stand.

"It carries life. The rain of this place…" he breathed.

Like the book, just like in the book. So much you don't understand.

Thad wasn't sure how long he stood there, but he

remained until he felt well enough to drive. He stayed long enough to fill a water bottle with rain. He stayed long enough to remember his wife and daughter and how much he loved them.

CHAPTER EIGHTY-THREE

Day 3 – 10:00 p.m.

FOR THE MOST PART they had driven in silence, Del watching the road and the young girl at his side clutching the box, unwilling to take her eyes from it.

"When She returns, do you think she'll want to go back to that place? Shadow Cove? I mean, they're still there, right? The ones who did this to Her?"

Christina remained silent, her fingers running across the carved box.

"I sure as shit would," Del confessed. "After what they did? They had no right, none whatsoever. Didn't they understand who she was? What she was?"

"That's why they did it, you bumbling idiot," Christina mumbled under her breath.

Del smirked. "It ain't gonna happen again, that's for

damn sure. Not while I'm on the job." Reaching over to her, he rested his hand on her bare knee. "Ain't that right, doll?"

Christina forced a smile before plucking his hand away from her knee and dropping it on the center console.

"Oh, I'm hurt," Del frowned. "You know, as Thad's agent I get ten percent of whatever he gets. I'm ready to settle up as soon as you are."

Christina rolled her eyes. "Watch the road, lover boy."

"You'll learn to love me. All the ladies love ol' Del," he stated.

Christina turned back to the window and calculated the remaining drive time silently in her mind. Not much longer now.

CHAPTER EIGHTY-FOUR

Day 3 – 11:00 p.m.

WHEN RACHAEL WOKE, HER groggy eyes opened upon new surroundings. No longer was she in her bedroom; they had moved her outside. The dark, cloudy sky stared down on her with contempt as cold, damp wind slithered over her skin. Her hands and feet were still bound, but someone had attached them to stakes pounded into the earth. A thick rain fell, hiding the faces of those around her. So many faces, far more than she had seen in the house.

"Ashley?" she cried softly. "Are you there, sweetie?"

Murmurs floated through the crowd, their voices unfamiliar but many, their numbers growing still.

The contraction hit her hard and a groan ripped unabated from her dry lips, silencing those around her. She wanted to clutch her belly, to feel the baby within her, but ropes held her firm. Her back arched, then fell back against the muddy earth with a wet slap as the pain receded.

She smelled something sweet in the air and noticed the bougainvilleas; thousands of them surrounding her. She was in the center of what was once her front lawn. These plants, these people, they had taken it all over; it belonged to them now. The ground around her had been plucked bare. Turning her head, she realized she was at the center of a large pentagram constructed from the thorny branches of the plants.

A hand stroked her hair. "Are you comfortable, Rachael?"

Eleanor. She had changed into a long black robe.

"I have to go to the hospital. Please don't make me have my baby here, I beg of you…"

Eleanor smiled. "Your baby shall be born of the earth, as it's meant to be. The onset of a new world in which She will reign again."

"You're sick!"

She only smiled.

Three of the minions darted past on her left, each dropping an armload of bougainvillea leaves beside her, vibrant shades of pink, red, and purple. They had created small piles all around her—they shimmered in the rain. Other minions worked their way through the crowd, adding to the existing piles. Under her also, a thick bed of blooms.

Eleanor knelt beside her and ran her fingertips across her belly. "Her energy is so strong, more than even I could have imagined. Are you ready to bring her into this world?" Reaching into her robe, she produced a jagged knife set in a carved wooden handle. The sharp blade glistened as she held it up to the light. Those around her fell silent and drew close.

"Behold, the knife of Glanding!" she shouted above the storm.

The wind and rain howled with excitement, stirring up the blooms at their feet.

To their left, a car door slammed. Rachael turned her head and spotted Del, her husband's agent, shuffling toward her, a young girl at his side. She held a small wooden box in her hands. The crowd parted to let them pass.

CHAPTER EIGHTY-FIVE

1692

The Journal of Clayton Stone

*T*HE YOUNG GIRL CONTINUED her tale. *"I was but fourteen when she first came to me. We lived in this very cabin—my mother, sisters, and I. My father had passed some years earlier, when I was just a child. I recall very little about him: his smell, his laugh. He died of consumption, so my mother told us.*

"She was a skilled healer, but she was unable to save him. All her knowledge and remedies, and it was not enough. We buried him in a small, nearby clearing and visited him often.

"On one such visit shortly after the break of spring, my sister and I approached his grave about an hour before dusk. We each carried wildflowers picked in the nearby woods, which we placed at his headstone. We then sat in

the moist grass and prepared a simple meal of bread and pudding we had brought in a wicker basket favored by my sister.

Father liked picnics, *my sister had told me on more than one occasion. She was two years older than I. She had been six when he died.*

This was our way of remembering him.

I was first to hear the cough. It was very soft, but I had always had exceptional hearing. It had come from the woods just to our west. As now, visitors were rare at such a distance from town and I first attributed the sound to that of an animal. When I heard it again, though, there was no mistaking it.

I rose slowly and approached the trees, my sister calling my name from behind.

He was lying on the ground, his back propped up against an old oak. A bundle of sorts was at his side. I imagined it contained clothing, personal items.

He was very old, perhaps the oldest man on which I had ever laid eyes. His skin was pale as paper and creased with lines. His bleak, gray eyes stared up at me with both fear and hope.

He uttered a whisper from cracked lips, but I could not make out the words.

He gestured for me to draw closer, but I hesitated.

Night was falling and dark shadows grew from the damp ground, weaving through the trees.

Pain filled his face and he whispered again, softer still than the first.

I knelt at his side.

It was foolish, I know, but I didn't see what harm he could bring. He appeared so weak, unable to stand, barely able to speak.

He grabbed me with the speed of a serpent attacking prey.

"Bagahi laca bachahe. Lamc cahi achabahe," *he breathed.*

I hadn't seen the bougainvillea clutched firmly in his other hand. Even if I had, I wouldn't have know its significance, not then.

Clickity, click.

I heard it as I tried to pull away. His grip tightened as he repeated the strange words.

"Bagahi laca bachahe. Lamc cahi achabahe."

I saw Her then, for the first time.

It happened quickly, faster than I could have possibly imagined—had I been able to imagine such a thing.

His life, this stranger's life, I saw it all. I witnessed every moment. His name was Ezekiel Crowley. He wanted to protect me, he wanted to keep Her from me. Yet, he could not.

I saw Her in his eyes, if only for a brief moment. Then it grew cold, so cold.

"Zeke, no."

Ice filled my veins from his hand, through my arm, my chest. It filled my head and all went white.

I woke to the sound of my sister's voice.

The man was dead, his fingers still wrapped around my wrist.

And I could feel Her.
I could feel Her inside of me.
This woman, this witch, had crept into my soul.

—Thad McAlister,
Rise of the Witch

CHAPTER EIGHTY-SIX
Day 3 – 11:15 p.m.

THE BOX SEEMED TO grow warm in her hands as she entered the yard, as her feet crushed the bougainvillea blossoms which covered the ground. "Wait here," she instructed Del as she stepped into the crowd.

Hands reached out from all around her, fingertips stroking the wooden case as she passed. Christina recognized most of the faces. Some dated back as far as her childhood. Others had come into her life more recently. She could see the woman at the center of the crowd, her aunt, hovering over her. The wife of Thad McAlister, Rachael, if she remembered correctly. She had liked Thad and was sorry he had to die, but there had been little choice. The witch had picked Thad long ago when she had placed her story in his mind. Only he knew the complete truth—where to go, what to do; his journey could only end in death.

Christina approached her aunt and placed the box in her outstretched hands. Her aunt smiled and nodded her approval. Christina then stepped back and remained still as those around her removed her clothing and helped her into a robe.

"It has been a long time coming, my dear niece," Eleanor said, her hand caressing the warm wood of the box.

Christina nodded. "That it has." She paused, closing her eyes. "She is with us now; I can feel her...so close."

"She's growing stronger as the hour draws near," Eleanor agreed. "Her energy flows freely among us." Looking to Del, she added, "You brought another?"

"He has served her well. I believe she has much more planned for him."

Eleanor nodded. "I sense that, too."

Lightning crackled through the sky, and Rachael McAlister let out a pain-filled groan.

Eleanor stroked her hair. "It is time."

Urgent conversation floated through the crowd as they found their positions, creating three circles with Rachael McAlister at the center. They reached out to each other, their fingers interlocking as they joined hands. Around them, the minions continued to gather bougainvillea leaves and stack them at their feet as the sky churned with eager anticipation. Rachael McAlister cried out once again.

CHAPTER EIGHTY-SEVEN

Day 3 – 11:30 p.m.

ASHLEY TRIED TO PULL her hand from that of the woman leading her through the crowd, but she would not allow it. Instead she dug her nails deeply into Ashley's soft skin, squeezing painfully. She gave her a look that said she would hurt her again if she didn't stop squirming.

Ashley forced back the tears welling up in her eyes. She was a big girl and refused to let them see her cry. Most of the faces were hidden beneath the shadow of their hoods, but the few she could make out were strangers. They passed out black candles.

The minions followed at her heels. She kicked at one but the little monster proved too fast for her, hiding behind the leg of the woman at her side. It looked up at her with a wicked little smirk on its face, its sharp teeth gleaming in the moonlight. Ashley wanted them to go away—all these people, too. She wanted her daddy to come home, and for her mommy and Buster to be okay. Why couldn't everything go back to the way it was just a few short days ago?

When her eyes fell on her mother at the center of the people, she tried to go to her but the woman pulled her back. "Put this on," she told her, holding out a black robe.

Ashley shook her head. "I don't want to."

The woman knelt down beside her and ran her fingers through Ashley's fine hair. "I'm not asking you, sweetie," she told her. "I don't want to hurt you, but I will."

Where did Zeke go? Why wasn't he protecting them?

The woman beside her beamed. "My dear child, your friend Ezekiel has moved on to a better place."

"Ashley…," her mother mumbled. Her voice weak, trembling.

When Ashley tried to reach out to her, the woman pulled her back. "Put on the robe, now," she ordered.

Ashley did as she was told and slipped the robe over her clothes. The woman at her side pulled the hood over her head. Her face shielded, she let the tears flow.

Candles burned around her, and the crowd began to chant.

CHAPTER EIGHTY-EIGHT
Day 3 – 11:35 p.m.

"***B**AGAHI LACA BACHAHE. LAMC cahi achabahe,*" the words flowed from Eleanor's tongue with ageless confidence as those around fell silent and still, only their breath on the chilled night showing any life at all.

The clouds above opened again, sending the storm's wrath down upon them. Deep thunder joined the wind's chorus as a single bolt of lightning cracked the sky. The rain pricked at their skin, as if attempting to burrow under their skin.

"*Bagahi laca bachahe. Lamc cahi achabahe,*" she repeated. At her feet, Rachael cried out in pain as another contraction ravaged her.

The baby will be here soon, Eleanor thought. After centuries of failed attempts, the baby would be here soon. She couldn't help but smile.

She placed the box at Rachael's feet atop a blanket of bougainvillea leaves. They had turned crimson in the rain, saturated with this life-giving blood. Christina approached and knelt before them. Reaching out, her hands drifted over the carved wooden surface, her fingers slipping over each groove, tracing the mazelike pattern until she reached the center at the top. Looking to Eleanor, she nodded, then pulled a small vial of incandescent blue liquid from the pocket of her robe. Removing the cap, she poured the contents into the center of the carving at the top of the box. She watched as the liquid raced through the labyrinth, filling every inch of the box, setting the wood carving ablaze in blue. It began to sizzle and smoke as the acidic liquid began to eat through the wood and lead, breaking the centuries-old seal.

CHAPTER EIGHTY-NINE

1692

The Journal of Clayton Stone

I **WATCHED IN SILENCE** *as the young girl continued.* "My sister carried me back to our house, to here. I do not recall the journey. Forced to carry me, she left our blanket and basket near my father's grave. Our mother spotted our approach and ran out to help.

"I had become feverish, burning to the touch. I was placed in bed and stripped of my clothing as mother prepared a remedy. My sister recounted what little she had witnessed; I heard her words but understood little, as if her language were foreign to me.

"Visions of other lives led filled my slumber—not one or two but dozens, hundreds. I witnessed birth and death, all through the eyes of others, the voices of others. None of the tongues were my own, yet I could comprehend them all. I knew not what my own sister uttered, yet these unknown languages made perfect sense.

More so, they were memories. I felt I had lived these lives, felt this pain; I had been to these places and times filling my thoughts.

"Nearly a fortnight passed before I regained my senses, before I awoke."

"The witch possessed you."

She eyed me warily. "I do not know that she is a witch. To this day, I do not know."

"She is an agent of the devil, that is certain."

"She is older than you or I could possibly imagine. The devil is but a child in her world."

I felt a knot tighten in my stomach. "She must be cast out, or you are damned."

She looked at me with both sadness and indignation. When lightning filled the room, it was the old woman in her eyes. I tried to pull away but her grasp was strong, her nails buried deeper into my arms.

A smile played across her rosy lips. "She is to leave me tonight, this has been foretold. More so out of necessity than desire, I'm afraid. I do not wish to see her go, but the arrival of that man outside has forced her hand. She had so much yet to teach me. Our time was so brief."

I tried to pull free but she was too strong, aided by the witch. Her other hand shot out and gripped mine, a stone-like grip of which I was prisoner. The scent of bougainvillea filled the air.

"I envy you, and the time you will spend with Her. I hope you will love Her, as I have."

Clickity, click, click.

—Thad McAlister,
Rise of the Witch

CHAPTER NINETY

Day 3 – 11:40 p.m.

THAD PARKED ABOUT TWO blocks from his house, then shut off the lights and engine. Thick rain fell from the dark clouds above, but he knew it wasn't the same as the rain in Shadow Cove; nothing could possibly be the same.

Thad raised the water bottle to his lips and savored the last few drops as they found his throat, breathing life throughout his tired body. The water surged deep, converging on his cells, somehow restoring the youth taken from him only hours earlier deep within that strange forest.

And cursed earth, his consciousness reminded him.

He would take his family back.

And he would put an end to theirs.

Thad climbed out of the car and gently closed the door. He then shielded his eyes from the storm as he peered toward his house. Even in the darkness he could make out the tangled mass of bougainvillea bushes covering his yard. How they grew so fast, he didn't know. He heard the voices a moment later, dozens, growing louder as he neared. Thad didn't care. He only wanted to find his wife and daughter, to know they were okay.

Del stood at a black sedan parked at the edge of the property. He stared ahead, his expression blank. No longer the man Thad had known for so many years, Del was just a shell. He belonged to Her now.

Thad knew Del had summoned her the moment they had spoken in the forest back in Shadow Cove. He recalled writing the words to the spell at a fevered pitch, much like the rest of the book.

It had all been Her.

He knew that now.

She controlled Del, maybe even Christina and all these others.

All of these people were somehow bringing her back to the world. Freeing her from the bonds that had held her for half a millennium.

Unleashing this evil, evil thing.

Rachael and Ashley.

The rainwater of Shadow Cove returned his strength. In many ways he felt stronger than he had in years.

He had no weapon.

No plan.

But somehow he would get his family back.

Thad started toward his house, oblivious to the storm churning around him.

"Christina!" he shouted.

CHAPTER NINETY-ONE
Day 3 – 11:41 p.m.

DEL HEARD THE VOICE through the rising storm and peered through the rain. He spotted Thad just as he pushed through the bougainvillea at the edge of the property, disappearing into the tangled mess of branches.

How is he still alive?

The man had looked like a dried-out corpse only a few hours ago. Christina assured him he would not survive.

Wasn't that the reason she had sent him to the tree in the first place?

She told him how the forest had been cursed centuries earlier, how the evil place stole life from anything crossing its threshold. The spell was strongest at the tree— its purpose wasn't only to keep people away, but also to keep Her prisoner.

Thad not only journeyed to the tree, withstanding the powers of this curse long enough to hand them the box—it appeared he somehow summoned the energy to pull himself behind the wheel of his car and drive all the way back home.

Home.

Could that be it?

Could the love of one's home, his family, be strong enough to give a person such drive?

No, Del thought. That was bullshit.

It was something else.

Kill him.

Christina's voice pushed through his thoughts, engulfed him. He felt the warmth of her press against his cheek.

Kill him and I will reward you so.

Without hesitation, Del started toward the house, toward the maze of wild bushes. His fists clenched at his sides.

He would enjoy killing Thad again.

This time, he would make it hurt.

CHAPTER NINETY-TWO
Day 3 – 11:42 p.m.

THAD PUSHED HIS WAY into the bougainvillea, feeling the tiny thorns rip at his arms and clothing as he went. The branches at his back reached for him, tendrils scraping at the air, like the fingers of famished prisoners stretching beyond their bars for a taste of meat, while the ones between him and his family weaved tighter together, entwined, twisted into a solid wall of living pain covered in little daggers craving his blood.

The mud at his feet fought him, too. The earth pulled at him with each step, holding him long enough for the branches to twist around his ankles into shackles of sorts. He'd rip himself free, only to be tangled again in an unforgiving embrace.

Thad groaned and pushed forward.

He didn't have much time.

They planned to summon Her.

Thad knew how this story ended because he had written it.

The bougainvillea, the rain…all so familiar to him.

He glanced up at the sky and searched for the moon beyond the thick, gray clouds.

The summer solstice would come to an end tonight. In the world of witches, this was the most powerful night of the year, the only night on which something like this could take place. Her soul, Her essence, was in the Rumina Box where it had remained for hundreds of years. They planned to summon Her, release that essence, bring Her back.

They needed a vessel, a host.

In life, She had been strong enough to take on any host with a simple touch; no longer, though. Being locked away for four hundred years had weakened Her; She would need a willing host. One who would accept Her without a fight, preferably an innocent.

They were after the baby. Nothing else made sense.

Even Ashley, at her young age, possessed the will to resist.

Judging by the height of the moon, they had already started. As he had written it, Her family would be gathered around his wife in a clearing up ahead. They would be preparing to open the box. The eldest among them would have started the spell, the others joining in.

If Thad closed his eyes, he could see their actions unfolding—the writer within him weaved the scene together like words filling a blank page.

His wife on the ground, surrounded by strangers. His daughter, watching helplessly from her side. A baby, only moments away.

Thad's eyes went wide as the idea rushed into his mind. It came to him much like all the others for his books; escaping from a deep, dark place in the back of his subconscious to the forefront long enough for him to grasp it and hold tight before the sliver of thought drifted away, a dream just after awakening.

She needed a host. A willing host.

Thad planned to give her one.

He had written this story. He could rewrite it.

Pushing his way deeper into the bushes, he began to mumble under his breath. He began to mumble the spell he had written not so long ago. *"Bagahi laca bachahe, lamc cahl achabahe."*

Above him, the sky cracked open again and the storm clouds unleashed their fury with a thunderous howl.

CHAPTER NINETY-THREE

1692

The Journal of Clayton Stone

I **EMERGED FROM THE** cabin to the waiting eyes of the Stranger and Tauber. Both poised at the edge of the clearing.

"Now!" I heard someone shout.

I felt the heat at my back, but I did not turn. They had set the cabin ablaze, as I knew they would. Attacking it from all sides with flaming torches, setting fire to the piles of kindling they had amassed while I lingered inside. This had been planned before we left town, the girl's fate determined long before I went to her. I had been a distraction, nothing more.

Tauber awaited her screams; I could see it in his eyes. He had burned witches before; they always screamed as the flames licked at their unholy bodies.

She did not, though. For I knew she was already dead.

The Stranger eyed me wearily, the wooden box held tight in his wrinkled hands. "You did well, son."

I ached, as if each muscle had been pulled taut and released, only to be stressed again.

I forced a nod.

I could feel Her inside me. The witch's breath, one with my own. There was an immense power flowing through my limbs, gripping my soul. I could see with Her eyes and She with mine. "She is winning this battle within me," I said.

The Stranger nodded and gingerly stroked the wooden box.

"By the Lord's breath," I heard one of the men exclaim. "His feet, they are no longer on the ground!"

I looked down and realized this to be true. I was floating above the earth by at least a hand, perhaps more. She was growing within me. I willed it to stop with all the energy I could muster and settled back to the ground. "Hurry," I forced out. "We haven't much time."

The Stranger's face was long, somber.

Tauber approached, a crucifix clutched in his fingers. "The moon is nearly full."

"Shackle him," the Stranger commanded.

The urge to flee nearly overwhelmed me, and I felt my feet once again lift from the earth. The hands of the other men grabbed at me in an attempt to hold me still.

"Shackle him now, or this beast will be unleashed upon the world again and we will all meet certain death!"

The jailer and a man I did not recognize approached with caution, iron bonds at the ready. It was then that I noticed the stake in the ground at the clearing's edge, the fire at our backs bathing it in light.

I felt an energy surge through my fingertips and I reached for one of the men at my side.

Clickity, click, click.

My touch sent him through the air. He crashed into a large oak with a deadening thud and puddled at its base, the life gone from him.

"His hands!" the jailer cried.

They gripped my arms and pulled them behind my back; I felt iron close around my wrists as they locked the restraints. Then they were at my feet and I was robbed of motion.

"Get him to the stake!" I heard the Stranger cry.

Thunder had begun to stir the night sky. Churning angrily, the threat of rain moments away.

Dragging me across the clearing, we reached the stake a moment later and they fastened my bonds to it with chains. I felt the witch gain strength, Her will pushing mine to a black void. I fought back, but she was so strong.

"Death cannot take me. You know this, Samuel." *The voice that came from my lips was not my own.*

The Stranger walked slowly around the stake as the others piled wood at my feet. When he stopped, he set the small wooden box on the ground and opened it, extracting a knife. Gilded edges glistening in the firelight, its handle black, carved with symbols. I felt the witch inside me shrink back, and a breath escaped me.

"I'm so sorry, my son."

"Hurry," was all I could say, for She returned with force a moment later and pulled at my bonds.

He raised the knife and slipped it across my neck. It sliced effortlessly and I felt little pain, only a warmth as blood flowed down my chest.

"Evocatio Valcyriarum Contubernalia Gladiaria!"

The Stranger raised the box to my chin. It was full of bougainvillea leaves, their scent sweet. I watched my blood trickle over them.

"Evocatio Spiritualis de Septendecim Valcyriis Mortiferis!"

I could feel the witch struggling within me, Her desire to escape clawing at my insides. She pulled at the restraints, wanting nothing more than to touch one of the nearby men, to flee my body for another. But they all stood just out of reach, as the Stranger had told them to do.

"Hexagramma et Pentagramma, Malos Spiritus Sigillent! Lagena Signatoria!"

The fight began to wane as a sleep drifted over me.

As my blood, Her blood, filled the box, the leaves grew black and crumbled, turning to dust.

I watched the Stranger close the cover moments before the world went black, and peace found me and wrapped me tightly in its arms.

"It is over," he told them. His voice was at the end of a long tunnel, then gone as all else.

—Thad McAlister,
Rise of the Witch

CHAPTER NINETY-FOUR

Day 3 – 11:43 p.m.

CHRISTINA'S EYES WERE WIDE as the liquid enveloped the box, each crease and crevasse coming alive in a brilliant blue glow. She could feel Her inside, Her spirit, Her essence, clawing to get out, to be free again.

Christina ran her hand across the top and spoke with a soft confidence, *"Bagahi laca bachahe, lamc cahl achabahe."*

CHAPTER NINETY-FIVE

Day 3 – 11:44 p.m.

DEL PUSHED THROUGH THE bushes with a fury.

Thorns lashed out, sending blood dripping down his arms and face. He was oblivious to the pain. Thad wasn't supposed to be here. He should have died back at the forest. She was done with him now. It was Del's turn to serve Her.

"Where the fuck are you, Thad?" he shouted. "Nobody invited you to this party, you resilient shit."

He knew he was close, he could feel him. The rain and this impromptu forest made it impossible to see more than a few feet in any direction. Where?

The tangled mass at his left opened then, the branches spreading wide, creating a path. She was guiding him. "Oh, here I come, buddy," he said above the storm. "Ready or not."

CHAPTER NINETY-SIX

1692

The Journal of Clayton Stone (Author Unknown)

*T*AUBER WATCHED WITH WONDER as the Stranger closed the lid on the small wooden box.

"An angel's kiss shall seal it tight,

"The Rumina Box a vessel born of this night.

"No seams to remain,

"No lid to raise,

"Closed for eternity

"Held tight by our faith."

The box glowed in the moon's half-light, a thin wisp edging across its lip. One moment there was a lid and clasp, the next it was gone, the box becoming a solid block of wood. Intricate carvings glowing all around. A spell of sorts; it was witchcraft, of that there was no denying.

"She's in there, isn't She? Her essence, you've somehow

trapped it?"

The Stranger looked at him for a moment but did not respond. His old skin was covered in sweat. Whatever was happening, it was draining him.

Tauber watched as he carried the box to a large oak at the edge of the clearing. There was a hollow at its base, one large enough to hold a man. With the box at his side, the Stranger dug with his bare hands. He dug with a ferocity found in younger men, dug until the hole was so deep it was nearly an arm's length from top to bottom. He then placed the box inside and filled the hole with dirt.

When he was done, he pulled out the knife he had used to kill the boy and slit the palm of his hand, watching as the blood dripped to the fresh earth.

"By scattered leaves,

"By blood of saints,

"Taint this ground,

"Earth, air, and place.

"Of life it's not,

"No life shall leave,

"Trapped for all time,

"In the bowels of this tree."

With these words, flowers at the base of the tree began to wilt and die. Before his eyes, Tauber watched a death spread from the base of the tree outward toward the forest. It engulfed the Stranger and he grew older in an instant, then older still. "From this moment, this place is cursed," he cautioned. "No man shall disturb it, no life shall exist upon it. To do so will bring certain death quickly, without fail."

The grass at their feet turned brown, then black. Tauber felt a pain course through his lungs. His legs grew weak. He began to back away.

"Run," he breathed, his eyes wide with fear. "Run from this place!"

The remainder of his men disappeared in the forest in the direction of town.

"You will keep them away," the Stranger said upon a gasp filled with death. "You will keep all away from this place from now until forever more."

Tauber ran after the others as the forest died around them. At his back, the Stranger collapsed upon the earth. He became dust, and he became one with this place as the wind scattered him among the trees.

The sky opened and rain tore through the night.

—Thad McAlister,
Rise of the Witch

CHAPTER NINETY-SEVEN
Day 3 – 11:55 p.m.

THAD SAW THEM NOW, just ahead. Rachael, at the center of the group on the ground, wasn't moving. Ashley knelt at her side, her face red with tears.

He spotted the box at their side.

He felt the witch, Her energy surrounding them, an evil so thick upon the air it grew palpable.

The blow from behind knocked him to the ground, sending the air from his lungs.

"We've got unfinished business, you and I," Del breathed at his ear.

CHAPTER NINETY-EIGHT

Day 3 – 11:56 p.m.

"**B**RING HIM HERE!" CHRISTINA'S voice echoed through the night, her gaze bearing down upon them. The others had turned, too; all now faced them. "Now!" she commanded.

Del swore under his breath and hauled Thad to his feet, pushing him through the remaining bushes until they reached the clearing.

"Daddy!" Ashley shouted.

A woman at her side reached down and held his daughter still.

"It's okay, baby. I'm here. I won't let them hurt you."

Del snickered. "Yeah, you're in control of this show. You're clearly pulling the strings."

Christina walked up to him and ran her hand down

391

Thad's chest. "You drank the water, didn't you? The rain in Shadow Cove?" She couldn't help but smile. "That is how you survived? The power becomes you, Thad. It really does. Your eyes are the bluest of sapphires."

Thad pushed past her to his wife.

Rachael's hand shot out and grasped his as another contraction came. Eleanor turned back to her and positioned her hands between her legs. She could see the baby's head now; only a few more moments.

"Push, my child," she told her. "Deliver her into this world so that She may breathe again."

Around her, the others drew near. Hand in hand, they watched in silent anticipation.

CHAPTER NINETY-NINE
Day 3 – 11:57 p.m.

THE BABY CAME WITH a shrill cry. With a final push, Eleanor took hold of the child's shoulders and pulled her free of her mother.

A little girl.

Rachael fell still. Although breathing, the last of her energy was gone; childbirth had drained her battered frame.

Christina spread a blanket at Eleanor's side and she placed the baby upon it, inches from the box.

Hands reached out and held Thad still.

CHAPTER ONE HUNDRED
Day 3 – 11:58 p.m.

THE KNIFE IN HAND, Eleanor cut the baby's arm and smeared a thin line of the blood on the child's forehead. "This child is yours, this life, this body."

With an almost inaudible click, the box popped open and a gray mist danced from beneath the lid. It rose high into the air, circling them, engulfing them.

She was here.

Thad gasped. He felt Her, this creature from his book. This witch of generations old. Her spirit rushed out upon them and filled the clearing with an energy unlike any he had ever experienced. The others felt it, too—enveloping them, her brothers and sisters, her children. She took form and rose high into the night, looking down upon them with ravenous anticipation.

She looked down upon his baby, his child.

Her sharp, yellow teeth glistened in the rain, her long fingernails rapping against each other.

Clickity, click, click.

CHAPTER ONE HUNDRED ONE

Day 3 – 11:58 p.m.

THE THORNY BUSHES HAD opened his arms in a number of places. Thad wiped at one of the wounds and smeared the blood on his forehead. "I am yours, this life, this body," he blurted out. "Why wait for the body of a child, when you can have that of a grown man?"

"No!" Eleanor cried, lunging at him with the knife in hand.

"Bagahi laca bachahe, lamc cahl achabahe," Thad chanted. "Come to me. Tamsalin, I am yours," he breathed. Her true name came from his lips for the first and last time.

The rain stopped.

The night fell silent.

For the briefest of moments, the gray swirl paused,

then raced for him, swallowing Thad in a cloud of darkness. The mist found his eyes and pushed inside, filling him with a chill that scraped at his bones and soul.

When Thad's eyes opened, She looked out upon the world for the first time in almost half a millennium. She looked out over those who had brought Her back, those who had rescued Her from Her fate. She looked out for the briefest of moments before Eleanor plunged the knife into Thad's chest with such force that the blade cracked his breastplate and tore through his heart.

CHAPTER ONE HUNDRED TWO

Day 3 – 11:59 p.m.

ASHLEY PULLED FREE AND ran to her dad, reaching him as he crumbled to the ground. Eleanor fell with him, twisting the knife as they went. At their backs, Christina screamed in protest. She reached for Eleanor and threw the old woman to the side.

Her hands fell upon the knife, but she knew there was nothing she could do; he was dead.

"He couldn't have Her," Eleanor cried. "He didn't deserve Her, he didn't earn the right."

Christina glanced around, eyes aflame with anger, at the men who had been holding Thad, then at Del and Ashley, glaring at Eleanor. "Where is She? Did She die with him or escape? Where is She?"

Eleanor realized the horror of what she had done,

and her face filled with agony.

"All of you were touching him at his death. Did she transfer to one of you?" Christina shouted in frustration.

Above, the moon appeared through the haze. The storm clouds broke and the night began to clear.

In the distance, a siren wailed.

Christina's glare shot to Del. He had his cell phone out; he had dialed the police. Her spell upon him had been broken.

Around them, the bougainvilleas began to wither and die. The minions that had been running around their feet were now nothing more than small piles of dirt.

It was gone, all of it.

She was gone.

Pushing past the others, Christina shed her robe and disappeared into the night.

DAY 4

CHAPTER ONE HUNDRED THREE

Day 4 – 7:00 a.m.

"MRS. MCALISTER? CAN YOU hear me?"

Rachael woke to a bright light. Her eyes fluttered open and she pinched them shut.

She was so cold.

"She's coming around," a voice said. "Mrs. McAlister?"

She groaned and hesitantly opened her eyes again, allowing them to adjust.

"You're at Morningside Memorial. Try to remain still; you've lost a lot of blood."

Rachael nodded, awakening a throbbing pain behind her eyes.

A small man came into focus. Balding with dark-rimmed glasses, he stared at her with concern, a penlight in his hand.

He offered a weak smile. "I'm Doctor Spalding. You gave us quite a scare last night, but you're out of the woods now."

"Doctor, if she can speak, I need to talk to her."

Rachael turned her head to find an older man in a rumpled suit rising from the chair beside the window. She pointed to a glass of water and the doctor handed it to her, helping Rachael get the straw in her mouth.

"Mrs. McAlister, this is Detective Jack Doulis. He's been waiting since they brought you in last night. If you don't feel up to speaking to him, tell me and I'll have no problem making him wait longer."

Rachael shook her head. "Where's my daughter?"

"She's in maternity. She is a little underweight due to the early birth but otherwise in good health. She should be able to go home in a few days," the doctor explained. "We paged Dr. Roskin; he's on his way."

"No, Ashley—where is Ashley?"

Spalding glanced at the detective. "I'll give you a few minutes." He left the room.

The detective cleared his throat. "We haven't been able to locate her, ma'am. The patrolmen recall seeing her when they arrived on scene last night, but she disappeared during the commotion. We issued an Amber Alert statewide and set up roadblocks at all the major roadways. There were a number of people at your home when the first car got there. They scattered. We were able to pick up a few, but most ran. At this point, we're not sure if she went willingly with one of them, was abducted, or simply wandered off. I was hoping you could shed some light on what happened. What were they all doing on your lawn?"

The images of last night began to flood back into her mind. Rachael gasped. "Thad?"

"I'm sorry."

Tears began to well up in her eyes.

"Who would want to hurt him? Were these people fans? Some kind of cult following? It looked like we stumbled onto some type of ritual." He ran his hand through his thinning hair. "The ones we picked up aren't talking. I mean, at all. They haven't said a single word. I'm not going to be able to hold them much longer unless someone gives me something."

He paused, then sat on the edge of the bed. "Your husband's agent was there too, Mrs. McAlister. Can you tell me why your husband's agent would be standing on your front lawn with a group of people in the middle of the night? He suffered a heart attack shortly after we arrived; he didn't make it to the hospital. Did he stab your husband? Did they get into an argument or physical altercation?"

Rachael just stared at him, her mind swimming in thoughts.

"Your dog was locked in the garage. As soon as we opened the door, he darted for your neighbor's house—the Nelsons. Aubrey and Jim. Nice people. They said they'd keep an eye on him until you returned home." He glanced down at a small notepad in his hand. "Aubrey said they've been gone for a few days visiting their niece in Ohio. Left on Monday and returned late yesterday. She said your landscaping changed completely in that short amount of time, not for the better. Seemed perplexed. You must have had hundreds of bushes planted and they all died. Any idea why? She was worried it would spill over into her yard."

A nurse stepped into the room. One glance from the detective turned her around.

"Rachael, you need to help me find your daughter," he told her.

E<u>PILOGU</u>E

CARMEN PEREZ WIPED AT her tired eyes and opened another energy drink. She chugged the beverage and tossed the can out the car window, watching as it bounced off the median into the grassy shoulder off Interstate 605.

They had been driving for nearly sixteen hours in silence. She had anticipated roadblocks, but they didn't encounter a single one.

The child rode silently beside her. Her eyes transfixed on the desolate stretch of highway, her tiny fingers knotted around the seat belt. "In a day or so, you will be among friends," Perez told her in Spanish. "There will be shelter, food, clothing. A place where you can grow unabated by the trappings of this world. A place where you will be safe until the day you wish to venture out. I won't notify the others, not unless you wish me to do so. I am yours to command; I am your humble servant, as are those at our destination. You will see. It is a good place."

The child understood the strange tongue, as she understood all languages.

She did not look at the woman driving the vehicle. Her gaze remained fixed on the surroundings, mesmerized by this carriage and the miles it effortlessly chewed up in their wake.

It was a lot to take in, Perez knew. So many years had passed, so much time spent in darkness.

She would guide Her. She would help her adjust to this new, fast-paced world.

Perez reached for the radio dial and scanned the channels; there was nothing but religious broadcasts and country music.

The child was staring at her, her eyes wide.

Perez understood. "We have the ability to broadcast messages over great distances—not only audio, video too. When the time is right, your messages will be heard by millions all over the world."

She switched off the radio. Perhaps the selection would improve as they approached Mexico.

The child stared as a minute passed, then nodded in understanding. The movement was mechanical, jerky. In time, she would grow accustomed to this body.

"The township of Shadow Cove, it still exists?" Ashley asked in Spanish.

The child's voice startled her. It was that of Ashley McAlister, yet wasn't. When she glanced over, the child was still looking out the window.

"It does," she replied.

"I wish to visit the township of Shadow Cove," the child told her.

Perez frowned. "It's not safe right now; they will be looking for you. We need to leave the United States for a while. Someday, you will be able to return—not now, though. It would be too risky."

The child's gaze did not falter. Her light blonde hair fluttered gently across her forehead and over her eyes. She made no attempt to move it. She remained rigid, unnervingly so.

"You wish to find those who trapped you? The deceptive ones?" Perez asked.

"He is still alive?" the child questioned.

Perez nodded. "He is not, but the others who were with him that night, they live."

"Then you will take me there," Ashley stated.

"When the time is right, I will."

The child's grip released from her seat belt and she stared at her tiny fingers; her thumb and forefinger rubbed against each other in a circular pattern, her nails snapping softly.

Clickity, click, click.

E<u>PILOGUE CONTINUE</u>D
Ten Years Earlier

A TINY BELL RANG as Rachael Adams pushed through the heavy wooden door into the store. She looked up and saw it hanging from the frame, still swinging.

Boxes littered the floor, many unpacked and empty. A few remained sealed, crumpled newspaper scattered about. Some shelves were barren, while others were overflowed with various items and knickknacks.

"Hello?" she called. "Are you open?"

Stepping inside, the door closed with a squeak at her back, sealing out the cool crisp air which seemed synonymous with coastal Maine in the fall. The room smelled of lemons and vanquished dust. Display cases and curios polished to a mirror finish surrounded her, and books lined the walls from floor to ceiling.

"Is there anyone here?" she said. This time, a little louder than the first.

Rachael was in town with her fiancé, Thad McAlister. They had spent the last four months touring the country promoting his first novel, *A Caller's Game*—moving from town to town, bookstore to bookstore. A blur of a trip they had both hoped would be an adventure, it had turned into hours trapped in his ancient Honda Accord surrounded by fast food wrappers and the constant need to find a new radio station as the previous one faded to static above the whir of tires churning away the miles.

She loved him, she was sure of that. She knew the moment they had met. She also believed he would succeed as a writer; he was very good. She had read his pages nearly every night for the past two years as he struggled to find the time to write between two part-time jobs. He had little trouble finding a publisher; they had even provided a small advance. It had seemed like a fairy tale at the time. She would often catch herself planning their life together—he the famous author, she the supporting wife raising their children in a picturesque house in a beautiful neighborhood.

It would all fall into place once the book was published.

Only things hadn't.

It had been out for six months now and sales were dismal. The critics tore the book to shreds. He sold a handful of copies on stops like this, but in many towns nobody turned up at all.

She couldn't bear to think of him sitting alone at a small table in the back of the bookstore again, surrounded by his novel, waiting for someone, anyone, to approach and request an autograph. She recalled one store in Illinois about a month into the trip, by far the worst. When they arrived, the clerk at the counter hadn't known he was coming; he didn't even recognize his name. After a phone call to management, he had gone to the back storeroom and pulled out the box of Thad's novel, sent in advance by the publisher—the box hadn't even been opened. Not a single copy had been set out. Thad had played it off with a smile, then spent the next two hours sitting at the table (it always seemed to be the same table), waiting.

It would get better, he promised her. His next book would be a blockbuster. He wasn't about to be discouraged. He wouldn't give up.

Each time his cell phone rang, though, she feared it was his publisher calling off the remainder of the tour, capping the advance, ending his dream.

Castle Rock, Maine, was their last stop in the United States. They were off to Montreal next—she shivered. She grew cold just thinking about the place. She missed their tiny apartment and the lumpy mattress on the floor of their single bedroom. The space wasn't much, but at least they could call it home.

"Ah, you must be Ms. Adams, the illustrious fiancée of the young author manning the author's corner table at Mr. Reese's bookstore on this wonderfully grand day!" a man's voice boomed from her left.

Rachael turned, nearly knocking a stack of picture frames off a nearby table.

He reached out to steady her. "I'm so sorry, Miss. I had no intention of startling you. Most hear my old, creaking bones coming from a mile away!"

His smile was pleasant, welcoming. His gray hair and mustache were groomed to perfection, his black suit tailored to a snug fit. Her eyes drifted to the pocket watch hanging from a belt loop by a gold chain. The metalwork was ornately carved, intricate, beautiful. He followed her eyes and reached for the watch. With a push of a small button on the side, the top flipped open, revealing the tiny hands slipping across the dial. The working gears were exposed beneath the glass—dozens of them. She found it mesmerizing.

"It was given to me by a man named Richard Habring many, many years ago on a trip to Austria. He made each component by hand; he is a master at his craft. I helped his wife with a small favor, and he gave this to me in return. A lovely couple; I miss them dearly. I do need to get back to the old country more often."

He snapped it shut, startling Rachael from her trance. "I...I wasn't sure if you were open," she stammered. "Well, the sign outside said you were, but I called out when I entered and there didn't seem to be anyone here. It looks like you're still getting settled in. I can come back."

He was already shaking his head. "Nonsense. You're only in town for a short time, and I'm honored you would consider spending some of it here." He reached out and kissed the back of her hand. "Allow me to introduce myself. My name is Leland Gaunt. I'm the proprietor of this soon-to-be fine establishment. I'm afraid you did catch me mid-unpacking, but don't let such a thing bother you. I'm sure I possess exactly what you need amongst this clutter."

Rachael thought about the twelve dollars she had in her wallet, the credit card which had exceeded its limit more than a week ago. "I don't need anything. I'm just looking around, trying to pass the time."

Gaunt leaned in a little closer. "Ms. Adams, we all need a little something. I've found it doesn't matter what you already own, or how much. There is always that elusive something out there we still want. Sometimes we don't know we want it until we see it, but nonetheless, it's out there, waiting to be found."

Rachael glanced around the store at the curious mix of objects. A shovel hung on the wall next to an electric guitar. The glass case to her side contained an assortment of matchbox cars, baseball cards, dolls—even a Rubik's cube; she hadn't seen one of those since she was a little girl. Walking to one of the bookshelves, she glanced at the titles: *A Christmas Carol, Dracula, The Original Adventures of Sherlock Holmes.*

"Each is a first draft, signed by the author," Gaunt told her.

She had picked up Sherlock Holmes and opened to the first page: *To my good friend, Rachael. May you find the clues you need to uncover the answers beneath.* Signed *Sir Arthur Conan Doyle.*

"It's signed to 'Rachael,'" she read with amusement.

Gaunt smiled. "A coincidence, I'm sure, but Fate is poking his head around the corner with a mischievous smirk. Perhaps such a book is precisely what you need to lift your spirits. He was a struggling author when he penned that one, much like your husband and the others on this shelf. At one point, all authors are unknown until the day they are not."

Rachael frowned. This man seemed to be in her head.

"I'm not a mind reader, Ms. Adams. I've just been around the block a number of times. I've known my share of struggling authors as well as the women in their lives. It can be a difficult life, particularly for those who don't know when to give up—the ones who keep plugging away, book after book without the sales to match their prowess."

Rachael felt a tear well up in her eye.

Gaunt produced a handkerchief and wiped it away. "There, there, Ms. Adams. That is not your Thad. I've read his book; he shows a lot of promise."

"You've read his book?"

"Of course!" Gaunt replied. "The instant I heard he was coming to town, I was down at Mr. Reese's little shop to buy the hardcover. I fully intend to ask your husband to sign it before he leaves today so I can add his work to my current collection." He gestured at the shelves. "I have no doubt one day he will be as well known as these greats. Perhaps he only requires the proper inspiration."

Rachael placed the book back on the shelf. She would like to buy him something, anything to lift his spirits. Although Thad wore a strong face, she knew he was as worried as she. "Do you have anything my fiancé might like?"

A smile again filled Gaunt's face. "A muse for a writer? I am sure of it!"

He walked across the room, his hand rubbing his chin. "I believe I have a box here which might contain the perfect gift. Now, where did I place it? That is the real question."

As he neared the window, he turned a sharp left and disappeared down a hallway. "I'll be back in a jiffy!" he called out. "Don't you go running off on me!"

Rachael considered doing just that. Regardless of what he found, she was fairly certain she didn't have the funds to purchase it. Thad wouldn't appreciate her spending money on something for him, not now.

Rachael turned and was about to head for the door when Gaunt returned holding a medium-size cardboard box. He struggled with the weight, setting it on the glass cabinet.

"I'm sure I've got just the thing in here," he said. With a small pocket knife, he cut the tape and unfolded the flaps.

Rachael tried to look inside, but he quickly sealed the top back up. "Now where's the fun in that?" he chuckled.

"Half the enjoyment of a place like this is discovery, but it shouldn't be rushed. There are three items inside—all of them would make an excellent present for your fiancé, but only one is the best. To make such a difficult decision, it's best to view each item one at a time rather than all at once. You'll know which is the right choice when you see it."

She didn't know what to say to such a thing, so she only nodded.

Leland Gaunt reached inside the box with both hands and pulled out a manual typewriter. An ancient thing of black metal. The keys were worn and almost unreadable. It must have been a hundred years old. Rachael had seen pictures, but in this age of computers they were very rare.

Gaunt placed his hand on the side and slid the carriage to the left. It glided with soft clicks rising up from inside. He tapped on a few of the keys. Rachael watched the gears jump and the letters appear on the faded yellow paper threaded through the machine. "It's a Corona 3; belonged to the late Ernest Hemingway. I suspect he used this when he wrote *The Sun Also Rises*, but there is no documentation to back up such a theory. He was such a promising young man, but his demons got the best of him. He never could give up the women and the drink; there is no telling where his career would have led him if he had."

She took a step back from the table. "Oh, Mr. Gaunt, I don't have much to spend. Something like this...I can't imagine what it would go for, but I'm sure it's outside my budget. I'm not sure I can get anything at all," Rachael confessed.

Gaunt smiled. "Don't fret about cost, young lady. We have two more items in this box—I'm sure your gift is among them."

Reaching back inside, his hand emerged, holding a fountain pen.

"Now this, this was truly a find," he exclaimed. "Many years ago, a number of writers gathered together on a stormy evening in Switzerland and decided to hold a competition to see who could write the best ghost story. They were all friends, you see; they spent many a night reading scary stories to one another and thought it would be a good way to practice their prose. The wife of one of the men in attendance, a poet in her own right, wished to participate. Lord Byron, her husband's friend—"

"*The* Lord Byron?" Rachael asked.

"Yes, my dear. Lord Byron gave his friend's wife this pen so she might write her tale. Her name was Mary Shelley, and she drafted *Frankenstein* with it on that miserable night." He held the pen up to the light; it glistened as if new.

Rachael smirked. "You can't be serious."

"Oh, but I am," Gaunt said. "I never jest about such things. Objects carry power, a life of their own. They are to be respected, cherished. I won't allow anything in my shop to fall into the hands of someone who wouldn't appreciate it. That's why I keep items like this boxed up; they're waiting for the right person, the right place to call home."

He handed her the pen and Rachael took it in her hand. "It should be in a museum somewhere—the typewriter, too."

"One day, perhaps, but right now that is not where they are needed."

She returned the pen to him.

"Not speaking to you?" he asked.

"Neither seems right," she told him. "Not for Thad, anyway."

Gaunt nodded and reached back into the box. "Then maybe this—"

His hand emerged, holding an old book.

"It's a journal of sorts, but an odd one indeed. Dating back to the sixteen hundreds—the witch trials, in fact. The cover is leather, but its pages are bound with metal much like today's spiral notebooks. I wasn't aware such a thing existed back then until I stumbled upon this one; I never found another. The leatherwork on the cover alone is extraordinary."

Rachael ran her fingers across the cover; it was so soft. "May I?" she asked.

"Of course, my dear," Gaunt replied, handing her the journal.

She set the book on the counter and opened to the first page with a delicate touch.

The Journal of Clayton Stone
Township of Shadow Cove, Massachusetts
1692

The writing was in perfect script, penmanship long lost on today's generation. She turned to the next page, then the next… Rachael frowned. "It's blank," she pointed out.

Gaunt looked down at it. "Why, yes, it is. Apparently Mr. Stone purchased this journal with full intentions to write upon the pages, but the words never came to him. Or perhaps the ink he used was of such poor quality it faded over the years. It's been almost half a millennia, after all…one could not be sure. Nonetheless, this journal is clearly in search of a writer to fill it cover to cover."

"This is perfect," Rachael told him.

Gaunt nodded. "I would agree. Such a book could easily inspire your fiancé to write an epic story. Imagine how his mind will just start whirring along when he reads that single page—I doubt he will have trouble filling in the rest."

Reaching into her purse, Rachael pulled out her wallet. Only ten dollars remained—Thad must have helped himself to two. "This is all I've got," she told him.

Gaunt looked down at the money and shook his head. "This isn't about money, my dear. This is about your fiancé's career, your very future. You can't assign a dollar value to something like that. What would you be willing to give to place Thad McAlister at the top of the bestseller list? To help him become the famous author you both see in your dreams? To possess the fame, fortune, and recognition which comes with such a post?"

"I'd give my firstborn," Rachael chuckled.

Leland Gaunt smiled back at her and rested his hand on hers.

A moment later, Rachael stepped back out into the crisp morning air and felt the sun on her skin for the first time since arriving in Maine. Gaunt had been kind enough to wrap the journal for her; she tucked the package under her arm and started down the street in the direction of the bookstore. She glanced down at the receipt before shoving it in her pocket—

Thank you for shopping at Needful Things.

ARRIVING SOON
Master of horror Thad McAlister's final novel,
Rise of the Witch.
Pre-order at amazon.com

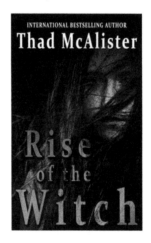

NOTES AND ACKNOWLEDGMENTS

Writing a book is a journey. Sometimes that journey ends at a destination. Bags are unpacked and life is resumed. Other times, you find yourself pausing at a rest stop along the way. You remain just long enough to grab a snack and take a break before resuming your trek. *Forsaken* was such a stop on a much longer wandering—a chance to tell a small piece of a larger tale. The people of Shadow Cove have many secrets, many stories left to tell. The Draper are still waiting for you in those woods.

Although *Forsaken* is a work of fiction, I borrowed heavily from the actual witch trials. Some of the people mentioned were, in fact, real. I can guarantee if I ever find myself in Salem, Massachusetts, I won't do so much as a card trick for fear of the consequences.

Many thanks to my First Readers: Anna Boehnker Cadieux, Laura Cartwright, Heath Howard, D.J. Roberts-Jessee, Peter Jung, Julie Meek, Summer Schrader, Violet Szilvas, and Nancine Thompson. Without you, grammar and punctuation would have run wild and the residents of Shadow Cove would have surely been carrying the wrong types of weapons while eating Big Macs instead of cuisine appropriate to

1692. I appreciate your feedback, commentary, and guidance throughout this project. Thanks to my editor, Jennifer Henkes, for pointing out all the things that can go wrong when you sleep through English class in school.

Jack Ketchum, you have my undying gratitude for putting up with my many emails, making introductions, steering me in the right direction, and lighting a path down a dark, unknown highway.

I would also like to thank Stephen King. Over the years, your books have provided countless hours of entertainment, inspiration, and many dead lightbulbs which I forced to burn far too long into the night rather than extinguish and face the dark after pouring through your prose. Thank you for allowing me to take a peek into the life of Leland Gaunt. It's nice to know his retail business is thriving in today's economy. Should anyone visit Castle Rock, Maine, I hope they take the time to stop in and say hello. Needful Things has a little something for everyone, and Mr. Gaunt will welcome you with a smile.

Most of all, I would like to thank my wife. Without her, this book would still be an idea on a post-it note and I'd still be writing "people that" instead of "people who." Thank you, PB.

I'll see you again soon.
jd

ABOUT THE AUTHOR

Jonathan Dylan Barker holds a BA in English from Beaumont University and currently lives in Shadow Cove, Massachusetts, where he is hard at work on his latest novel.

Are you ready to pick a side?
The battle for our future is about to begin.

The witch of Shadow Cove lives.
Her story has been told.
Her numbers are growing.
Whose side are you on?

www.jdbarker.com/sides

Lightning Source UK Ltd.
Milton Keynes UK
UKHW02f0801071117
312329UK00011B/389/P